One Week in Greece

International Affairs

Demi Alex

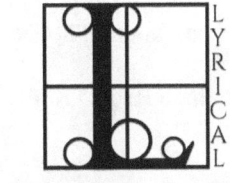

LYRICAL PRESS
Kensington Publishing Corp.
www.kensingtonbooks.com

LYRICAL PRESS BOOKS are published by

Kensington Publishing Corp.
119 West 40th Street
New York, NY 10018

All Kensington titles, imprints, and distributed lines are available at special quantity discounts for bulk purchases for sales promotion, premiums, fund-raising, educational, or institutional use.

Special book excerpts or customized printings can also be created to fit specific needs. For details, write or phone the office of the Kensington Sales Manager: Kensington Publishing Corp., 119 West 40th Street, New York, NY 10018. Attn. Sales Department. Phone: 1-800-221-2647.

Lyrical Press and Lyrical Press logo Reg. U.S. Pat. & TM Off.

First Electronic Edition: June 2017
eISBN-13: 978-1-5161-0202-0
eISBN-10: 1-5161-0202-9

First Print Edition: June 2017
ISBN-13: 978-1-5161-0203-7
ISBN-10: 1-5161-0203-7

Printed in the United States of America

A thousand reasons why three is the luckiest number . . .

Bethany Michaels is headed to the sun-bleached island of Mykonos on business, not pleasure. But an unexpected face from the past will introduce her to a brand-new desire . . .

Proving her business acumen to her demanding father is Bethany's only goal as she boards a ferry for Mykonos—and the beautiful resort she's determined to acquire for her family's hotel chain. Gorgeous Greek hunk Paul Lallas stands in her way—alongside his lover, Justin Bentley, who broke Bethany's heart into a million pieces years ago. When the two men make their very personal interest in her clear, mergers and acquisitions are suddenly the last thing on Bethany's mind. Could the chance to live out every one of her forbidden fantasies lead to a future more blissful than she ever imagined?

The International Affairs Series by Demi Alex

26 Hours in Paris

Four Nights at Sea

One Week in Greece

Published by Kensington Publishing Corporation

One Week in Greece is never enough...
so as we add time to our stay, we add gratitude.

An extra special thank you to my original editor
of the International Affairs series,
Peter Senftleben.
So grateful you believed in and enabled my virtual passport.
So grateful you then urged me to travel beyond my borders.
I'll miss you. Even more, I wish you all the best.

To my new editor, Martin Biro, for a smooth and painless transition.
And to my friends for life, Christine Maye and Tiffany Tergeson,
for more than handling my neurosis on deadline.

xoxo,
Demi

Chapter One

Alas, once again, Bethany Michaels had allowed work to take priority over her lady needs.

Ha, lady needs, she silently repeated.

Like she even remembered what lady needs were. Her personal life was non-existent. Sex life? Did she even know what that was any longer?

No. She had no clue. But it didn't matter. This time, work suited her. She was on her way to Mykonos, and regardless of the reason for the trip, a week on the gorgeous Greek island would do her good. Greece had always been a bucket list destination, and now she had the opportunity to make it a permanent part of her life. Bethany was sure as heck going to make it happen.

The sexiest scent of man lured her attention from the spreadsheet and had her surveying the café for its source.

Holy smokes!

Bethany couldn't stop sniffing the air. Her mind clouded. Her heartbeat raced. And she inhaled deep like a woman taking her first breath after breaking the surface from the longest free dive possible.

She began on her left, scanned in a slow and circular pattern, and didn't realize her mistake until she'd missed her opportunity to glimpse the men's faces that had thrown her olfactory system into overdrive. She should have started directly behind her, because by the time she'd located them, they'd walked straight ahead.

She released a breath and settled for appreciating the view of the duo strutting to the bar. Wide shoulders knocked as the ferry swayed, and deep laughter drifted in the air, wrapping around her and heightening her senses.

Yes, fine male specimens in Greece, she thought. *Damn fine.* She licked her parched lips, forced her throat to swallow, and kicked her libido back into hiding. Reprimanding her body for its reaction, she reminded herself of the purpose of her trip.

Heading to Mykonos for work. Not personal pleasure. You have one week in Greece to accomplish the deal of your lifetime. A deal to make the real life you want.

Still, no matter how much the sensible part of her mind repeated *business commitment, business reason, business*, she couldn't help but gawk at the testosterone-loaded display. Broad backs, one in a black tee and the other in what looked like a striped button-down, matched large and nicely shaped hands, motioning their emphasis just right, and two perfectly toned backsides, both showcased in well-worn jeans, completed the yummy display.

She listened closer, and made out the voice of the brown-haired man, which was holy-smokes deep enough and strong enough to roll over her and coax her repressed desires for a man, or two, to the surface.

She shook her head and closed her eyes. She really didn't need the distraction.

Bethany had practically begged her father to consider this venture, and she couldn't lose sight of her goal. She'd give anything to make her dad proud. And putting it simply, her dad would only be proud of professional accomplishments...a successful deal.

Lustful thoughts were off the table.

She needed that successful deal.

Making a very conscious effort to avoid the men at the bar, she flipped up the cover of her MacBook and checked her email. Earlier in the morning, she'd emailed her father and suggested he come visit before the anticipated signing of the contract.

Bethany planned on familiarizing herself well with Mykonos, and she wanted to show her dad the island and all she'd learn about it. If he came early, they could have a few days to enjoy each other's company. Maybe bond. But even as she'd composed the message, she'd known she was setting herself up for disappointment. He wouldn't come an hour earlier than needed. He was too busy for a leisurely lunch by the sea with his daughter.

Sure enough, she'd been correct about her dad's actions. He hadn't bothered to reply. His assistant had sent new files, which itemized the costs required to outfit the Mykonos resort with kitchenettes in each room that didn't have one and a proper timeshare office on the premises, as well as a projection on the timeline for the conversion.

She hit reply and typed out a response, stressing what she really wanted from the endeavor.

While this is a profitable project, my research on the property suggests we evaluate the possibility of continuing to operate the property as a family-friendly resort.

She explained how most of the resorts near the beaches were known to be party spots and not very kid-appropriate. The Lallas property had maintained a reputation for striking a perfect balance between luxury and casual, welcoming all ages to the beautiful seaside. Keeping it family-friendly seemed the way to go.

An instant response from the assistant flashed across the screen.

The board of directors, (aka Bethany's father) *has given distinct directives for the property to be evaluated only as a timeshare location. Please forward observations at your earliest convenience.*

That was a virtual slap on Bethany's hand. She didn't appreciate the tone, but she knew when to stay silent. After all, she was repeatedly reminded she was being held to the same standards as any other employee and needed to prove herself. Not only as her father's daughter, but as a true executive worthy of power. The big problem being that her father had always attached personal requests to her proving her professional prowess.

Releasing another long breath, she decided to ignore the negative emotions and continue with her strategy. And truth be told, her earliest convenience wouldn't be for at least a few days. She hadn't even made it to the island, was still on the ferry, and Bethany had such grand plans for Mykonos.

She wanted to make Greece her home base and she planned to make the most of every minute spent on Mykonos. Even without seeing it, she knew she'd love it. She loved everything she'd seen of Greece: the landscape, the people, even the food. The idea of spending lots of time at the new Luxury Homes Away From Home property put a smile on her face.

She lowered the lid on the computer and sneaked a glance back at the men. Being a woman, she deserved a little dreamy pleasure.

Her breath caught in her throat and her skin flushed.

Justin, her J, stared clear into her soul. Adrenaline shot through her, and every one of her cells launched a revolution. She considered how quickly she could escape. But her body wouldn't cooperate. Her legs wouldn't move.

Recognition flashed in his eyes and his mouth turned up in a smile. He stood, nudged the lighter-haired man's arm, and motioned for him to follow. Those well-worn jeans came her way, and Bethany melted into her pleather seat.

She hadn't seen Justin in years. She wasn't sure she could handle seeing him at all. The man had walked away and broken her heart.

"Bethy," he said, reaching her and pulling her up on to legs that had turned to jelly. She fell forward, and he steadied her against his chest as he tucked her into a full embrace and lowered his face to the curve of her neck. His breath tickled and his lips heated, causing bumps to rise on her skin. "I'm happy to see you."

"Me, too, J," she rasped, failing miserably at finding her balance while breathing in his familiar scent. That was the sexy smell that had distracted her in the first place.

"J? Bethy?" The other man's surprised voice penetrated the haze and she somehow found the strength to stand. "Your Bethy?"

"My Bethy," Justin said, only a slight question in his gaze, maybe searching for her acceptance of his touch, before he smoothed a finger down her cheek and dropped a kiss on her forehead. "Bethany, this is my boyfriend, Paul."

She had no time to process Justin's words as Paul wrapped his arms around them, both her and Justin, and pressed his lips to the side of her temple. "Such a pleasure to finally meet the elusive and beautiful Bethany."

Stunned, she didn't know what to do or how to react. She went with a simple smile. "Hello, Paul."

Paul, her once-lover's boyfriend, held her in his embrace like a cherished friend. Snug against his muscular body, she realized it had been his scent that had added an edge of sophisticated roughness to her dreamy olfactory experience. She looked up at Justin, who kept on grinning like he'd just won the lottery, then over to Paul, who tightened his hold and squeezed her closer. What was she supposed to do?

"You should sit," Justin said. "You look a little shell-shocked."

A little! Was the man crazy? She dropped on to her seat and stared up at the man who had once shattered her world with a breakup phrase. *I can't stay here.*

Not only had Justin moved on, but he'd moved on with a man. And yes, they'd discussed love for the sake of love; love not limited to heterosexual or homosexual love, just love. And yes, the fact that Justin had a boyfriend was not news to Bethany. But meeting the gorgeous man was.

Paul squatted beside her, placing his large palm on the side of her thigh. "From all Justin says about you, I feel like we've known each other for years. I know so much about you, but I can honestly say I'm totally stunned at how little justice his sweet words did for you. You're even more beautiful than I've imagined."

Well she didn't know anything about him—other than the fact that his touch did things to her a stranger shouldn't. That was a lie. She also knew he was more beautiful than she'd imagined a man could be. If you could call a handsome man beautiful?

Bethany forced another smile. She gazed at Justin and recalled her last conversation with him.

"I'm not signing away our life," he'd said. "I can do it on my own. Be my own—"

"I don't want to hear anymore. I can't hear anymore."

"Give me a chance to explain," he'd urged. "Staying isn't the—"

"No. It hurts too much," she'd said, then begged him to stop speaking. "Just go. This isn't working anyway. We're done."

Over the months that followed the heartbreak, she'd erased all the messages he'd left on her phone without listening to them. She'd deleted each unopened email. She'd even transferred schools and had given the house staff specific instructions not to share her forwarding information with him. It simply hurt too much.

Shoot, she wasn't fooling herself trying to be all civilized and calm. Her world had been royally fucked and turned inside out. She'd been ready to make a life with Justin and had believed he'd been ready to make a life with her. They'd gone out of state for school together, but he'd left only a couple of weeks into the semester. She'd transferred to a new school in January.

"How long has it been, Bethy?"

She knew exactly how long. To the month. To the day. To the hour. She checked her phone, then realized she was in a different time zone. Nope. She wasn't going there with him.

"It doesn't matter," Paul said, coming to her rescue. "We're just happy to reconnect. Amazing good fortune to run into you today. It's happenstance."

Happenstance her ass. It was a curse.

"I kept trying to reach you," Justin said. "You vanished. You were impossible to find. No one, not even Sheridan, would tell me where you were."

Of course her sister wouldn't tell him. While holding her hand and telling her to release her anger by slashing his bicycle tires, her sister had held Bethany's head in her lap and had played with her hair so she could actually get some sleep.

"The only thing that helped was that your father said to leave you alone," Justin continued. "To me, that meant you were okay. So I reapplied to my original choice of schools, a university I could afford, and enrolled the following year. I've kept my same phone number, just in case you ever wanted to contact me. You never did."

Nothing he said was news to her. He'd never blocked her on any social network, so lurking had always been an option and the way she'd learned of Paul's existence. Taking a deep breath, she kept her smile big as shit and concentrated on not letting a single tear slip. Those professional poker players had nothing on her.

"No worries," Paul said. "You're together now."

Traveling to one of the sexiest places on earth, a past lover at her side, and his current lover at his side, did not mean "no worries." It showcased the life of solitude that haunted her existence. No matter how Bethany had tried to drown her hurt in meaningless physical relationships, she hadn't managed to put Justin out of her heart.

"So where are you going?" Paul asked.

That's right. A tiny bit of hope crept through her as she realized the ship made more than one port and had a full route. She might not be subject to hormone-overload for the rest of the week. And it was hormonal…that was her story.

If she were to be subjected to so much tempting testosterone when it was off-limits, it would be pure torture, and her body and mind would be in constant turmoil. She couldn't handle the turmoil already brewing inside her.

Body: Go for it.

Mind: Are you crazy? Stay away!

Body: Go for it. Orgasms guaranteed.

Mind: Heartbreak guaranteed.

Body: Fantasy come true.

Mind: Shut the fuck up, body. We don't like him anymore.

Bethany had to stop feeling and start thinking. What was it? The itinerary hit three different islands before returning to Piraeus. Maybe, just maybe, the boat would reach Mykonos, she'd disembark, and the men would continue on.

"Work," she blurted. "I'm working on Mykonos for the next week."

"We're here for a week." Justin slid into the booth beside her and draped his arm across the back of the seat. "Sort of for work, too."

"Sort of?" Bethany asked.

"No. It's work." Justin shrugged, and dark waves of hair fell across his forehead.

She had to stop herself from reaching up and sweeping them off his brow. She loved the feel of his hair on her fingers.

"We'd rather it was play, but it doesn't matter. We have a chance to spend some time with you. A real chance to put the past behind us and move ahead." He met Paul's gaze. "And you finally get to meet Bethany and see how amazing she is in person."

The pit in her stomach swelled, and her insides twisted with dread. Why did fate mess with her in such an evil way and subject her to two handsome men, Justin and his boyfriend, when all it would do is remind her of her current solo status?

Despite her confident and suave reputation, she had limited experience in honest relationships. Sure she'd had her share of lovers, but she wouldn't classify any of them as relationship material. She'd always managed to leave before the sun came up or they'd wanted to chat. Then their calls would be diverted to voice mail and they'd eventually stop calling. Guess the effort wasn't worth it.

Maybe she wasn't worth it? Maybe it was her doing that Justin had gone gay?

Ludicrous. Nobody made anyone any way. They were or they weren't. And if she was honest, like she had been when they'd been together, Justin never defined love by gender. He loved who he loved.

More likely, her real issue was that she was doomed to be lonely and alone.

"What's wrong?" Paul sat across from her and placed his arms on the table. For a split second she thought he'd reach for her hands, so she tucked them under her thighs. "What are you thinking?"

"Nothing." She shook her head, hiding her emotions. "It's a work thing. Conference call." She inched across the seat and out of the booth. "I need to go."

"Where are you staying?" Justin asked.

Straightening, she shrugged, collected her files into a neat pile, and placed the computer in its case. "Not sure. The info is in my cabin," she lied.

"A phone number?" Justin persisted, but she just couldn't do it. She couldn't give him her new number, and definitely couldn't place her heart and soul on the line to have them blown to smithereens again. But his gaze wouldn't waver. "Want my number?"

"I remember it." Another shrug.

"That's great," Paul said, standing beside her and giving her a reassuring smile. He pulled a card from his back pocket and handed it to her. "Plus, you now have my info, too. Local and US cell numbers. Both phones are on. Call either, any time."

He closed his hand over hers and squeezed as if he understood her predicament, and her traitorous hand didn't pull back. She liked it. She actually wanted to step into his arms, knowing darn well he'd welcome and comfort her.

Mind: Walk away now.

Body: Just let the man do what he can do.

Mind: I said now!

"Let's shoot for meeting up before we disembark," Paul said, the glint in his amber-colored eyes holding her as much as his touch. "But if the signal is bad onboard, or we don't meet up before we dock, we'll wait for you on the pier by the Sunset Café."

"Okay." She turned and walked away, waving over her shoulder because she didn't dare meet Justin's gaze again. If she did, her resolve to stay away would crumble.

Chapter Two

Justin had heard her, but didn't believe her. Bethany had smiled. The smile hadn't reached her eyes. She'd intentionally avoided sharing her number, so once again, he feared she'd disappear.

"I'm sure we'll see her again," Paul whispered, as if reading his mind. "We're on a ferry. In the middle of the Aegean Sea."

But once upon a time, he'd also thought he'd had logic on his side. He hadn't. She hadn't returned any of his messages. No matter how he'd tried to reach her, she'd never responded. He finally had the opportunity to make her respond and tell him why he'd fallen short.

He wasn't going to fail.

Paul draped his arm over Justin's shoulder and whistled beneath his breath.

"She's gorgeous."

Justin nodded, still watching her weave her way through the passengers. "Even more today than in the past."

"Seriously," Paul said, squeezing his shoulder. "Don't worry. Even if we don't see her on the ferry, Mykonos is an island. It's my island. We'll find her. Give her a chance to get over the shock of seeing you where she least expected it."

"I thought she was good with it." He rubbed the heel of his hand in the center of his chest. "Then she bolted. Like I did her wrong."

"You didn't," Paul insisted. "But are you sure you can handle it this time around? They shredded you."

Justin had to believe she had no say in what had happened. He had to. Otherwise everything else was a lie. And nobody could lie for years. "She's not a liar. And no matter how she ran in the end, she was happy to see me. Did you see her eyes?"

"I did."

Bethy's eyes spoke volumes. She couldn't lie because her eyes always gave her away. And when she'd recognized him, it was like coming home.

"Yup. You can't erase years of love. It may change, but it doesn't go away." Justin knew it was the romantic in him speaking, but he didn't care. "She also liked you. She was comfortable with you."

"I felt that, too." Paul shuffled and stared at his feet. "There's still a lot of chemistry between you."

"Yup." Damn, he needed to use more words to express himself, but he didn't think them necessary.

"You sure you're okay with it? What if she's married?"

"She wasn't wearing a ring," Justin noted.

"You checked. So you're still interested," Paul said.

"I'm not dead," he said. "You just said how gorgeous she is." Snaking his hands around Paul's waist, he pressed his *interest* against his thigh. "Interest enough?"

Nodding, Paul grinned. "More than enough."

It may have been a while, but they'd played with others in the past. Not often. Never for long. And never with anyone who'd been married. So checking for a ring was reasonable.

"It's a natural response," Justin said. "And as for checking for a ring, anyone would check if she was taken. Clearly, she's not. And she may need friends around to look after her while on the island. The place can get wild."

"It can," Paul agreed. "If she is with someone, he'd be a huge asshole to let her come here on her own. She'll be propositioned at every turn."

"Yup."

"Yup," Paul mimicked. He shook his head and laughed. "Okay, the chemistry is still there. And since you're good on being with her, what do you think of asking Bethany to get to know us—well me, she already knows you—better? She can join us at the resort while she's here and you never know where it may lead."

"No," Justin objected, panic tightening his chest.

"What is it with the two of you and all these no answers?" Paul sounded almost amused, but his confident nature faded. "Something wrong with me? You don't want to share her with me? Do you want to be alone with her? Without me?"

"No," Justin said in a low voice, remembering how he'd shared Bethany's ménage fantasy they'd never gotten around to making a reality with Paul. Taking his lover's hand, he returned to the table. "No matter what you may think, I always want you. Always."

They sat and Justin released Paul's hand as he rested his leg against Paul's. They were good with additional lovers, but they'd never needed or developed an emotional connection with anyone else. Nobody had mattered like she mattered.

"Sharing Bethany would be pure ecstasy. But, Bethy is different. It's not about me. It's about her. We cannot do that. A sexual relationship would not work with us."

"Justin, are you blind? Or have you forgotten all you've told me about the two of you?" Paul pointed to his own groin. "When I first saw her, I could have pounded nails into a concrete wall."

"No argument here." Justin raised his palms forward to stop Paul from elaborating. He was in full agreement when it came to chemistry. They had an abundance of it and there was no way to deny it. However, they could ignore it. "But then she spoke. I saw your reaction. Felt what moved between the two of you. You looked into those hypnotic dark eyes, and she suddenly became more than a sex partner."

"She's beautiful, sweet, a little skittish because you interrogated her, but perfect for us." Paul raised his broad shoulders. "She was coming around to the idea of me...of us. So why not pursue something more?"

"Because Bethany is not a temporary kind of woman." And that was their deal.

Temporary. No strings attached.

From the very beginning, they'd agreed to keep their real life uncomplicated. No responsibility of pleasing a third person.

"Not temporary?" Paul's features turned stoic and hard. He sat back on the seat and rubbed his chin. "We don't do long-term with others."

"I know." The other sex partners they'd invited into their bed knew from the get-go that it was only physical. No emotional attachments.

"It's not who we are," Paul said, folding his arms across his chest.

"I know."

"And you're saying she could get hurt," Paul added.

"She could," Justin agreed. "Either one of us could get hurt, too. Both of us could get hurt. We can't invite her into our bed, so get those thoughts out of your head. Think of how you had to change your physical relationship with Kathryn when we got involved."

"Kat and I have been friends forever, convenient lovers when it suited us, but when you came into the picture, the latter had to change," Paul said. "Even if you'd agreed, which I honestly didn't think to discuss, Kat and I weren't going anywhere. It wouldn't be fair."

"Exactly," Justin said. "That's how it is with Bethany. We may be fantastic together, may not be able to get out of that bed, but I'm not letting her off the hook by handing her ammunition to tell us it's too much for her to handle. I'm not letting her out of our life. She will be in our lives forever, so she can only be a friend."

"That's if she agrees," Paul said.

"Why wouldn't she?"

"Seriously, Justin, think about it. That's a lot to ask when there is so much sexual tension between us. Then, when it comes to the emotional part, she was taken aback with our meeting and she didn't look too happy about it." Always practical and efficient, Paul had regained his composure and was too pragmatic.

"She'll agree." Justin fisted his hand at the thought of her denying him again. No fucking way. He had to make it right with her. Wipe that hurt from her sweet face, and see her smile in earnest. Without a doubt she was the most loving and generous girl he'd ever met. "She's not a girl any longer. She's a grown woman."

"I'm not sure what you're thinking, but whatever it is, it's leaving an unsettled feeling in my gut," Paul said. "She's adorable. Gorgeous. Sweet. I've already said that. But you can't think she's still the girl you knew in high school. She's not. Do you really believe she can handle rekindling an explosive past with a simple friendship?"

"She really took to you," Justin said. "And that's huge because Bethany rarely reaches out to people. She reached out to you."

"Careful," Paul warned, toggling a finger in the air. "You threw a bucket of ice water on the physical. Her reaching out was a physical connection. Don't misinterpret the facts and set yourself up."

Whatever.

She'd be back and a definite part of his and Paul's life.

The three of them were meant to be in each other's lives. And because she'd insisted on pushing him away in the past, this time he'd bring her in on his terms.

Selfish?

Maybe.

But it would work.

"You can't bulldoze her," Paul said, once again reading his mind.

"You like her," he said, looking into his lover's eyes and searching for more than hope. He found it.

"I said as much, so you know I do. What's not to like?" Paul said, reaching for him and trailing a finger over Justin's forearm in a cautious, but caring manner. "She's fucking breathtaking. But, Justin, you just told me that Bethy isn't a temporary option. That means we'd need to commit to her, and we can't."

"You still on the sex stuff?"

"No," Paul insisted. "I'm on commitment. We can't change our whole life. We won't. And you can't just show up and demand she let you close on a totally different level than she knows. The woman isn't happy with the past."

"It's not about the past. And I didn't show up. She did." Justin leaned back, crossed his arms over his chest. "Seriously, Paul. Let's not overanalyze. I'm not in the mood to dissect this right now. Seeing her after all these years of a Bethany-blackout is totally messing with me. I'm not delusional about picking up where we left off, nor am I unhappy with my life. Actually, I'm very happy with my life. Our life."

"Good to hear."

"Never doubt that, love. Never."

He'd never lied to Paul. He trusted him, more than trusted him, and couldn't imagine a life without him. So no lies. Ever.

"I don't know how, and I need some time to figure where she'll factor into all of this, but I want her back in my life," Justin said. "Since she's very important to me, I need to know you're okay with that because it means she's going to be in your life."

Paul nodded, but didn't speak.

"Even more than time," Justin continued, "I need you to stand with me."

"I do. Always." Paul didn't hesitate. "I'm open to your Bethy in our lives. The connection between the two of you is obvious and solid, and I know the more I get to know her, the more special she'll be to me. Just be careful, babe. Don't reopen wounds that won't heal."

Chapter Three

"Mykonos is the perfect place to find love," Paul said, attempting to distract Justin as the iconic *Kato Milli* marked the ferry's way into the harbor. But not even the view of the windmills caught his attention. There was no reply from Justin. The man didn't even bother to glance over his shoulder. He stared at his phone, supposedly checking emails, only looking up to scan the deck.

Paul wanted to wrap him in his arms and tell him everything was going to be okay, but they didn't lie to each other and that wasn't something he knew for sure. The truth was that within the span of a few hours, Paul's own problems had multiplied. Not only was he concerned about his uncle throwing away his life's legacy, but he was seriously worried about Justin being able to deal with seeing Bethany again, and possibly being rejected, again.

No matter how much Justin insisted he was good with seeing Bethany, tension rolled off the typically calm and collected man.

Paul inhaled the fresh sea air, then wrapped his arm around the pensive man at his side, hoping some of his strength and optimism would transfer to Justin.

"Babe, stop checking email. Take a freaking break. You can't miss this view. It's like the windmills are welcoming us home." And even though Paul was sure Justin was still preoccupied with Bethany, he gave him major credit for pretending, almost convincingly, to shift his focus back to *City Wings* work issues and their original reason for visiting the island.

"Agreed," Justin finally said, looking over his shoulder. "We should've sent someone to Mykonos for *City Wings*. We could have made the Valentine's *Best Place to Find Love* competition a three-way. Kat, Charlie, and..."

"Our ladies did good. The articles were perfect. And all our goals were met."

At last, Paul struck a chord and brought Justin out of his funk. They both adored their girls. And they were happy Kat and Charlie had accomplished individual professional goals. And if he were honest, totally honest, his objective had been more than gaining great features.

"Kat had to have her chance with Marko, and Charlie needed to break out of her rut," Paul said, outlining the true objectives of the Valentine's contest.

"And your ludicrous, manipulative, and totally unprofessional ploy worked," Justin said. "Kat and Marko are together and married." Justin looked at the shore as he spoke and pointed out some of their favorite spots. "Charlie is free of all bullshit and really happy with that hunky barista fiancé of hers."

"Ford isn't exactly a barista, but he is crazy for Charlie," Paul said, happy that Justin was smiling again. "It's all good."

"I agree. You and Marko were over the top devious with the way you set it up. And I don't think you could have gotten away with such a scam if Kat and Charlie weren't friends and more than professional acquaintances. But it worked."

"Sometimes you need to get creative to help your friends," Paul said. "They both got their bylines and more."

"They're great journalists, so they would have gotten their bylines anyway," Justin said. "It's the more that matters. Kat was always in love with the Frenchman, but the force of that love terrified her. But Marko had balls of steel to last so long without her. I'm so glad, for both of them, that he went all He-Man, stopped pussyfooting around, and made her see the truth. Those two belong together."

"True. Very true. And how weird is it that Charlie found her perfect match on that cruise?" Paul asked, laughing at how the singles cruise had unraveled the pretty little bundle of nerves. "Straight-laced girl finds love on kink cruise. You know, I would have hand-picked Ford for her if I had known him."

"Yes, he unleashed the beast in Miss Prim and Proper," Justin said, shaking his head. "He gets her, identifies with her uppity upbringing and history, and knows how to deal with her in order to make her realize what she wants."

"They're a perfect fit," Paul added, considering how well the couples complimented one and other.

"Like us," Justin said, settling his arms around Paul's waist and pressing his torso against his chest. "We fit." He leaned in and touched his lips to Paul's in a soft but strong kiss. "Fuck, I love you."

"I love you," Paul echoed, pulling him closer and deepening the kiss, wanting to reassure Justin that he was with him in every step of life. He had his back. Would always have his back. No matter what came their way.

Broad shoulders lifted and Paul felt Justin's smile against his lips. "Maybe I've already found love—"

"Or love found you," Paul offered, running his palm down Justin's chiseled bicep, all the way to his hand, and interlacing their fingers.

"Doesn't matter. The point is I have love," Justin said. "So maybe I can do a spin-off of the girls' articles and try my hand on writing a piece featuring Mykonos as a romantic getaway? This place has magic. The light. The energy. Love pulses in the damn air here."

"Yeah, that's rather poetic," Paul said, hesitant to encourage Justin, even if it kept his focus off what looked like a doomed rekindling with the woman he wanted back in his life. He went for easy-going and carefree. "Maybe you should keep to your spreadsheets, number magic, and leave the writing to the professionals?"

Paul had seen his man's attempts at writing, and either the articles were flat and boring, or embellished with imagery and big words. It would be professional suicide and *City Wings* would take a huge hit. The readership would tear them apart for publishing flowery prose and have a field day with it on social networks. He shook his head and prayed he didn't need to elaborate.

"Whatever," Justin grumbled.

Paul touched his lips to the side of Justin's neck in order to hide his smirk and keep from making a smartass remark. He knew this newfound desire to write about romantic getaways was because of Bethany. Their reunion had done a number on him. He also knew what the woman had once meant to him. No need to poke at old sores.

The ferry entered the port, and he singled out the quaint homes, with brightly painted wooden doors, occupied by friends. The labyrinth of narrow whitewashed streets in town held some of Paul's favorite places on Earth, and he was itching to get on land and start convincing his uncle to keep the resort, but first he had to address Justin's pain.

"I'm sorry Bethany hasn't shown," he said, tempering his own concerns.

"Kind of expected. She was spooked. We'll wait for her at the café. Hopefully, she'll come and we can drop her at her hotel on the way to the resort. We can even go to the bakery together." Justin searched the deck again, just like he had for the past hour, but Bethany was nowhere to be seen. "She loves honey, so she'll love the Mykonos cheese pie. You know, the special one that sweet grandma makes for us with the honey inside. And she'll fall in love with freddo cappuccinos."

"What's wrong with a classic frappé?" Paul was relieved, but at the same time concerned, that Justin was talking about it, so he tried to keep the conversation light. He chuckled and stepped around Justin, giving his shoulders a playful squeeze. "I promise we'll stop at the bakery on the way to my uncle's."

"Good," Justin said. "But you know it's not as cool to drink a frappé as it is to have a freddo cappuccino. Need to get with the times. Frappé is passé."

Frappé is passé? Since when did his traditional and ultra proper man speak in rhyme? "Screw that. If I want a classic frappé, I'm having it."

Justin laughed and shook his head. "You've always liked what you like."

"That's true," Paul agreed. "I like my frappé, and I like this place. I get to share the two with you. What else could I ask for?"

"I can't believe Kosta is considering giving this up." Justin's face turned sad, and Paul knew that in spite of spewing all that stuff about supporting his uncle, Justin really didn't want the resort sold either.

"He won't," Paul mumbled. "I won't."

"Land of hot sun, hotter sand, and hottest opportunities. I'm going to miss it," Justin said.

"We're not going to miss anything. We're going to remind *Theo* Kosta how much he loves this place," Paul said, knowing that his uncle Kosta had an insane love affair with the resort. The man had built buildings with his own hands, landscaped the grounds, and poured his heart into every nook and cranny of the physical structures.

"I'm sure your *theo* remembers," Justin said.

"The first step is to get him to admit it. Then we'll implement new practices that will allow the resort to run with a minimal amount of overseeing. There are devoted and capable employees that can step up to more responsibilities with the proper training. Once all that's done, he'll forget about letting a huge conglomerate ruin our place."

"You can't dictate his future. It's not right, so don't force it," Justin said.

"Sounds familiar," Paul retorted, recalling what he'd said about forcing Bethany to accept them. "Good advice." Advice Paul knew neither of them would follow.

Since he'd only just met her and his instant attraction for her was physical—fuck it, it was pure lust—he'd been able to think with his brain once she'd left them alone. And once the long-term reality of the tempting Bethany had really sunk in, he'd made a conscious decision to dismiss the possibility of what he knew would be a very satisfying tryst.

It was unlikely that he'd be hurt by a fling. But he didn't want her hurt. He didn't want Justin hurt. If she ever did show or call, they'd need to find a way to be friends.

Caution played in his mind, and his thoughts meandered back to the resort.

"Look at the hustle on the port," Justin said, seemingly calm and collected. Maybe, just maybe, he really did believe things would work out.

Trucks backed up to the loading area, island shuttles lined the street, and the cafés emptied of the local innkeepers waiting to collect new guests.

"It's amazing how Chora can have so much traffic around it and still look so picturesque," Paul said, deciding he had to trust Justin on Bethany and not obsess on how he'd handle it. Justin was smart, strong, and rarely wrong. Paul would concentrate on what he was good at: their business, the local industry, and family. "I know it's one of the most popular party destinations in the world, but there is something so comforting and homey about it." The ship bumped against the dock and he widened his stance to brace himself. "It has a unique energy."

"I feel it," Justin agreed, rubbing his hands up and down his arms. "And I'm not just talking about the wind whipping into my pores."

"It's extra gusty today." Keeping an arm around Justin, Paul leaned down and reached for his backpack and heaved it on to his shoulder. It held both of their laptops and a booster for the WiFi, just in case. But he still felt the wind at his back. "The *meltemi* winds are the reason the windmills were so genius and successful throughout history."

"The Venetians were smart to harness that energy. Made life easier," Justin said, leaning over the railing and peering into the water. "And today, damn if the *meltemi* doesn't make the heat on the beaches enjoyable, gusty or not. The sun sizzles on your skin. The breeze cools you down."

History and meteorology aside, Paul knew he was coming home. He also knew there was no way he'd let his uncle sell the resort. "I spent many summer afternoons on those winding paths," Paul said. "Good memories."

"Paradise for sure." Granted, Justin hadn't enjoyed the place to the degree that Paul had, but they'd spent hot and sultry afternoons on the beach—Paradise, Super Paradise, and "their" beach. The nights were even better. Justin rubbed his tight butt against Paul's groin in an obvious attempt to get his mind off the sad possibility of the sale. "You going to promise me at least one night of hedonistic pleasure before we lose ourselves in work?"

"Promise," Paul replied. "Tonight is all ours. No resort talk. Just you, me, and the beach bar of your choosing." He tightened his hold around Justin's finely sculpted abdomen and held him against his chest, pressing his mouth to Justin's neck. He inhaled the familiar scent and closed his eyes.

"Justin, I'm sorry that things didn't go as smooth as they could have with Bethany. Are you okay?"

"She'll come around," he said. "I know she will."

What was Justin expecting from the woman? She'd jumped at his touch and shrank from his attention. She'd even looked to him, a stranger, for understanding. And Paul hated to admit it, because he felt like he'd betrayed Justin, but she'd found it. He felt the tension. He even felt the attraction. Trying to establish a new type relationship would be awkward.

"Are you okay?" Paul repeated.

"I really am. I'm not worried about Bethany, if that's what you're thinking. It'll work out," Justin said. "I just wish we were here on vacation and not to help facilitate the sale of the resort. It's not going to be fun. You're not going to be in a good mood. And there will be stress galore with your uncle if you push it."

"I'd never push anything on him he doesn't want. But I will try to help him remember why he chose to make a life here in the first place. And we'll come back." Paul said. "Maybe later in the summer. He won't sell. So we'll be back for more fun, and next time, under better circumstances."

"I didn't hear that." Justin turned and curled firm fingers over Paul's shoulders. "You're going to make yourself sick trying to make it happen when we both know that it's going to be difficult. Plus, the timing is bad. We have too much going on in New York, and we can't stay past the next release of *City Wings*. This summer is too close for a return trip."

"I didn't really have a say in the timing. I had to come for *Theo* Kosta. He's always been there for me, and it's my turn to be there for him."

"I know. I get it," Justin said. "And it's not about the short timing. I'm concerned we left things up in the air. We have a business to run and a magazine to get out."

A life to live.

In spite of Justin's attempt to minimize his objection, Paul heard the unspoken words and wanted to argue for a life, a summer life, on the island. But they'd had that discussion before they'd left home. Justin, even more so than Paul, didn't want to change their life. He liked the carefree existence that allowed them to grow professionally and enjoy personal time. In truth, they had it good.

"The July issue is ready to go, and August's is under control. Plus, we have a competent staff," Paul insisted, thankful Justin was back to business mode.

From the looks of what was going on, he was going to have a bad case of emotional whiplash over the next few days.

"We can do all of our daily tasks electronically, and we can oversee production from anywhere in the world. I've already checked to make sure the internet connection at the hotel is up to par. It'll be okay."

Encouraged by Justin resting his linked hands in the small of Paul's back, Paul rubbed his thumb over the dark stubble shadowing the handsome face he loved.

They needed a break, and they needed each other.

The rapid growth of the millennial-based travel publication had consumed too much of their time, placing their international travel plans on the back burner. It had taken his uncle's call for help for Paul to book the flights. The hotel needed to be properly presented to the Luxury Homes Away From Home executive—regardless if Paul didn't want the sale, *Theo* Kosta was more than considering it. And if Paul couldn't convince his uncle to hold on to the property, he'd damn well do his best to protect his uncle's interests.

Since losing his wife, Kosta Lallas carried the weight of the world on his shoulders. Paul would see if new procedures were needed for the operation of the resort. Then maybe his uncle would not feel it necessary to sell. The resort, Vaso's Dream, would still be his...theirs.

"Don't think so hard. It'll be okay." Justin consoled Paul.

Whiplash.

"I'm over the bad timing. I'll get Bethany to come around. All will go well. We're here, and it's sinfully gorgeous, so let's get to your uncle, settle our asses in the room, and deal with the rest as it comes."

"That's why I love you, Justin. You see the light in every situation. You're so fucking good for me. You being here means everything to me." He made a silent promise to schedule their return for a real vacation as soon as possible. "I'll make it good."

"I know you will. And no matter what you're thinking, I do want to be here," Justin said, giving him a handsome grin.

"Because of Bethany?" Shit. That sounded catty.

"No. And yes. I'm happy she's here." Justin kept grinning, clearly having grown comfortable with the situation. "Trust me when I say you'll like her. And no, because you're kind of stuck with me…always. I go where you go. I'll take advantage of your determination to win your uncle over and set up the office while you try to convince him. When the sun goes down tonight, I'll hold you to the promise of a hedonistic night. Actually, we could spend the majority of our time here in the same pattern. Work in the daytime. Party at night."

"I'll do my best." Paul immediately regretted saying that, because it bordered on one of those lies they never told each other. He feared doing his best wouldn't be enough. They'd be too exhausted to party much. He met Justin's gaze and once again silently vowed to make the most of their situation. "Any special requests?"

Justin's fingers held tight and he leaned into Paul, sealing their lips in a long passionate kiss with a different kind of promise. Paul immediately reacted, grinding himself against Justin and deepening the kiss.

"Thank you," Paul said, sucking Justin's tongue into his mouth and swirling his own over it. "I'm going to thank you properly the moment we get to our place."

"Holding you to that," Justin said, bringing his mouth to his ear. "By the way, I like your appreciation best when you're on your knees."

"Fuck me." Paul groaned, adjusting his jeans as his erection swelled.

"That'll work, too," Justin said, surprising Paul. "I live to please."

Damn. Sweat beaded on Paul's brow and his heart hammered in his chest. "Babe, anything you want."

While their sex life had always been good—phenomenal actually—Justin rarely made the first move or took control. When he did, he commanded complete surrender. It was one of the few times Paul was able to lose himself. He relished the times he bottomed.

"Remember you said that, Paul."

"Anything," he repeated.

"Good." Justin inclined his head toward the staircase, which led into the ship's belly. "You get the car. I'll check the cabin for anything left behind. Meet on the pier."

Chapter Four

"This is absolutely nuts." Justin glanced over his shoulder at the motorcycle that swerved past the produce truck at a ridiculous speed. "They're driving like maniacs."

"Yes they are." Paul downshifted into second and beeped the horn before taking a hairpin turn, immune to the vehicles barreling down the opposite side that didn't seem to take into consideration they were sharing the road. "Relax. You're going to pull the handle off the door. They know this road like the back of their hands. Know every pothole, every twist and turn. They drive it all the time."

"I know. I can't get used to it, though." Justin looked down the angry-looking serpentine road, then glanced back at the serene and hypnotic blue of the water. "I give you mega credit for keeping your cool. I can't drive here."

"You can't drive back home, either. You can't drive period. But you don't have to worry," Paul said. "That's why you have me."

Another NASCAR-worthy turn, and Justin welcomed the comfort of Paul's hand on his knee. He rolled down his window, letting the crisp morning air soothe his nerves, then leaned back in his seat.

They were back on Mykonos, and no matter the reason, Justin couldn't deny the excitement of visiting the beautiful island and having the chance to reconnect with Bethany. And he would, just as soon as he found her.

"Office concerns and work for the hotel aside, I'm really glad we're here."

* * *

Twenty minutes later, they walked into the small office Kosta used just off the resort's main dining terrace. The man, a total workaholic, had devoted himself to building a magnificent hideaway for all types of travelers. Unfortunately, he'd lost his zeal for the beautiful place when he lost his wife to a quick battle with breast cancer.

"*Theo*? Where are you?" Paul called.

Kosta was stretched out on a sofa, watching the early afternoon news.

"*Kalispera,* good afternoon," a slightly grayer-haired version of Paul's uncle replied, bracing beefy hands on his knees to rise from his place. "I wasn't expecting you so soon."

"We managed to catch the early ferry," Paul explained, closing the space between them and embracing his uncle. "Happy we made it before lunch."

"So am I," Justin added, accepting the tight hugs and pats on the back like the converted Greek he was.

During his first trip to Greece, he'd learned that Greek families were more touchy feely than his own. He'd also learned to accept and welcome the hugs and kisses from everyone. There was no question or discomfort over the loving attention bestowed on them by the loud and boisterous uncle.

"It's so good to see you both. So good. I've missed you," Kosta said, taking Paul's cheeks in his hands and smothering them in kisses like he was greeting a young boy. He turned his attention back to Justin, but toned down the smooching noises as he kissed both his cheeks in turn. "Welcome back, *Americanakia*. It's good to see you boys. Thank you for coming. I really appreciate your help."

"We'll only help if you stop calling us boys," Paul said in a teasing voice. "Just because you look like a jolly grandpa, doesn't mean you get to treat us like kids."

"Fine, fine. You're all grown up, and you're super-successful, but I'm forever your proud uncle. And," he raised a finger for emphasis, "I will keep the boys reference for when we're alone."

He laughed, and with an arm draped over each of their shoulders, Kosta led them past the open doors to the restaurant on to the terrace overlooking the sea. "I don't look like a jolly anything. I'm still as good-looking as the day I went into the army. You're just jealous of my genes."

Justin couldn't help but smile. Kosta was as handsome as they came, and he had no qualms about reminding them. "Okay. You look like an older and rugged Thomas Magnum."

"Better," Kosta said, squeezing Justin's shoulder in approval.

"And why would I be jealous? I share in those good genes," Paul added, puffing out his chest and standing taller, with a huge grin on his face.

"*Nai, nai*," Kosta agreed. "But just like wine, they get better with time, my boy. I have some time on you."

They all laughed, and Justin felt the relief roll off Paul's shoulders at seeing his uncle joking again. He gave him a quick nod and mouthed a silent "much better," before returning his attention to the older Lallas man. He flattened his palm over his abdomen and let out an exaggerated groan.

"Are you going to feed us or what?"

"Of course. I asked Katerina to have your favorites ready," Kosta said, stopping by the open kitchen and pointing to the stuffed tomatoes and stewed green beans behind the glass display. "*Gemista* for Paul—only tomatoes, no peppers. *Fasolakia* for you, my boy. But the beans would be much better if you added a few pieces of veal to your dish. I don't know how a tall man like you lives on vegetables."

"I'm not a vegan. I eat fish and dairy," Justin said, chuckling when he recognized the old conversation. The man never gave up. He lectured Justin on the virtues of red meat before every meal they shared.

"Your man needs meat, red meat, to be virile," Kosta said to Paul, pinching his index finger, middle finger, and thumb together, and shaking his hand before turning back to Justin and bringing that same index finger to his temple. "You will remember that when you need more strength to make babies one day. Or," he raised a thick brow and leaned his head toward Paul, "are you going to let this guy do all the work for you?"

More laughter, and Paul cleared his throat. "*Theo*, don't worry about babies. We're not thinking about making babies. We like things the way they are. Nothing tying us down, no one but ourselves to worry about, and our time is our own."

"When you turn thirty-five—"

"That's a couple years away," Justin interrupted.

"Whatever." Kosta feigned disgust and shook his head. "There is no reasoning with the two of you. Maybe because you don't have a reason to be reasonable. But you remember my words, when the time is right, you will not think about all those silly things you're saying today. You are family men. You will want children. I'm not a scientist, so you will need to find some modern way to make that happen." He led them away from the display and past Katerina's potted herbs. "Let's have a drink and some lunch to get this visit started properly."

The said visit kept throwing curveballs at them. Justin had no idea why Kosta was on a baby binge, but he did agree with the family men statement. He could see bringing a little child into their life one day. They'd be great dads. So much love to give, and so many children that needed a good home. He knew it wasn't the right time, but he'd look into the adoption process and everything required in the future.

Paul seemed oblivious to the child/baby conversation though. He was back to the original purpose of their trip.

"You know this is more than a typical visit," Paul said, clearly hesitant to ruin the good mood his uncle was in, but not willing to put off the inevitable.

"First, we eat," Kosta said, stopping at a table and pulling out the wooden chairs on either side. "Then, you get settled in your suite. Then, we'll talk business. I promise."

Justin grinned. *He promised.* That was where Paul had gotten the phrase. They always promised when something was important. And they always delivered.

"Okay," Paul said, the little twitch at his temple giving away how difficult it was for him to refrain from launching into a full argument on the topic. "But remember that I'd like to review a few things with you before you meet the representative from Luxury Homes Away From Home."

They sat and dropped the business talk while they ate the specially prepared meals. It wasn't until the watermelon was on the table that the conversation returned to the sale of the resort. Feeling slightly out of place for the first time in Kosta's company, Justin only half listened as Paul tried to convince his uncle things would get easier if only he allowed new measures. Since Justin wasn't blood, he didn't think he had a legitimate say, so he abstained from commenting.

"I'll computerize as much of the operations as possible, and I'll set up ways to help on the overall management from the States," Paul explained. "You'll have more time for yourself and the hotel will remain…"

"It doesn't work like that, my boy. The resort operates just fine," Kosta insisted. "Everything runs well, and I have more help than I really need. But with your aunt gone, the joy of this place is also gone. It's not a matter of profits."

"It's too soon for you to make any decisions," Paul insisted. "It's only been a few months, and understandably, the pain is very real and still raw. I can't even imagine what you're feeling with losing her. But I do know that *Thea* wouldn't want you to change your whole life and stop living your dream."

"It was *our* dream, not my dream. I bought this place and made it what it is today because of your aunt."

All true. Justin had heard the stories of how they'd started with the Sirens' building and a small café. They'd built up slowly, adding a villa or two each year, and putting in a lot of the physical labor themselves during the long winters. And from the end result, Kosta's construction background and meticulous planning was obvious.

The older man pressed his fist to his chest. "It's not the same without her."

Justin motioned for a time-out and looked between the men. "Kosta, no one disputes the fact that Vaso held the heartbeat of this place in her hands. We all miss her, and we can't even begin to imagine how much you miss her. I think Paul is concerned that it may be too soon to make such a drastic and permanent decision. If you sell to Luxury Homes Away From Home, this place, and all it means, will be in the past. You can't ever get it back."

With a look of utter despair crossing his face, Kosta shook his head. "I know, my boy. I know. I simply can't do it without her." He pinched his fingers together and tapped them to the middle of his chest. "I do not want to do it without her."

"So it's not at all about needing the money?" Justin asked. Maybe he wasn't blood family, but he was a financial analyst and he did want to make sure Kosta, who he did consider family, was comfortable and secure.

"*Eh.*" Kosta shrugged and wiggled his hand in a so-so gesture. "*Etsi kai etsi.* The money is good. It will make things easier, but it's not the most important thing."

"Then give me some time to come up with an alternative," Paul interjected. "Instead of making me report to the Luxury executive, give me a few days to explore all avenues. Perhaps we'll decide on something that won't have us losing a part of our souls. I'll look at the operating plan, Justin can review the books, and there may be a different solution that will satisfy you."

"You take it," Kosta said.

Justin's breath caught and his chest grew tight. He stared at Kosta in disbelief.

Kosta's hands moved from his heart toward Paul. "I'm not joking. You run Vaso's Dream."

Warning lights flashed around him as he looked from one Lallas to the other. That would change their life for real. If Paul agreed, he'd have to spend summers on the island. More than the summers. "He can't. It's impossible."

Paul wouldn't, couldn't, consider it. They had a business to run, a life in New York, and they didn't need the complication of being separated for months at a time. But Paul wasn't objecting. He was rubbing his hand over his chin as if considering his uncle's proposition.

"You take the resort and do with it as you please," Kosta repeated.

The wind stilled and the atmosphere bloomed with stifling heat. Guests and servers faded into the background. Tension pulsed at his temples and pressure built in his ears. He didn't dare blink as he watched his partner's face for a hint of what he thought.

"We can't," Paul finally said, and Justin exhaled. "*City Wings* is doing well, but not that well. We're standing on our own, realizing a profit, but the cash flow just isn't there yet. There is no way we could match Luxury Homes Away From Home's offer."

Kosta held up his hand and pointed a finger. "I didn't ask you to match their offer. I said you can take it. If you send me a check for my monthly expenses, I'll be able to do what I need, and the resort will remain in the family. It's simple."

"Not that simple, *Theo*," Paul said, acknowledging the difficulties of the situation, but not completely negating the possibility of assuming control.

Justin mentally called for him to meet his gaze, but Paul didn't. He was lost in his thoughts, most likely searching for a way to leave their carefree life behind and commit to a job that would require more than their free time at best, and keep them apart at worst.

And, yes, regardless of the good memories or how much Paul loved it, the gorgeous vacation spot would become a job.

"Again, allow me to evaluate the management procedures, while Justin reviews the figures and compiles his reports. We'll sit and discuss it before anything needs to be signed."

Signed? That was just under a week away. Was Paul losing it? They couldn't possibly entertain the idea of changing their life overnight. It was insane.

"Good. We'll talk next Monday," Kosta agreed. "The representative is already here and doing her work, so I'm sure she'll need some clarification of what I've given her in the meantime. I've promised her you'll walk her through all the departments and details of our resort. You know, just in case you decide to let the place go."

"I don't think we should discuss options with Luxury Homes Away From Home," Paul said. "This possibility needs to remain between us."

"I know," Kosta said. "We don't discuss family business with corporations. I offer the resort to you because I know how much you love it." He turned and looked at Justin. "You love it here, too. It is a good place for a young family to grow a life together."

"Our permanent residence is in New York, Kosta," Justin said. "We don't intend to change that."

"*Nai*, my boy. I know that. Most of the young people do not live here all year." He twirled his finger in the air. He had clearly intended to say year-round. "The winters are harsh, and the island's infrastructure is not ideal for school-aged children. The families with kids spend only the summers here. They go back to Athens after The Feast of the Theotokos."

"The Virgin Mary," Paul said for Justin's benefit. "August fifteenth."

He nodded his understanding, but decided to redirect the conversation. "You asked us to present Vaso's Dream in a positive light. We should have no problem with doing just that since the resort has made numerous Top Ten Island Destination lists the past few seasons."

"All that is left is to verify a healthy bottom line." Justin knew that to be the case. It would be easy for the Luxury executive to appreciate the balance sheets.

"We have that," Kosta said.

"I know," Justin replied. "It's a matter of providing proof to the rep."

"We've always kept excellent records, but even more so now with all the new government audits and regulations." Kosta turned in his seat and scanned the other tables.

Justin followed his gaze, then stopped. She was here. Bethany was at Vaso's Dream.

Ridiculous as it was, Kosta flashed a charming smile and motioned Bethany over.

Chapter Five

"I know we agreed to eat and enjoy each other's company," Kosta said. "We were supposed to hold off on business till later, but we already broke that agreement. The representative checked in a little while before you got here. I've been speaking with her for weeks. She's a smart and sweet girl. When you meet her, you might decide it's okay to sell. You'll see." *Theo* Kosta pulled out a chair and waited for her to reach them.

Once again, Justin was speechless.

He blinked, unable to believe his eyes. Bethany had joined her father's team, and her father had obviously expanded his hotel business to timeshares. After all the talk about making a difference in establishing an eco-friendly world for future generations, Bethany was now peddling international luxury properties for her money-grubbing dad.

How had Justin missed it? Maybe because he didn't do his homework on the company, didn't even do a damn Google search. He was too concerned about his precious vacation, the limited time to let off steam, and justifiably, the stress it would cause Paul and Kosta.

"Not only is the girl smart and sweet, she's very pretty," Kosta added.

Actually, she was stunning, but she wasn't a girl. Dressed in a white linen sheath and a pair of sensible sandals, the material swayed in a sultry song as endless legs carried a perfectly sculpted body to them. She wasn't small, but she wasn't large. She was just right. Rounded hips, tight waist, lush chest, and a killer smile promised any man she chose ecstasy in her arms.

Paul's foot landed on Justin's shin, and Justin glanced at him. *She's the competition*, Paul mouthed. "And it's not polite to gawk," he added in a low voice.

Kosta's laughter filled the air. "Gawk." Apparently, he'd overheard and understood the word. "There's been a lot of that happening since Bethany arrived. She's a beautiful girl."

"She's not a girl," Justin repeated aloud. She was definitely beautiful. But she was all woman.

"Good afternoon, Mr. Lallas." All three men stood, waiting for her to take her seat. She smiled, but didn't greet Justin or Paul as he expected. Instead, she looked into Justin's eyes, pleading for silence.

"I'd like to introduce you to my nephew, Paul, and his partner, Justin," Kosta said. "The bo—Paul and Justin are here to help us with the presentation."

"Pleasure to meet you," Bethany said, extending her arm for a formal handshake.

What the hell? Why is she acting like she doesn't know us? Justin thought.

Pressure pounded in his head, and he wanted to shake the woman and wake her. He did not want to shake her hand in fucking greeting.

"Nice to meet you, Bethany. I'm Paul Lallas, your official source of information and resort tour guide." Obviously, Paul wasn't thrown like Justin was, and he accepted her outstretched hand. "Justin Bentley is our financial analyst. We're both pleased to meet you."

"Bethany Michaels, Associate Director of Property Acquisitions," she said, releasing Paul's hand and offering her own to Justin. "So glad you could make it over and take some work off of Mr. Lallas's plate. From our correspondence, I believe he enjoys taking care of his guests rather than dealing with paperwork."

Her gaze stayed on Justin, begging him to play along, as he closed his fingers around her trembling hand. Bethany was playing a game he didn't understand, but he wouldn't betray her and make her look bad or feel worse.

"On point," Justin said, searching for common ground and finding it in Kosta's preference to deal with his guests. "We'll provide you and your company with all the tedious information you need." He reluctantly released her hand, and moved behind her to guide her chair.

"Now that we all know each other," Kosta said. "No more Mr. Lallas. Call me Kosta. Okay, Bethany?"

"Okay."

"Well, *Bethany*, with the fancy title," Justin said, "has Vaso's Dream impressed you so far?"

Seemingly unaffected by his sarcastic tone, she raised her shoulders and spread her arms to indicate the colorful landscape and the endless view of the sea. "It's amazing. Heavenly," she said. "Everything and everyone is wonderful. I can't imagine a better place on earth to recoup and recharge from the burnout of daily life."

"I told you the girl is smart." Grinning, Kosta drummed his fingers on the table as if he had a point to prove.

"Thank you." She tapped a dainty finger on the older man's forearm and his face brightened with appreciation. "Your uncle has made my job easy. He's been a real pleasure to work with. Thank you, Mr. Lal—"

Kosta cocked his head and raised his brow.

"Thank you, Kosta," she finished.

"The patriarch of our family on this side of the Atlantic," Paul said.

"Not for long," Kosta said, clearing his throat. "After this summer season, I'm buying a place near my brother's and exploring America with him—that is when his work allows. It's a long overdue adventure for me and a much needed break for him. He works too hard. His wife is going to leave him if he doesn't slow down."

It was said in jest, but while Paul's dad did work a lot, he was a model patriarch. Nothing like Justin's dad had been. Paul's mom was an absolute doll. She doted on the family, and Justin as well. No complaints with the Lallas family, who was Main Street worthy and could star in the next family sitcom on a *Big Fat Greek Life*.

"You deserve anything you desire," Bethany said, giving Kosta an empathetic smile. "We all do."

And there it was.

She said it: anything you desire.

She flashed that brilliant smile, and issued what was probably a subconscious invitation to Justin and Paul with the twinkle in her eyes, effectively pulling Justin out of the verbal ping-pong match in his head.

What Justin desired was the opportunity to get Bethany back into his life. And while he wasn't certain why she'd pretended not to know him, he knew it pissed him off.

Contrary to his earlier warning about Bethany being the competition, Paul also appeared more than a little interested in her. The conversation eased on to the amazing scenery and the magical location. They didn't discuss business again. They ate sweet watermelon, paired with savory feta cheese, and discussed everything Vaso's Dream offered. Everything she'd begun to love about the place, and everything Paul was worried about losing.

When a reception attendant came for Kosta, and he left the table in order to assist the front desk, Justin confronted Bethany about the bogus introduction.

"Suddenly you don't know us?"

"What?"

"Bethany Michaels, Associate Director of Property Acquisitions. Pleasure to meet you." Justin mimicked her earlier presentation.

"You don't understand—"

"Understand what?" He fisted his hand, trying to calm the quick beating of his heart. His voice rose, proving he'd failed to control his emotions. "You're embarrassed to know us?"

"No," she said, worrying her lower lip as she always had when she was anxious.

"You avoided us on the ferry. Didn't meet us at the café. And now you fucking introduce yourself to me like we've never met? Me? I've known you for well over a decade. I've known your secrets, your dreams, your every fucking desire. Hell, I know your freaking food allergies, your cute-as-hell obsessive quirks, and every freckle sprinkled across your gorgeous body. But suddenly, you don't know me?"

"It's not like that," she insisted, lifting her chin and straightening her shoulders. "This has nothing to do with our personal relationship."

"Like fuck it doesn't." Justin smacked the wooden table, before bringing his hand to the back of his neck and massaging the stiffness. "Why would you do this, Bethy? Why? What is wrong with knowing us? Knowing me?"

"Nothing," she said, pushing back her chair and standing.

She placed both hands on the table and leaned down to speak to him in a low voice so as to not be overheard by other guests.

"But you really do not understand." She enunciated each word in a painfully slow manner. "I told you I was working. This is business. Business, Justin. My damn food allergies and childhood dreams have nothing to do with the success of this deal."

She gave Paul a quick nod, then grabbed her tote. "Leave the past out of it, and deal with today, Justin. This is fucking business."

He watched her strut off the terrace without even a look back. The pounding in his head rose to a painful level and he pressed a finger on each temple. The woman had the nerve to rant on him and then walk away. She was in the wrong. He wasn't. There was nothing wrong with knowing her. No shame in their past.

"She's right," Paul said, waving a hand in front of his face to get his attention. "You've met in different circumstances. You can't bring the past back."

"She can't walk away like that."

"She did," Paul said. "And if you want her in your life, you better find a way to fix the mess you just made."

* * *

Bethany's dream project had turned into a personal nightmare.

If her father ever found out who she'd been negotiating with and realized Justin's connection to the family, he'd accuse her of manipulating company resources. She closed the door to her room and leaned her back against it, grateful for the support of the strong structure.

A sob escaped her lips and she buried her face in her hands. She slid to the stone floor and pulled her knees to her chest. A good cry would relieve the heaviness in her chest. Tears she'd fought while walking the path to her room wet her cheeks.

She didn't know how long she sat there crying, but she did know the haze clouding her mind allowed her a strange kind of peace.

Consumed by the gray cloud, the sound of her cell phone singing that her sister was on the phone, barely registered in her mind. Wiping the back of her palm across her cheeks, she let it go to voice mail.

Sheridan called again and again. On the fourth call, she knew that Sheridan wasn't going to give up. She had no choice but to answer.

"You okay?" Bethany asked, clearing her throat and hoping Sheridan would miss the misery in her voice.

"The question is…are you okay?"

"What are you talking about?" Bethany pushed her palm on to her belly, trying to calm the nervousness that had settled there. She'd never been able to hide anything from her baby sister, but she couldn't imagine how Sheridan had learned so quickly about her predicament. Maybe Luxury Homes had learned as well?

"I've been stalking all your personal pages since the moment you left for Greece. Two days of post after post of gushing commentaries and incredible pictures, then there's only an eerie silence since last night. You haven't tweeted, posted, snapped, or shared anything, anywhere, since you left Athens."

Bethany blew out a relieved breath, tucking her feet beneath her and wiggling in place. Her sister had the intuition of a good witch, with the most enchanting social media skills to confirm her suspicions. And while Sheridan didn't know about Justin and Paul, didn't know they were on the island and were part of the Lallas property, she knew something big had rattled Bethany. Specifically, something had put a damper on her great adventure.

"It's not fair, Bethy. You blow up the net with posts, tease us with snippets of information, and make me sleep with my phone for more, then nothing—*nada*." Sheridan paused, and Bethany could hear her sipping on something. Most likely the sparkling mineral water she carried everywhere. "Does it suck that bad?"

"No," Bethany said. "It's gorgeous."

"Then what's the problem?" Sheridan asked.

She didn't know how to break the news without appearing pathetic. Sheridan had put her heart back together piece by piece after Justin; she'd been her lifeline, and she'd had a little more than some responsibility in the party girl image Bethany had worked to cultivate back then. Summing it up, Sheridan had taught her to hide her devastation and act like she didn't give a shit about the man.

"I saw him," Bethany said.

"Who?"

"Him."

Chapter Six

Okay, so maybe Bethany could use a lesson in tactful communication.

She rose from the floor, her phone still pressed to her ear, and walked to the small refrigerator. Opening it, she discovered a gift basket wrapped with a blue ribbon and loaded with local wines and cheeses. Pulling a chilled bottle of rosé from its place, she sighed in victory.

She rummaged through a draw of utensils in search of a bottle opener and after locating one, she moved to the table. It displayed even more welcome gifts: a loaf of bread and a bowl of assorted fruit made for a tasty centerpiece. As the resort's numerous reviews had indicated, Vaso's Dream's authentic hospitality put a smile on her face.

"Are you still there?" Sheridan asked, her patience waning.

"Give me a second," Bethany said. "I need a glass of wine to go with this talk."

"Should I pour a glass of wine?"

"What time is it there?"

"Almost eight in the morning," Sheridan replied.

"In that case, I'd say no. Warm up your coffee, or grab another mineral water, and get comfortable."

As her sister grumbled about being stuck with coffee while Bethany got to have wine, she studied the translucent rosé. After pulling the cork, she inhaled the sweet aroma of berries, and poured a healthy serving. Then she sat cross-legged on a chair and readied herself to share.

"Not too classy, but I poured enough for both of us."

"Good. Now talk. Who did you see? Who is there?"

Bethany took a long gulp of the chilled wine and swallowed. "Justin."

"Justin? J?"

It was more of a shriek than a question, and understandably so. Bethany held the phone away from her ear.

"Yup. J is here with his drop-dead gorgeous boyfriend. A boyfriend he's been with for years." She took another sip. The glass was only half full now. "I met them on the ferry ride over."

"Hold on. Back up. His boyfriend?" Sheridan asked, but didn't wait for a reply. "Does he still like women? I mean is he into both? Just gay? You know Mykonos is one of the most popular gay vacation destinations in the world, right? J is gay? That's difficult to believe."

"Stop, Sher," Bethany said. "You can't put a label on Justin. J is who he is and he loves who he loves. That's J. Always has been. That's what I loved so much about him."

"No wonder my Bethany-Trouble alarm has been going off like all night," Sheridan said. "Are you okay?"

"Not really. It was really messed up." She closed her eyes and replayed their meetings. On the ferry, she was in shock and barely able to react, so she'd run. At the resort, she'd panicked and sprouted prickly quills of defense. "You'd think it would have been awkward, and it was, but what really threw me was that I actually liked feeling J's arms around me and his lips on my skin."

"Lips on your skin? You can't do that, Bethy. You can't."

"Not like that." Or was it? She'd gone all warm and tingly, and had wanted to melt into him.

"But, wait. It gets worse," she insisted, setting the stage for the real shocker. "I liked Paul, too. And if he wasn't with Justin, I could see myself giving him my number and waiting for him to call."

"What? Hold on. Seriously. I'm not following you. Is he gay? Bisexual?"

"Not a question I typically ask on first contact, so I'm not sure." Bethany rubbed her fingers over her forehead and massaged away the tension. "What I do know is that he's hot. There's something about him that just makes me melt."

"Bethy, do you hear yourself talking about giving Justin's boyfriend your number?"

"I take that back. I wouldn't give him my number and wait for him to call. I'd get his number and call him."

She heard her sister's shocked inhale and laughed, feeling better at her admission.

"Seriously. He's hot. If I met Paul under different circumstances, without J, I'd be all about jumping his bones. And I get the feeling he'd be good with it, too."

"I like it when you laugh," Sheridan admitted. "I like it even more when you're finally talking about jumping a drop-dead gorgeous man's bones again. Your choice of words, not mine. But do you think you may be in over your head with this?"

"Totally." Bethany poured a second glass of wine. Less this time. She had no right to thoughts of such a carnal nature with either one of them. "Actually, he did give me his number."

"Holy shit, sister. The only two men you've ever gushed over are hooked up and you've got their numbers. Bethany, listen to me." The concern and alarm in Sheridan's voice were impossible to miss. "They. Are. Committed. To each other."

"I know," she whispered, running her finger along the rim of the glass. "While I'm not sure if Paul has any interest in women, let's say for argument's sake he does . . . I'm not about to make any moves on Paul... or Justin. I don't go after taken men."

"Taken or not, you steer clear of that train wreck. You don't need heartache. Remember what happened last time you let yourself fall for J?"

"Of course I do. I'm not senile."

"I hope you didn't tell them where you're staying."

"I didn't, but—"

"At least you can hide in the resort, bury yourself in work, and avoid them," Sheridan said. "Get this deal signed, then get your ass on the first plane home. We'll hit the South Shore for a week, and Justin and Paul will be a distant memory. Real distant."

Bethany twisted her wrist and watched the delicious pink liquid swirl in the glass. "It's not that easy. There's more."

"Go on," Sheridan urged, more than a hint of hesitation in her tone.

Bethany considered the ludicrous coincidence of her dilemma and raised the wine to her lips. She took a long sip. "Maybe you should pour a glass of wine for yourself. This is more absurd than you could ever imagine."

"Just spill, sis. Now."

"You've read up on the resort acquisition, right?"

"Of course I have. Daddy is throwing every pretty project on my desk, hoping I'll sign on permanently. He thinks my personal aspirations are a passing phase," Sheridan said.

"Sugar, he doesn't get careers with a creative twist...other than that they lead down one path. The path of the starving artist."

"Excuses. But we're not talking about Dad," Sheridan said. "I can see that the Lallas property is a no-brainer. It's obvious why you want to get it."

"J's Paul is Paul Lallas." She didn't bother easing into the problem. Her sister knew the implication of the connection. She simply sucked down more wine. "Vaso's Dream is owned and operated by Paul's uncle."

"Fuuuuuck," Sheridan groaned. The sound of opening and closing of cupboard doors traveled through the silence of the phone. "I need something stronger than wine."

"There's a bottle of Jack in the side table, right behind the little monkey statue," Bethany offered. "Add some to your coffee."

"You know, if people could hear us, they'd think we're raging alcoholics."

"If we were raging alcoholics, I doubt a splash of Jack and a few glasses of wine would be enough."

"Who cares what people think," Sheridan said. "What are you going to do?"

"Did you pour the Jack yet? The story gets even more twisted."

Bethany waited for her sister to moan her response, indicating that not only had she poured the Tennessee Honey, but she was already drinking it.

"We're freaking sharing an infinity pool."

"You're rambling. What are you talking about?"

"One of those heavenly pools that looks like it overflows into the horizon." She stood and strolled to the large window, no glass pane, just blue shutters folded back against the white walls, so she could smell the sea in the cool breeze that swept over her wet cheeks. "They're staying in the suite next to mine."

The background noise became muffled. Either Sheridan had thrown the phone on the couch or had crushed it between her cheek and shoulder. Bethany waited, knowing that when her sister was on a mission, there was no way to call her off. It would be useless to try and get her attention. Sheridan was probably formulating a rescue plan. A plan she'd shoot down.

She didn't need rescuing.

Bethany sat on the cushioned window seat, mesmerized by the natural beauty before her. She leaned the side of her head against the blue window trim and waited, softly speaking into the phone as if she had no care in the world.

"The view is surreal." The intense blues of the sky and the sea contrast with the stark white of the island structures, pink and red of bougainvillea blooms sprinkled in the scenery. "You'd love it."

"What are you rambling about?" Sheridan asked.

"I was just saying how pretty it is here." She so wanted to swim in the pool, to reach her arm up, touch the sea, and lose track of time.

But she didn't dare. What if one of the guys showed? What if Justin demanded they speak? What if Paul sided with her instead of Justin?

Friction.

Tension.

Drama.

She unfolded the shutters, linked them together for privacy, and retreated to her seat at the table. Tapping the phone's screen, she placed the call on speaker and topped off her wine. She managed to munch on a corner of the bread and a few grapes from the fruit bowl before getting back to the conversation.

"I've got this," Sheridan said at last. "I'm booking a flight to Athens. I'll get there as soon as possible."

She hurriedly swallowed the sweetest grapes of her life. "No."

"Why not?" Sheridan asked. "You need me. You fell apart when Justin broke your heart. Honestly, sis, you have no defenses when it comes to him. And now there's that guy, Paul, yanking your chain. How are you going to get through this in one piece?"

"I will." She heard the words she spoke, but needed to repeat them for her own assurance. "I will...get through it just fine. I'm not an inexperienced kid any longer. I'm a true professional who knows how to separate business and personal relationships. I've already relegated them to a business-only relationship. I made certain Justin understood this is a strictly business week, and that he has no hold over me."

Her sister didn't respond, and the silence was deafening. Trepidation crawled over her skin and her stomach tightened so hard, she had to press her palm to her belly in order to relieve the pressure. She knew Sheridan didn't buy her declaration.

"I'm not going to give into the urge to see him again—not like that. Besides, there's that issue of his boyfriend."

"How did Justin react?"

"Not good. He was more than a little pissed that I pretended not to know him in front of Mr. Lallas. I explained that it was because of our circumstances. I had no choice," Bethany added. "Paul gets it better than Justin. He agreed that this week is about business."

"Paul agreed with you?" Sheridan asked.

"Of course. He seems reasonable, and he knows how to separate business from pleasure. I get the impression that he's not a pushover or a go-with-the-flow-just-because kind of guy."

"Paul backed you over Justin?" Sheridan voice rose an octave.

"Yes. He speaks his mind. And it wasn't the first time he made Justin back off."

"Shit, sis. You're in big trouble," Sheridan said, her words laced into a long moaning sentence. "Fake an illness—bad summer flu—they're the worst. Tell Dad to send a replacement. Get home."

"I'm not running away because of a man," Bethany said, glancing at her suitcase.

She really should unpack and make it clear she wasn't going anywhere. She stood and walked over to her suitcase, before lifting it to the luggage rack. She unzipped it and threw back the cover.

"Hello…it's two men," Sheridan said.

"No. I'm staying right here and getting what I came for. I'm the one who found this place. I'm the one who's been speaking with Mr. Lallas for the past two months. And I absolutely adore Greece. I honestly believe that Luxury Homes will have a diamond in this property, and Dad will finally acknowledge my business savvy."

"No argument there. It's your heart I'm worried about."

"What heart?" Bethany found the white bikini Sheridan had given her for the trip and pulled it from the case. She held up the crocheted bottom and studied it. "I'm using my head for the deal and having a blast with the rest of me. Bethany Michaels, aka party girl, will be making appearances at off-property pool bars during off-work hours, and I'm going to have a carefree and amazing week."

"That's a fictional character you're talking about," Sheridan said. "I should know. I made her up. You may have fooled everyone else with that supposed wild streak, but I know you've been celibate for almost a year now. You're not going out to party."

"Well your girl is putting on her bikini and heading to the Enigma beach bar." She tossed the suit on to the bed, then pulled her dress over her head and lobbed it on to a shelf in the wardrobe closet.

"That's the wine talking," Sheridan insisted.

Yeah, the wine was talking. Bethany reached for the new Max Mara dress she'd carelessly tossed aside and carefully settled it on a hanger. There was no use in abusing her clothing to prove a point.

"But it's not just the wine. I've decided to let loose and have some fun."

"You're such a fake," Sheridan said. "You think that just because you hooked up with a few guys in the past century I can't see right through you?"

"What are you talking about? I'm a heartless bitch who has no problem enjoying a man and walking away in the morning," she lied.

"Right. Remember the Swede we met at Dana's Fourth of July party?" Sheridan asked, but didn't give her a chance to answer. "I saw him again at a Labor Day BBQ. He wanted to know where my friend, Leah, had been hiding. Then that guy from Stephen's Halloween party?"

"Yeah, Luke," Bethany said with a longing sigh. She remembered Luke well. Charming and extremely well-built, he had been wonderfully adventurous, making her rethink her one night only policy. "He had lots of talent."

"Right," Sheridan quipped. "Luke wanted to reconnect with the beautiful Mara."

Laughing, she almost choked on her wine. "So?"

"Listen, you geek, not being real with handsome men doesn't make you a cold-hearted bitch. It makes you a wimp."

Sure she had a thing for *Star Wars* characters, and maybe she did take the easy way out of explaining who she was, but she wasn't a wimp. She was a Jedi. Raising a pretend lightsaber, she slashed doubt in half and cut a doorway to opportunity. The geek in her couldn't help but giggle. She liked it.

Bethany laughed more, and felt relieved and much better than at the beginning of the conversation. And she almost had Sheridan convinced she could handle the fiasco when they disconnected. She smiled at her reflection in the mirror and gave herself a thumbs-up.

"I'm going to make this deal happen and have a good time doing it— right after I sleep off the wine."

Bethany dove on to the plush mattress, pulled a feather pillow against her body, and closed her eyes. But once again, the quiet didn't last.

* * *

"Bethany, are you in?"

She pulled a second pillow tight around her ears, choosing to ignore him.

"You know I can see you through these shutters," Justin said. "Come on, open the door and let me in. I come bearing a peace offering."

Just wonderful. He could see her, sprawled on the bed, still in her panties. "Turn your back to the door and give me a minute."

She glanced at the narrow opening between the shutters, and when she was sure he had turned away, she got up and pulled the dress she'd worn earlier off the hanger. Slipping it over her head, she walked across the room.

"What can I do for you, Justin?" she said, pulling on the heavy door.

He turned and offered her a frothy iced coffee. "Freddo cappuccino? Sweet and with plenty of extra milk."

"Thank you," she said, accepting the treat. "You didn't have to."

"I did. Actually, I had to have an excuse to knock on your door," he said, looking every bit as heart-stopping as he had earlier. The difference was the humility in his eyes. "I know I was off-base during lunch, but I didn't see a problem with our knowing each other. I still don't. However, I do see your point and accept it."

Holding the tall glass, she folded her arms across her chest and looked into his chocolate-colored eyes. The same loving and sincere man she'd known stared back at her, melting away any opposition she had to him. No hidden agenda. No ulterior motive. He was here to make things good between them, and she hated she could see that.

"I get it," he said, tipping her chin up with a finger when she tried to look away. "Your father will be his typical asshole self and give you a hard time about my relationship with Paul. Considering our past, and my relationship with Kosta's nephew, he'd give you a lot of shit and make you miserable. I'm sorry I added to the drama."

"It's not drama yet," Bethany said. "The drama is what I'm trying to avoid."

"I do get it. Seriously," he said, motioning for her to come out and join him at the little blue table poolside. "Can we talk?"

Taking a deep breath, she nodded. He'd come to apologize, something she knew he rarely did. Something he rarely needed to do. And, he'd remembered how she liked her coffee. She couldn't stay annoyed with him, but she wouldn't allow herself to be susceptible to his charm again.

"We can talk, but you need to accept that this is going to be a trying week for both of us. We need to get along, no matter our past." She pulled the door behind her and walked to the table, placing the iced coffee in the middle. "Can you do that, Justin?"

"I can do that. I will do that," he said, pulling over a chair for her to sit on.

She swore she could see hope in his handsome face. He actually looked happy about the situation. She sat, and he placed a hand on her shoulder.

"Now let's enjoy our coffee and cookies, and we'll be caught—

"Cookies?"

"Cookies," he said with a grin. After reaching into the large pocket of his cargo shorts, he retrieved a baggie with mountain-peak-shaped powdered sugar sweets.

"But not just any cookies." He unzipped the baggie and the delicious aroma of rose water and almonds filled the air. Leaning over her, he removed each cookie and placed it on the makeshift plate from the plastic bag. "*Amygdalota*. Think of an almond marzipan cookie, with a Mykonian twist."

"I love almonds."

"I know."

Chapter Seven

"I went through hell convincing the resort's baker to let me carry his precious *amygdalota* in a baggie, so we're going to eat every last crumb." Justin raised a fingertip covered in powdered sugar to his mouth and licked it. "They're a specialty on the island, and a treat in the afternoon."

"I can smell how good they are," she said.

He squatted beside her and brushed a sugar-coated thumb over her lips. "Taste."

It was intimate and familiar, and her need argued with her common sense, but he wasn't totally off base. Her pulse raced and excitement sizzled to her core. Heat flushed her cheeks, but she didn't pull back. She tasted, and he smiled.

"Don't look so scared, sweetheart. I promise that I won't ask anything of you you're uncomfortable with," Justin said, pressing his thumb to her mouth to keep her from objecting. "You've chosen your career and your father's ambitions for yourself, and I respect that. By us breaking up all those years ago, it's clear you don't want an intimate relationship with me. We cannot be lovers as we once were, and I respect that, too."

Pride battled want in her brain, and she was honestly thankful he wouldn't let her speak. She would probably blurt out the truth and sound pathetic, because as far as she remembered, she hadn't said anything about not wanting him. Yet, his assumption helped her save face. She'd take it.

"Before we were lovers, you were my best friend. When you wouldn't speak to me, I thought I'd lost you forever." He cupped the side of her face and stroked her cheek with gentle fingers. "I miss you terribly, Bethy. I miss my friend, my confidant, and I want to have you in my life again."

She missed him, too. She leaned into the assurance of his palm. "Do you really believe we can be friends after all that's happened?"

"I do."

"And what about Paul? Won't he mind?" Worried she'd find the answer in the strong set of his jaw, she let her gaze wander over his shoulder to the blue of the sea.

"No. Paul won't mind anything at all when it comes to you," Justin said in a contemplative tone. "Look at me, sweetheart." He moved his palm from her face, down her arm, and took her hand in his. "I have never lied to you, and I'm not going to start now. So, I will admit that we do have a very real problem."

The nervous flutter filled her belly again, and she tried pulling her hand back, but he held tight and squeezed.

"Look at me," he repeated.

She met his gaze and shook her head. She could lie to herself all she wanted, but the truth stared her in the face. He mattered to her. He mattered big.

"Okay," she whispered, wetting her lips and tasting the remnants of the sugar. His gaze dropped to her mouth, and for a second, she thought he was going to kiss her.

He didn't.

He cleared his throat and sat back on his chair, tugging her slightly forward as he kept her hand in both of his. Justin had never shied away from physical affection, so it wasn't a surprise when he fit their joined hands between his knees and rubbed his thumb over her wrist.

"I know this will be difficult, but it will only be difficult for the next week or so. Once the resort issue is settled, we'll be just fine. We'll get past this together."

"It can't happen if it makes problems for you and Paul. I'm not a homewrecker."

"Stop," Justin said, his dark gaze going darker with annoyance. "Don't ever think I would disrespect you in such a way. I would never ask you to compromise a tiny shred of your integrity or values."

Still holding her hand with his left, he reached for the coffee with his right and offered it to her. When she accepted it, and had taken a sip of the creamy concoction, he reached for his own drink.

"First, Paul is very open-minded. Second, I love him with no limits. He is my partner in every sense of the word, and I see myself spending my entire life with him." Justin's demeanor calmed, and the brightness in his eyes when he spoke of Paul put that love on display. "Third, he already knows everything about you and me."

"Everything?" Bethany interrupted, her cheeks heating at some of the memories of their intense lovemaking marathons. Embarrassment flamed at the remembrance of her admission to wanting to know what it would be like with two men. Two men exactly like Paul and Justin.

As if reading her thoughts, he chuckled and leaned in, brushing his lips over her forehead.

"Everything," he repeated. "And there is nothing to be bashful about. He gets it, and he really, really, really appreciates it. After you left us on the ferry, he was all into making that double-teamed fantasy of yours a reality."

"He knows?"

Justin shrugged, dismissing any concern. "Sweetheart, Paul and I have been together a long time. We share everything. A scenario like that fantasy is one of the biggest turn-ons for both of us. Why wouldn't we talk about it? Is there something wrong with three people sharing something so phenomenal?"

"No," she said in a whisper, excited at the scene playing out in her mind. "But—is Paul into—ah, I can't formulate it right."

"No worries," Justin said. "He was openly interested in making that fantasy real for all of us, but I explained it was not an option between us. There is too much of a past between us to entertain a temporary physical relationship."

"Why is that? Is he or is he not bisexual? Is it a one-time fantasy for him to be with a woman?"

"Paul has been with women, can appreciate women, and would absolutely please a woman." He reached for an almond peak and popped the whole thing in his mouth, giving her time to digest his words while he ate. "It simply cannot work between the three of us."

"Why not?" She hadn't meant to speak aloud. She covered her mouth the second the words were out and regretted her innate openness when she was with Justin. *Control,* she thought. *Keep your daydreams private.* "Scratch that. Just speaking to myself."

His intensely dark gaze swept over her, but thankfully he didn't respond immediately. He swallowed, took a deep breath, and reached for his coffee.

"Sweetheart, there is nothing temporary when it comes to you. You're an everything and forever kind of woman. Too precious. Too addicting. Too real."

Studying his body language, she could see he'd been just as surprised by her question as she'd been when she'd heard her own words. She wished she could take it back, but she'd put it out there and he wasn't the kind of man to ignore it. Maybe, just maybe, she could get what she truly wanted if she went about it carefully.

Since Paul was into it, and Justin and Bethany already knew how good it had been between them in the past, maybe they could make a casual relationship work? Maybe a fling for while they were on the island?

Sipping on her freddo, she considered how and if she should continue sharing. She was a mature woman. She had wants and desires. She didn't fall apart because sex didn't lead to a happily ever after. Instead, she'd learned to live in the moment. Why not?

"J, I've changed, grown, a lot in the past few years," she said, nibbling on the delicious cookie and choosing her words carefully. "There's nothing intimidating about a physical relationship. I'm a big girl now. In spite of this uptight professional appearance, I know how to enjoy my time off, and I do. I plan on enjoying every moment I have to myself in this gorgeous place. Don't go making assumptions you have no clue about."

Nodding, he stood and pulled his shirt over his head, exposing a perfectly sculpted chest. Her mouth went dry, and she swallowed at the reminder of how great it would feel to run her fingers over that sprinkling of dark curls. Time had been good to him. Really good.

"Go get your suit on," he said, "and we'll continue this heated conversation while we swim. Or we don't continue the conversation and just swim. Your choice."

Within five seconds, a decade disappeared. He flicked the button at his waist and let his shorts slip past his slender hips. He wore a bathing suit, but the outline of his impressive package wasn't lost in the simple blue material.

"Okay," she said, needing the distance to calm her own reaction. She stopped and turned back to face him. "Snapshot?"

"What?"

"Sheridan is worried. Want to let her know we're good," she said, sidling up next to him and holding her phone out.

He laughed and took it from her. "Pirates?"

"Pirates," she agreed, and smiled for the camera.

He took the snap, selected Sheridan's contact, and hit share. Before she'd managed to take her phone back, her sister's reply flashed on the screen.

WTF?

* * *

Tempted, but not fooled, Justin tore his attention from the beautiful woman and walked to the pool's edge.

He had to think with his head, not his cock, and watching those sweet curves for the few feet it had taken for her to disappear inside the door was difficult. Large pupils, flushed skin, and hard nipples all meant she was just as susceptible as he was, so he had to be the grownup and make sure their reunion was permanent. No matter how much he wanted her beneath him—again.

After diving into the cold water, he swam the length of the pool and willed common sense to return. While Bethany had spoken the words every man fantasized about, carnal ecstasy, with no commitment, he knew better. He knew her.

No sex. No ménage. No fantasy.

It didn't matter how perfect it would be for him to make love to the two people that mattered most in his life. The need to protect her from potential pain resurfaced and took priority. He found the resolve to stay strong.

Making a flip turn for the fifth lap, he glimpsed her approach in his peripheral vision and swam toward the dark-haired beauty in the crocheted bikini. "You okay?"

"Yeah," she replied, sitting on the edge of the pool.

He fit himself between her legs and placed a wet hand on her waist. "No matter what you think, Bethy, I won't gamble on you. You're too important to me. I want you around. And if having you as a best friend is how I ensure that, I'm going for it."

"Bethany, best friend to her ex-lover, who is now gay."

"You know I'm not gay. You know my heart and body are open. But to make us, the three of us, a sure thing, we can't involve the physical." He studied her face, saw the regret and relief in her eyes, and he knew he'd made the right decision. She'd be hurt if they had to end a relationship again. He'd be devastated as well. "No matter how our bodies react, we need to listen to our hearts. Nothing between us is casual."

"You're right," she said, smoothing a hand over his shoulder. "We need to keep it real and be friends…if possible."

"It's possible," Justin said, happy the sexual tension hadn't killed their sensibilities. "Do you want to be friends? To reconnect and be there for each other?"

"Yeah," she said. "I miss you, too. So no matter how, I want you back in my life. I'll trust you on this one."

She'd always trusted him, which was why he hadn't been able to understand why she'd reacted as she had when he'd written to her about her father's puppeteer attempt to control their lives. He'd been so angry with the bastard. But she wasn't her father. She was his Bethany.

"Okay. That's the end of that conversation," he said, unable to move away, regardless of his mind telling him that the lack of physical distance between them wasn't typical of friends. "We're not typical."

"What was that?" Bethy asked, bending down to bring her ear closer to his mouth.

Her scent clouded his mind and he closed his eyes to savor it in private. It was going to be the hardest thing he'd ever do to be just friends with her, but he was up to the challenge. Then with Herculean effort, he inched back into the water.

"There is something we need to discuss. Something that may cause us problems."

She placed her palms on his shoulders and pushed him farther. After sliding into the pool, she swam to the opposite side, and turned to smile back at him. "Spill."

"You want to buy the resort. Paul doesn't want Kosta to sell it."

"And you're stuck in the middle," she offered, her posture indicating her defensiveness had once again been activated.

"No. I'm not," he insisted, gliding close to her and refusing to allow her full retreat. "I'm just the numbers man. I was asked to review and prepare the financial presentation. I will do that and nothing else. Nothing will make me choose between your wants and Paul's. And I know, when this is over, you and Paul will find common ground. So I'm not going to get stuck anywhere. I'm with both of you, but I will not help either one prevail over the other."

"It's business," she said, then turned and crossed her forearms on the pool's edge, looking out at the sea. "What are your personal feelings?"

"I love this place," he said. "I want Kosta happy, and I don't want him making a decision he may regret. Even more, I do not want your father getting his paws on this wonderland. He'd taint it."

"I would be running it. Not Edward Michaels. I want this place."

Justin cupped her head and placed a kiss on her damp temple. "I'll have the reports ready for your review in two days."

"No more business talk between us?"

"None. Not my place," Justin said. "But sweetheart," he continued, his mouth still against her silky hair, "I'm not too proud to entice you with cookies and coffee every afternoon. And I'll even wake up early, have that first cup of coffee with you, and watch the sun rise."

"Since when do you wake up at the crack of dawn?"

"Since it means I get to spend more time with you," Justin said. "Paul is an early bird. Would you like it if he joined us?"

She smiled and nodded. "It would be nice to get to know him—outside of business hours of course."

"Good. One final warning," he said, holding up a finger. "I will not deny who you are to me. Not to Kosta or anyone else who happens to cross our paths."

Chapter Eight

Still annoyed. Still frustrated.

Paul had left his uncle on his own and had attempted to tame his irritation with physical labor. It had been a stupid idea, because it had also been years since his summer construction stints. Working out at the gym or playing a few games of handball every week simply hadn't prepared him for the Greek sun.

And the only things he'd gained from taking out his frustration on whitewashing the rooftop terrace in the midday heat were aches and pains.

He rolled his shoulders, wanting a shower and some muscle relief almost as much as he wanted to make his uncle understand he was making a mistake. The man belonged here. They belonged here. This spot of heaven on earth was theirs. No one should make life-altering decisions so soon after losing the love of his life. And *Thea* Vaso had been Kosta's one and only.

He opened the door to the suite and walked into the welcomed cool. "Justin?"

No reply. The sound of running water in the bathroom told him exactly where he'd find his man, and he immediately thought of a different way to expend his energy. He pulled off the sweat-dampened T-shirt and continued toward the shower, growing hard with the decision on the new way to release some steam.

Stepping into the large floor-to-ceiling tiled room, he was immediately rewarded. His body reacted with pleasure at the scene before him.

On the other side of the glass divider, a naked Justin stood beneath a steady stream of water. Eyes closed, head back, suds down the center of his back to the curve of his ass, he looked like a damn Greek statue on display for his pleasure.

"You're just what I need," Paul said. He kicked off his shoes, shucked his jeans, then rounded the glass partition. "Want company?"

"Always," Justin replied, attempting to turn and look at him. "I need to speak to you."

Paul placed his hands on Justin and kept him standing exactly as he wanted him. Fitting his erection along his tight, soap-sleek, and perfectly toned ass, he wrapped an arm around Justin's torso and skimmed a work-roughened palm down sculpted abs.

Either he wanted to talk about the office setup or his rendezvous with the beautiful Bethany. The talk could wait. He couldn't.

"I need you. Okay?"

Fuck did he need.

"Yeah," Justin groaned, guiding Paul's hand south. "More than okay."

"It's been a rough day. You can make it better," Paul admitted.

"I'll make it better," Justin replied. "You want it strong and quick, love? Or slow and long?"

Paul didn't reply. Justin would read his desire.

He wrapped his fingers around Justin's shaft, and he went fully erect with only a few strokes. Rounding his thumb over the smooth head, he moved down the thick length and tightened his grasp and pumped.

He brought his mouth to Justin's shoulder and bit as he ground himself along his ass, thrusting his hips in tandem to jacking off his lover. He set a punishing rhythm, feeling his climax build and his knees grow week. But when he felt Justin's balls draw up, he dropped his hand and pinned him up against the cold tile with his groin.

"Don't come," he commanded, moving his hips faster, and watching his cock slide up and down the sleek valley Justin's cheeks created. "*Gyrna.*"

The Greek word for 'turn' had become part of their sexual vocabulary. Somehow more guttural and wanton in a groan than the word turn, it seemed fitting.

"Give me room," Justin said.

Paul pressed him harder. "You make it happen."

Justin didn't hesitate. He turned and ground himself against Paul. Cock slid against cock, and Justin crushed his mouth to Paul's lips and took what Paul offered.

Control shifted, and Justin applied insistent pressure on Paul's shoulders until he succumbed and lowered to his knees as Justin required.

Trailing kisses along Justin's chest, past his sculpted abdomen, Paul sent up silent gratitude for Justin understanding his need. Knowing *him* so well. He was tired, overwhelmed, and needed to be in the passenger seat.

Justin had taken the wheel.

Fingers tangled in his hair, as Justin encouraged him to keep kissing and go lower. Paul did, and once at eye level with a glorious erection and the most perfect pair of balls he ever knew, he was in heaven. Like his cock, Justin's balls were large and heavy, and he leaned to the side and licked first one, then the other, until Justin pulled on his hair and thrust against his face.

He was so amazingly handsome.

Closing his hand around Justin's base, Paul leaned close, licking and sucking, while working his hand up and down. Justin's hips bucked and he tugged harder on his hair, directed his mouth where he wanted it, and pushed past his lips.

"Open wide and take me all," Justin said, cupping the back of Paul's head and holding him steady as he drove into him, swept over his tongue, and nudged at the back of his throat.

It was Justin's turn to set a brutal rhythm, and he did, allowing no mercy as he filled him.

"I told you I like you best on your knees, and I do."

Paul placed his hands behind Justin's thighs, relishing each thrust. He nodded, relaxing his throat to take him deeper, enjoying the way Justin used his mouth for his pleasure. Unrelenting, rough, hard, and quick, he didn't allow opportunity to think or react. Justin claimed him. Marked him. And all Paul could do was accommodate the man.

Justin pumped faster and groaned as his climax neared. He tugged on Paul's hair, and ordered him to stop sucking and stay open as he released himself, shooting warm and steady streams of oblivion and ecstasy down his throat.

When he was done, and Paul had swallowed every drop, Justin sat on the tile beside him and wrapped him in a comforting embrace. Holding him securely against his chest, he pressed his lips to the side of Paul's head. "I love you."

"I love you more," Paul replied. "Thank you."

"I'm also proud of you," Justin said. "You're handling everything so well and doing wonderfully. It'll all work out for the best."

Feeling Justin's arms around him and hearing his reassurance was the best anti-anxiety medicine Paul could ask for. He nodded, and turned his face up for a kiss.

"Not here," Justin said, his voice commanding and unyielding. "The lube is by the bed. Place some on your finger and apply it where you know you'll need it. Then squirt some in your palm and warm it there. Position yourself on the bed, on your knees, shoulders flat on the mattress, ass high in the air. Stay like that and wait for me."

Yeah, Justin knew what he needed, and he gave it to him. Making love to him for almost an hour, getting beneath him, taking him in his hand, his mouth, and bringing him to the edge and then pulling back, he cleared Paul's mind of everything except what he made him feel.

But Justin kept him suspended in desire, and didn't let him come down.

Paul throbbed with need. He pleaded for release, but instead of allowing him to come, Justin teased him more by lubing up his finger and preparing him to take him.

"Come on, Justin. I'm so fucking ready."

"Do something better with that mouth than talk," Justin growled and returned to stand at the side of the bed.

His knees ached, his back hurt, but he kept his rear up and available. With fingers stretching him and mouth occupied, the yearning within Paul grew and need kept him hovering in a heated haze of passion. Justin moved, disturbing the status quo, and Paul groaned in agony. He lifted to Justin's fingers, but they were gone.

"I'm here, Paul," Justin said. "I'm going to give you what you need now."

Justin spread Paul's knees farther apart. Paul felt more lube drip on to his skin, and then Justin entered him in one smooth thrust.

"That's it, Paul. Just feel. Let it all go and feel."

Justin curved over Paul's back and finally wrapped his strong fingers around Paul's need. Slow and steady, with patience and tenderness, Justin took them over the edge together, and with the volatile climax raking his body, Paul experienced the euphoric liberation he needed from the day's stress. He fell to the mattress, entangled in Justin's embrace, and let the welcomed relief lull him to a peaceful bliss.

"Sleep, love," Justin said.

"No. Give me a minute to catch my breath, then we'll talk."

"It can wait," Justin said, spooning Paul and pulling him tight against his chest.

From the pressure of his touch and the tone in his voice, Paul knew the talk had nothing to do with the office setup.

"Tell me what happened with Bethany."

"We worked it out," Justin said, smoothing his hand over Paul's hair and breathing against his ear. "We agreed to be friends, and will be such forever."

"That's great. I'm looking forward to getting to know her once this bullshit is all behind us." Paul hugged Justin's hand against his chest.

"Paul, she's in our life for good."

"I know, babe. I expected as much. I know how much she means to you, so I'm happy you made up. You'll make special memories together this week."

"Yes. We will," Justin said, landing a tender kiss on Paul's neck. "Now go to sleep, love. We're picking her up for dinner in two hours."

Chapter Nine

Justin pulled his phone from his pocket and checked the screen for the time. "We have fifteen minutes. Mind getting a move on?"

Paul spit mouthwash into the sink, then met Justin's gaze in the mirror. The few hours Paul had spent in the Greek sun had already taken effect. By the end of the week, his brown hair would be highlighted with blond, and his sculpted abs and golden tan would rival any Hollywood leading man's beach body.

And in order to enjoy their time in Greece, Justin had to find a way to get him past the turmoil with the resort and settle his unease. The sale was beyond his control, and in all the years Justin had known Paul, rarely was anything not in his control.

"I'm ready." Justin buttoned his white linen shirt and smoothed it over his chest. "Whereas you're still naked."

Paul wiped a towel over his face and turned toward him with a dismissive shrug. He leaned his butt on the marble countertop and folded his arms across his chest. "Babe, I'm tired. I have a really long day tomorrow. Go on ahead without me."

"Hell no. You're not playing it like that."

Justin needed Paul and Bethany together, interacting and getting to know each other. Maybe he was being self-centered in pushing Paul when he was so preoccupied, but he truly felt it would do him good to get out. And, he wasn't going to settle for two independent relationships. Paul and Bethany had to connect.

"You said you could handle this new relationship. You're supposed to be able to separate business and pleasure. Separate. Then dress. I'll meet you next door in a few."

Justin strolled out of the bathroom, and five seconds later out the door. Walking away was all he could do to keep his own anxiety from messing with Paul. He glanced at the dark window next door and wondered how Bethy was handling it all. He so badly wanted them to get along. They were the two most important people in his life.

Having a few minutes before they were supposed to meet, he made his way through the moonlit grounds to the hotel bar and was met by a gorgeous Bethany, in a sexy as all hell light blue sundress.

No. He couldn't think of her as sexy or gorgeous. Fuck no. She was only a friend.

"You look very pretty tonight," he said.

"Hi," she said, patting the seat next to hers. "Christo is pouring me some ouzo. Want one?"

"Christo?" Justin raised a brow at the known womanizer, then situated himself between Bethany and the bar. No need for Christo to enjoy the view and get any funky ideas about her. "Liquid courage from Paul's cousin, the island's lothario?"

"The Island Lothario?" She winked at Christo and raised her shoulders. "Impressive title. Well this lecherous and handsome man is treating me well and very professionally. No complaints to the management." Lifting the ouzo, she smiled. "Cheers."

The ultra-powerful shot disappeared in a single gulp.

"*Yia mas*," Christo called.

"Don't you have work or something?" Justin motioned toward a new couple that had arrived, but Christo didn't leave. He chuckled and pretended to wash glasses while remaining within earshot. Justin didn't care what the other man overheard; neither did he worry about Paul's cousin misunderstanding, so he turned his full attention to Bethany.

Being complete and honest friends was hard. He didn't really want to know she considered other men handsome, and he didn't like anyone flirting so brazenly with her and her liking it.

And she didn't need to drink ouzo for courage. She was going to be with him, so he'd be her courage. That was their deal. Had always been their deal. But when he turned back to reassure her, he had to force himself to breathe. She was tracing her tongue over her full lips and smiling at the taste of the ouzo.

He wanted to taste those lips.

"Best taste ever," he said, groaning as she turned those lips up in a sultry smile.

"Want some?"

He did. He really did. But, no.

If he got one tiny little taste of her, he'd pull her back to his room, force Paul to kiss her, and assure that they were both equally addicted to her taste and both in agreement about tearing up their temporary agreement. Because that's what she was…pure and simple addiction. So addictive he'd fallen for her all over when he'd seen her on the ferry.

"Nah," he said.

"Yeah, it's a little hard to stomach," she admitted, placing her hand on his shoulder for what he was sure was balance as she sat back down on the stool. "The first shot really burned. This one went down easy."

"You won't feel the third at all," Christo said.

"She is not having a third," Justin said, waving him off.

Bethany laughed and smoothed her hand down his chest. "I'm fine, J. This tastes like licorice, and you know I adore my Good & Plenty. Plus, I wanted some luck for tonight."

"And from the sound of it, she'll need it." Christo raised the bottle, but didn't have a chance to pour again.

Justin grabbed the neck and with a growl pushed it away.

With an amused grin, Christo shrugged. "That's telling."

"She doesn't need any luck. I got her. Go away," Justin said, leaving no room for the other man to argue. "Bethy, this stuff sneaks up on you. The first shot burns. The second and third go down smooth. The fourth makes you forget. Trust me. Ouzo on an empty stomach is not an option."

"I'm safe with my new BFFs."

He let out a long, slow breath. He wasn't worried about her safety, because he and Paul had agreed that no matter how attracted they were to her, no matter how they might want her, or how their bodies reacted, they were going to keep the relationship platonic.

But if she lost her inhibitions, would they be safe?

"You're right. *You're* totally safe, Bethy."

After reaching for a bowl of bar nuts, he popped a few in his mouth, then offered some to Bethany. Thankfully she accepted.

"So how are you doing with the jet lag?" Pulling the stool behind him, he sat and went for casual. It was safer that way.

"I'm good," she said, sucking on a salty almond, before biting down on it. "It was a little difficult the first days in Athens, but I think I'm over it. You?"

"Coming over doesn't bother me. I can nap in the afternoons." He raised a finger and called for Christo to return. "No real Greek goes out for dinner before ten, so it's like an early breakfast for us Americans."

Greece was seven hours ahead of New York. Every night was a late night party.

"Almost." Agreeing, she laughed and chewed on another almond. "Yeah, I see what you mean by the ouzo sneaking up on you. I'm feeling it all of a sudden."

"Want to have a snack on the terrace before we go? I'll text Paul to meet us there," Justin suggested.

"Fine" she said, lowering her feet to the ground. "Let's get something to soak up this booze, J. Don't want to be tipsy getting to know Paul and make you look bad."

"That can never happen." He stood and offered her the crook of his arm. Telling Christo to put it on Paul's tab, which was non-existent because they were family, he visually communicated Bethany's off-limits status.

Loud laughter was Christo's response.

"Seriously, Christo. *Ochi*," Justin said.

"*Ochi*," she repeated, threading her hand through his arm.

"*Ochi* means no," he explained, placing his hand at the small of her back and leading her away. "Christos is a nice guy, but he gets carried away with beautiful women. I want him to know he can't mess with you."

"Why not? I may not mind him messing with me. Have you seen him? He's gorgeous."

He shrugged off the sensation of red ants marching up his spine, and refused to answer her. "I mind."

Chapter Ten

It had been a while since anyone other than Sheridan had expressed such a highhanded minding of Bethany's personal business. Instead of being annoyed at Justin, she liked it.

She knew he cared, sensed how much he still wanted her, and that made her feel just a little bit guilty, because she also knew he was in a committed relationship. While she respected his position, she was having a difficult time adjusting to their new friend status. Tugging on his arm, she urged him to stop walking.

"J, you were right. I was looking for liquid courage."

It had been a running joke that alcohol had given them and their friends liquid courage, but once they'd gotten together, they'd had each other to lean on. No alcohol required. She no longer had him as her courage. Her relationship with him wasn't the same, and most definitely neither was her tolerance for alcohol.

She rarely drank hard liquor, and adding the earlier two glasses of wine to the equation, her stomach felt it and her courage wasn't much better.

"I'm more than a little nervous about tonight."

Justin traced his finger along her jaw and tucked her hair behind her ear. Her body responded to his intimate touch, but her mind fought and screamed for her to catalogue the caress in the "we're just friends" section. Unfortunately, she needed his support, craved his approval, and wasn't crafty enough to hide it. She'd need to trust him to do right by the three of them.

"What if he doesn't like me?"

"Impossible," Justin said immediately. "He already likes you." He caressed the side of her neck, trailing over her shoulder, and closed his hand in a comforting squeeze on her arm. "He likes you, sweetheart."

"What if he holds the fact that I'm your ex against me in the resort deal?"

"He's not petty like that. Paul adores you, knowing exactly who and what you are to me. As for the resort, he doesn't want it sold. Period. But if anyone has a chance of seeing eye to eye with him on Vaso's Dream, it's you."

"Why is that?" she asked, searching his handsome face for answers, but only seeing the cocky confidence that had originally attracted her to the man. J was holding out on her, and he thought it was for her own good.

"That's something the two of you will have to discover," Justin said, kissing the tip of her nose and confirming her suspicion. "Don't worry. We're going to have a great time tonight."

Resuming the short walk to the restaurant, he pulled out his phone and texted Paul. When the reply came, he squeezed her arm again. "He'll be here in a couple of minutes."

Countdown.

It worked or everything was screwed.

Those stupid butterflies fluttered in her stomach and she wasn't sure how she would make it the next five minutes until Paul arrived. Even more, she sure wasn't sure how she would make it once Paul had arrived.

Justin guided her on to the terrace.

"Table for three," he said, holding up three fingers. The waitress smiled and told him to simply pick one. "Thank you." But instead of leading her to a seat, he pointed out Katerina's prized herb garden. "Go ahead. Let those smelly things do their job and calm your nerves. I'll wait for you by the table."

"Herbs," she corrected. "But come with me."

She'd been wanting to check out the garden potted herbs since she'd first seen them, but she hadn't wanted to overstep the cook's hospitality and look as if she was being critical.

"I'd feel better with you there."

With Justin leading her to the pots, she didn't feel like she was intruding. He belonged to the resort. He wasn't judging or assessing Katerina's work.

She squatted, careful not to soil her dress, and touched herb after herb, releasing the variety of scents into the night air. She recognized the mint, basil, oregano, rosemary, and even some mini carnation flowers and many citronella plants in the garden. But the herbs were her favorites. Spicy, peppered, and even sweet, their intensity surprised her. She repeatedly inhaled and exhaled, as if meditating the stress away.

When she'd found her confidence, she rose and went up on her toes, and touched a kiss to his cheek. "Thank you."

"For what?" Justin asked. He was asking what someone who didn't know her would ask. Acting ignorant didn't let him off the hook.

"First. For knowing that I needed time to collect myself, and knowing that a few seconds with the herbs would do that for me." Then, just to make sure she hadn't misread him, she wrapped her arms around him and placed her head on his shoulder. It looked innocent, but her suspicions were immediately confirmed.

He held her close, very close, against his hard body. And it was impossible to miss that there was a lot of hardness.

She affected him every bit as much as he affected her. "Second. Thank you for giving us both a chance to regroup. You needed quiet time as much as I did. But you sacrificed your own comfort for me, because I could see that time apart from me is what you truly need."

"I do not," he said. "Why would you even say that?"

"Whether you want to admit it or not, we have a second problem. A huge problem." She pressed her belly up against his hard length and looked him straight in the eyes. "I don't know how this is going to work, and I'm scared out of my mind that we're playing with fire and are going to get hurt. We need to figure out how to deal with the chemistry between us. If we don't, this friendship stuff is doomed."

"It'll work," he said, releasing her and taking a step back. "Our bodies still remember, so that's not going to stop overnight. But we're not kids any more. We will make it work. And fuck it, Bethy. Of course I'm going to get excited when I see you looking so gorgeous and sexy. I'm a man."

"A man who is committed to another man," she pointed out.

"Sweetheart, you don't get it." He rubbed his chin, frustration evident in his handsome face. "No matter how Paul or I feel, we're never going to risk your comfort and protection. I've discussed it with Paul. We're putting our wants aside and doing what is right. Nobody will get hurt. We'd never hurt you."

She had no idea what he was talking about, but she thought it best to save her questions for a different time. Just a few hours ago, she didn't even like him. Now she was concerned about making this friendship work.

"And don't even think that I'm about to let you bail on me," he continued. "You're not disappearing again. You're going to find a way to deal with these kinds of physical reactions." he took her hand and placed her palm on his erection, "and so am I. So get over it. This conversation is now done."

This was the second conversation he'd declared done. They'd need to have a talk about him being so demanding...when he was in a more receptive mood.

"Good thing you're facing away from the terrace." She pulled her hand away and shook off the scorching heat of feeling him pressed against it. "You don't need to be so blatantly honest, Justin. I don't know how to handle this."

"Then don't," he said. "Just accept it. It will work out."

"Fine," Bethany said. "I'm letting you take the lead on this one because I'm totally lost."

"I'll take care of it. Promise," he said. "Take a few more minutes and check out the herbs while I order us a snack. Everything will be okay."

She took more time than needed touching the fragrant leaves. When she thought he'd had enough time to calm down, she headed to their table. They'd make it work. He was right. They weren't kids, but mature people who could separate sexual and platonic relations, just as much as they could separate personal and business relationships. Plus, they had been friends for a long time before they had been lovers.

The server approached with the bread as Justin rose and held out her chair for her as if nothing monumental had happened a few minutes earlier. Justin asked for a serving of spicy cheese dip and some cucumber slices.

"You'll love the *kopanisti*. Creamy and with just the perfect amount of heat."

"Awesome," she said, twirling a sprig of fresh basil. Then she smiled big and waved, relieved to see Paul's uncle. "Just awesome. The man has perfect timing. Now you have to behave."

Justin chuckled. "Everything is awesome when you're around."

Kosta came over, leaned down, and kissed each of her cheeks before he acknowledged Justin with a pat on the back and a request for him to scoot a chair over closer to Bethany.

"Glad you kids are getting to know each other," he said, raising his hand and indicating for the server to return with some wine. "I knew you'd be a good fit and become...how do I say..." He interlinked his fingers in demonstration. "Ah. I know...tight fast."

"Actually," Justin started, but Bethany held up her hand for him to stop.

"Actually, I owe you an apology, Kosta." She moved her hand to her heart, more to regulate her breathing than to show sincerity. "I'm very sorry. I lied to you earlier about knowing Justin and Paul. We'd met prior to you introducing us. Much earlier where Justin is concerned. Paul and I met on the ferry ride this morning." ·

Kosta looked from Bethany to Justin, but didn't ask what he was undoubtedly thinking. However, his gaze did ask.

Why?

Those Greeks. So expressive, they held full conversations with their eyes.

"Justin and I grew up together. We've known each other since sixth grade," Bethany confessed.

Her free hand reached for the small carafe of wine the waiter brought, and she moved it closer to the men, indicating she didn't want any. Justin set it before Kosta, and then covered her hand with his, relaying encouragement for her to continue.

"We were inseparable during high school, but we grew apart during college." Grew apart was bordering on a new lie, but she didn't elaborate.

"Then why the secrets?" Kosta asked.

"Her father is a bit of an asshole," Justin said.

"Justin!"

"It's true, sweetheart," Justin said, obviously putting the issue behind them once and for all. "While he is a brilliant businessman, Edward Michaels is very Bethany and her sister, Sheridan. He has very specific expectations and ambitions for his daughters, and he is sometimes difficult to deal with when it's about them. Demanding. Off-putting. An elitist asshole."

"There is nothing wrong with a father wanting wonderful things for his children," Kosta said. "I may not be a father, but I'm an uncle who wants nothing but the best for my brothers' children. I can understand that."

"So can I," Justin said. "But Michaels is very judgmental—"

"That's just part of it," she said. "You see, Vaso's Dream is my dream as well. I want the resort in the company portfolio. Acquiring this beautiful resort was my idea, not my dad's. From the first day I discovered this place, I fell in love with it." She took a deep breath and worked to keep her voice calm and steady. "This trip is a business trip. I'm here in a business capacity, and I didn't want to make it personal. I was worried my dad would think I used my past relationship with Justin as a bargaining chip if he learned about Paul and Justin being involved in any way."

"That's ridiculous," Kosta said, waving a dismissive hand. "We've been speaking for months. You and me. You just met Paul this morning. You said you haven't seen Justin in what …at least six years?"

"October will be nine," she corrected, scraped her lower lip in a nervous habit, but immediately made herself stop.

"It's okay. We're straight now," Justin said, clearly not willing to allow the evening to go down the drain. "Kosta knows all about overbearing fathers. The island is full of them."

"I do," Kosta agreed. He pretended to look out at the water, but the man managed to see Justin still her hand beneath his, and it seemed like he'd nodded in approval when Justin smoothed his thumb over her knuckles to reassure her. "Enough said. It just proves that I was right."

Kosta poured a tall glass of water for Bethany and two short glasses of wine. He offered one to Justin and took one for himself as if he had no care in the world.

"Right about what?" Justin asked.

"My feelings about our girl. I knew you three would get along well. Be there for each other. That's all."

He sipped on his wine, clearly attempting to hide a satisfied smile and pleased chuckle.

"This wonderful woman is a best friend for life," Justin said.

"That's a start," Kosta said under his breath, but not low enough so Justin wouldn't hear him. He spread *kopanisti* on a piece of bread and offered it to Bethany. Then he mumbled something in Greek and didn't bother to hide his laughter.

"I heard that," Paul said, walking up behind his uncle, clamping a hand on his shoulder, and winking at Bethany as he shook his head.

"Then get a move on," Kosta challenged.

Paul leaned down and looked his uncle in the eyes. *"Stamata, Theo."*

Chapter Eleven

Paul couldn't hear what they were discussing, but they really looked good together. He stopped at the terrace's entrance beside the jasmine, enjoying the view and indulging in the fantasy of having them both in his bed.

He'd allow the thought for one minute; then he'd be the supportive lover and friend he was expected to be.

Breathtaking, Bethany sat on the edge of her chair. Her leg moved in a nervous bounce and the rigid stance of her spine relayed that the conversation was a serious one. However it was the pink blush on her chest that added an alluring softness to the hard nipples outlined against the blue material of her dress that held his attention.

Damn fucking temptation...temptation he didn't want to refuse. His cock hadn't gotten the friends memo and pushed eagerly against the zipper of his jeans, but the voice in his head reminded him to protect her heart. He swiped a hand down his face, admitting he had the added responsibility of protecting Justin's heart. Whether Justin knew it or not, they were in for a bumpy ride.

Scraping a row of perfect white teeth over her lower lip, she glanced at Justin in a silent request for help. Damn. But something was wrong. Concern for her outweighed his sexual desire, and he walked on to the terrace, keeping his eyes on them as he weaved between the tables.

A touch from Justin soothed away her worry and brought back the business professional they'd encountered in the afternoon.

Paul slowed his step, confident in how easily Justin covered her hand and beamed his approval, stroking his thumb over the back of her palm the whole time she spoke to *Theo* Kosta. He wanted to watch their interaction. Learn.

Theo listened, appeared surprised, maybe even annoyed, but suddenly his features relaxed and he seemed to be enjoying himself.

Time was up. Nearing the trio, inappropriate thoughts of the beautiful Bethany in their bed effectively extinguished, he forced the friend vibes to the surface.

By keeping his distance, he was missing out on something good. And regardless of what that good was, he wanted to be a participant and not an observer.

"Stupid, stupid boys. If you don't wake up, she's going to be stolen from beneath your noses," his uncle said in Greek.

"I heard that," Paul said, squeezing his uncle's shoulder and earning an unapologetic response instructing him to act. He leaned down and looked the matchmaking man in the eyes.

"Stop," he replied in Greek.

He stretched across the table, and rubbed Justin's nape as their gazes met and he formally greeted the trio. Paul then walked to Bethany and kissed her cheeks, her sweet citrus perfume reminding his body of its carnal desires, but his mind thankfully reminding him of reality. Sometimes you can't have what you want, no matter how right you know it could be.

Resigning himself to the physical discomfort in his groin, he sat in the chair directly across from his man and next to the woman that belonged between them, although fate wouldn't allow her to be. He decided to redirect the conversation and act the proper host. "I hope you're saving room for dinner, because I'm starving. We're going to *Kalos Psaras*."

"Nice. The tavern lives up to its name of The Good Fisherman," his uncle said, spearing a piece of cucumber and eating it like it was the greatest delicacy on earth.

"Would you like to join us?" Bethany asked.

"I would like it very much, my dear, but unfortunately, I can't." Kosta smothered another piece of bread with the spicy spread and handed it to Bethany. "I've already had dinner," he said, with an exaggerated sigh. "Besides, the night is for the young. You kids go. Have fun, because tomorrow you have a lot of work to do."

"I know." Excitement colored her face, and the woman looked even prettier with added pink in her cheeks. "I'm so looking forward to the formal introduction. I'm itching to get the feel of the resort from the front desk, or as Christo keeps correcting me, reception," Bethany said. "He said to meet him at eight."

"Don't bother getting there before nine if you're supposed to meet Christo. He needs two cups of coffee to wake up. And if he said he'll see you at eight, it means nine," Paul said, touching her forearm and regretting the instinctive contact because the connection sizzled straight through him.

He'd meant to settle and reassure her; instead he'd thrown himself into a state of excitement. He had to stop touching her. His body's reactions were not easy to control.

Friends, friends, friends.

"No work tonight, though," Paul insisted. "We have a deal. We're focusing on your friends agreement."

"Thank you." She tapped her hand to her chest in a show of gratitude. "It means so much to me, to us," she said, gesturing toward Justin and including him in the heartfelt acknowledgement.

Paul read between the lines, and nodded, acknowledging her private thank you for giving the three of them a chance.

Then she gave him a wicked smile. "But tomorrow, tomorrow the gloves come off. I plan on making you see that we're the right choice for Vaso's Dream. Luxury Homes Away From Home will wow you, and you'll have no doubt, Paul. I promise."

That was his line. He was the only one who got to promise. Especially when it came to his resort.

He wasn't going down without a fight. The resort belonged in the family, not with a huge conglomerate.

"We'll see," he said in an indifferent tone. "But not tonight. Tonight we're friends. Okay?"

Obviously, the irony of the conversation wasn't lost on Justin, who grinned and pushed back his chair. He walked around to Paul, squeezed his shoulder in approval, and leaned down to place a kiss on Paul's neck. "We're ready to go when you are, love."

"I'm ready," Paul said, accepting the change in subject. "Hope you've left room."

"We have," Justin said. "Let's get this pretty lady to Little Venice for a taste of Greece." He held out his hand and waited for Bethany to take it.

Paul's thoughts moved from business antagonist to sexy temptation in three seconds flat.

He wasn't sure he could do it. A drop-dead-gorgeous business nemesis cozying up to his partner—and being polite and agreeable with him—was not something he was familiar with. Not to mention his body's reaction to her. Thinking of her with Justin, thinking of her with him, thinking of her between them. Fuck, he was in trouble.

She stood, and the flowing material of her sky blue halter dress played around her ankles, complete with a thigh high split up the right side. He adjusted the growing ache at his groin, hoping to disguise the evidence, before standing to join them.

"Paul, thank you." She surprised him with a quick hug, and his body stiffened further. "I can see why J loves you. You're not just a good-looking man; you're compassionate and wonderful. I'm really looking forward to tonight, and I'm glad we can be friends," she said, flashing a radiant smile, and accepting Justin's offered hand.

"Me, too," Paul replied, moving to his uncle and gently patting the older man's shoulder, when what he wanted to do was pull Bethany into his arms and hold her close. But what if he couldn't keep it all in perspective? Touching his uncle was safer. "We'll see you in the morning, *Theo*."

"Wait. Take my car," he offered. "It's roomier than your smart rental."

Paul and Justin both held out their hands, and Kosta laughed.

He looked at Justin. "You're willing to drive on our crazy streets?"

"I am, if I get to drive one of your vehicles." He turned to Bethany. "Kosta has a collection of the coolest cars. A wet dream on wheels."

"You're not driving," Paul said, pushing Justin's hand away and waiting for his uncle to drop the keys into his upturned palm. "You can't freaking drive to save your life. You suck at it. You prefer public transportation. Remember?"

"I'm with Paul on this one," Bethany said, pulling her hand from Justin's and stepping next to Paul. She touched his forearm in a show of unity. "I know what he's like when he drives."

"Drives slower than my *yiayia*," Paul said.

"Grandma," Justin translated.

"Scarier than his driving speed, I remember what it's like to be in the passenger seat when he makes a left turn." Her sweet laughter filled the air. Looking at Kosta, she raised a finger. "I vote you give the keys to Paul."

Paul smiled at the playful gleam in her eyes. She was going to be fun.

"Told you she's smart." Kosta laughed and dropped the keys into Paul's palm. "And your grandmother doesn't even have a driver's license."

"Case and point made." Unable to resist the easiness of her touch any longer, Paul wrapped his arm around her. "I got the girl, and I got the keys. You coming?"

"Whatever. I'm coming," Justin said, pretending to grumble. "I don't think it's nice that the two of you are ganging up against me, but I'm going to overlook that because I'm hungry."

Fuck me. This is going to be some sweet hell, Paul thought, caressing her hip like they'd all been together forever. And for that very reason Paul knew he had to tread more carefully than he'd originally planned.

Acknowledging that a friendship for Justin's sake wasn't the only motive in getting to know Bethany, he set a mental timeline and reviewed it continuously as Justin played tour guide on the drive into town.

One week to sign or not sign papers. Hopefully not.

Five days until her douchebag father arrived.

Twelve hours before spending a full day with her and explaining the intricacies of the resort.

Less than ten minutes of concentrating on the road, before he couldn't look away from her beautiful eyes, brown eyes that were as tempting as the dark chocolate he loved.

Resigned to a night of mental conflict, he parked and exited the car, managing to keep his distance from Bethany and Justin as they walked to the waterfront tavern.

Justin holding Bethany's hand was not the picture of friends reconnecting. Not by a long shot. Paul didn't miss how tight his or her fingers interweaved, nor how Justin stroked over the back of her hand, which rested so naturally in his, nor how obvious the connection was for everyone to see.

It was a connection of lovers. They had been lovers, were still in their hearts and would be once again. And what was most unsettling for Paul was that he liked the idea.

The end of summer flashed into his mental timeline. The fate of the resort would be settled by then. They wouldn't be under the spell of a magical island any longer. And he would be able to revisit the possibility of asking Justin to consider inviting Bethany into their bed with clarity.

Friends with benefits.

They'd need a crash course in FwB101 if the perpetual outline of Justin's erection was any evidence of how badly he wanted her, too. She leaned into him, welcomed his touch, and clearly enjoyed his kisses. And if it weren't for the expected decorum of their arrangement, Paul would have accepted the flare of her nostrils and widening of her pupils as the invitation—and interest toward him—they truly were. Bethany was an open book, and he was an exceptional reader.

The end of the summer it was. Without the business conflict, there would be no reason for him not to participate. Justin's need for the woman would be impossible to placate by then, and he would want to bring her into their bed. Plus, by then, she'd have grown comfortable enough with Paul to wholly trust him, mind and body.

Sating their needs, temporary or not, was the best way to ensure a friendship.

He knew it in his gut.

He just needed to give them time to realize the same.

Chapter Twelve

Another table for three. This time by the seawall, and looking up at the lighted windmills standing guard over the island. Surprisingly, Bethany didn't feel like the third wheel, but rather like she was a princess snug between two princes. The lights reflected on the water, music drifted in the air, and the world was just perfect.

She met Paul's gaze and raised her glass. "To new friends." She turned to her left and clinked her glass against Justin's. "And old, forever friends." Then she brought the chilled wine to her lips and sipped.

"To friendship." Justin tapped Paul's glass, and they raised their glasses together.

"To friendship," Paul echoed, his golden gaze growing heated.

While the men's words and actions were proper, the underlying chemistry set Bethany's body on fire.

She fanned her face with her hand and leaned back in her chair. Looking out at the water, she wondered how the hell this chaste arrangement was ever going to work. The sexual energy wrapped around her and smothered her senses more than the heady sweetness of the night blooming jasmine.

Being with Justin and Paul, on any level, made her skin flush and her mind cloud. She needed to get a grip on her hormones. Maybe find a sexy man—not one of them—and get laid.

She pasted on a big smile and accepted her fate: friendship with the only two men in the world that made her crazy enough to climb walls for an orgasm at their hands. But she wasn't going to cause them any problems. And she'd keep reminding herself until the guilt of her thoughts eased from her mind. They were just thoughts.

They wanted a platonic relationship. Friendship it was. Pure friendship. *Yeah, you keep telling yourself that*, she thought.

"I've had Greek salad with feta cheese, but this seems to be done up in a different way," she said, gesturing to the dish in the center of the cozy table and steering the conversation to a safe subject.

"That's not feta, but a special version of Mykonos's own white cheese. It's called *xinotiro*. It has a slightly creamier texture and is a bit tart, even sour, compared to Feta. They make it like the *kopanisti* you tasted earlier. The dish is called a *dako*," Justin said, surprising her since it had been Paul who had rattled off their order in Greek and appeared to be the food expert.

"Toasted whole-grain rusks are soaked in water to soften," Paul explained, moving a large spoon through the salad. "Then they're broken into pieces and topped with tomatoes, onions, the cheese, capers in this case, and local seasonings."

"It's drowned in olive oil," she added.

"Yup," Justin said. "The stuff is addicting. You'll crave it long after you get back to New York."

While Justin arranged a forkful of the *dako* and handed it to her, Paul scooped into the dish and heaped a serving on her plate. They worked together with such ease and efficiency, it made her mind drift back to the naughty fantasy she'd once whispered to Justin in the privacy of their bed.

She blinked to clear the vision, moved in her seat to shake the sensation, and redirected her thoughts, again, to the meal they were sharing.

She slipped the fork between her lips and savored the taste of the unique salad.

"This is *taramosalata*," Paul said, breaking a piece of the crusty bread and running it through a pink dip. "Think of a doctored version of caviar." He held it for her to take, and she gladly accepted it from his hands. Tasting the lemony fish spread, she sighed in contentment.

"Everything is full of flavor and just delicious," she said. It wasn't even fishy.

The waiter arrived, brings servings of golden calamari and tiny fried fish.

"*Aitherina*," Justin said, squeezing fresh lemon juice on the fish. "I called those tasty little suckers fish chips the first summer I spent here." He popped one in his mouth and chewed. "Yum."

"Eww. They still have heads and tails," she exclaimed, shaking her head and folding her hands in her lap.

"They're too small to debone. You eat them whole." Using his fingers, Paul picked one of the thinner fish, bit off the head, flipped it over to eat the tail, and then offered it to her.

"No," she said, leaning back from the table. "I'll pass."

"Give it a chance, Bethy." Paul's words rolled over her as he looked into her eyes and held the fish to her lips. "You'll like it."

Holy smokes. It didn't feel like he was talking about fish. He was speaking about them. She twisted her hands in her lap, wondering why she wanted to make him happy, and why it mattered so much to let him know she trusted him.

She swallowed her objection and parted her lips. He fit the fish between her teeth and tilted his head in approval. She chewed, pleasantly rewarded by the fresh and delectable taste of sea.

"It's good," she whispered.

"Yeah, I know," Paul said, smoothing his thumb over her lower lip and down her chin. "Want another?"

"Okay," she said, motioning for him to eat the head and tail before offering it to her again.

Strange as it was for a friend to feed her, his attention warmed her. She relaxed and listened as Justin and Paul recalled the last time they'd eaten at the restaurant. The water had been rough, and waves had sprayed over the sea wall. No one had sat at the first row of tables. But the weather hadn't stopped them from enjoying the appetizers and the fresh-off-the-boat fish, just as they were doing together.

"It seems like a lot of people's socializing is centered around meals or coffee breaks," she said.

"It is," Paul said. "Greeks make time for friends and slow down for meals. Sometimes dinner can last hours. So much is done at the table."

They ate family style, with Justin and Paul explaining the how and what of the best-tasting seafood and sides she'd ever had. No fillets. No neat plates of sectioned off food groups.

Horta, boiled greens, were piled high as the table's centerpiece. The calamari disappeared quickly, and the iridescent remnant of the oil on the white plate testified to its freshness. The grilled octopus cut with a fork and melted in her mouth. The crisply fried small local *barbouni*, the sweetest red mullet fish she'd ever had, was the biggest pain in the ass to debone. She waited—impatiently—as Paul meticulously cleaned it for her, but it was so worth the wait. And last, but not least, Justin's favorite side, French fries, sat amidst the table of seafood.

"*Koukla mou*, you want me to prep another *barbouni* for you?"

She was startled at Paul calling her his doll. She knew the meaning because Mr. Lallas had also referred to her the same way and she had

Google translated the term earlier. She pushed her plate forward. "I think I'm done. Totally stuffed."

The whole dining experience had been so strange, so comfortable, and definitely *not* a night out with a new friend.

Truth be told, she'd expected the comfort level to be easy with Justin. She trusted him, loved him, and knew him. And because of the comfort she knew she'd find in Justin, she'd feared things with Paul would be awkward.

Not so. Both men put her at ease, an ease that had her stomach doing somersaults.

The surprising feelings of comfort and belonging with Paul made her question her sanity. She wasn't just drawn to him. She was connected... linked. She wanted so much more of the man standing between her and the business acquisition she'd worked hardest for in her life.

"You don't need to be so nice to me," she said.

"You're easy to be nice to," Paul replied, expertly cleaning the last *barbouni* with his knife and fork.

Like a surgeon making an incision, he sliced through the crispy fish, cut off the head and tail, pushed away the rows of tiny bones at the top and bottom of the body, lifted the ribcage with his fork, and lastly removed the main skeleton. After checking for stray bones, he glanced up at her.

"You sure, *koukla mou?*"

"No, thank you. I'm good."

He moved half the fish on to Justin's plate, and Justin squeezed lemon over both of their now filleted fish. "Thanks, love."

"Seriously, you're making me comfortable, showing you care about me, and treating me like family. You don't need to do any of it. I'm not family."

"You are family," Justin said, his easygoing demeanor gone. "You're part of me, and that makes you part of Paul. He may not need to do any of the shit you're babbling about, but he does it because he cares. And we both want you in our life. Easy or not."

"J, a sincere and honest friendship is one thing, and under different circumstances it could have been easy. But it's not now. The rest of this week is going to be a bitch. Paul and I want the same thing."

"Don't fool yourself, *koukla mou.* This," Paul said, extending his arm and circling a pointed finger around the table, "thing between the three of us and what is happening here is what has you agitated. Not the rest of this week. The way you're feeling has nothing to do with the resort. It's this. It's real. And it will not go away."

"Paul," Justin said in a warning tone.

"Don't deny or candy-coat it, Justin. It is what it is." He looked from Bethany to Justin and back again. "It's not going away because you choose to ignore it."

Confused, because there was clearly a point she was missing, Bethany sucked in a breath and considered her words carefully. "Something is getting lost in this conversation. What I said was simple. You being nice won't make me change my position on the resort."

"I don't expect your position on the resort to change," Paul said, his amber-colored eyes growing dark and his Adam's apple moving. "I'm talking about this energy between us. It's here. We all feel it. We all want it. But we're denying it."

Still baffled, she rubbed her fingers against her temples. Did he want her out of their life, or was he talking about more than a friendship? The thought of the latter had crossed her mind, had even starred in her afternoon shower fantasy. But Paul didn't even know her. What if he didn't want to share Justin with her?

"I'm sorry. I'd never want to come between you and Justin," she whispered. "I didn't mean to imply that. We don't need to do this if you don't want to be friends."

"I want to be any kind of friends to make us all happy," Paul said, lowering his voice. "Baby, the more I get to know you, the more I like you. So much so. Don't think for a single minute you're doing anything wrong. You're perfect. We're the screwed up ones." He waved his hand between himself and Justin.

"Maybe it's screwed up, but it's the safest and surest way for us to be together," Justin said, not hesitating to take her hand.

"As long as it doesn't cause problems between you guys, I'm okay with it," she said, keeping how frustrating it would be on her hormones to herself.

"Paul and I are together on this. We want to be in your life, sweetheart."

She squeezed his hand. "Good. I like you there." Then she reached for Paul's hand and did the same. "I like you there, too. A lot."

"The feeling is more mutual than you could imagine," he said, lifting her hand to his lips and placing a kiss in the center of her palm. "I'm sorry. I didn't mean to imply it was you. Trust me, it's me. But I'll do what it takes to keep this good."

"I can take it. Let's clear the air, so we can move forward," she said. "Any other questions, clarifications, or anything? Let's not leave any skeletons in the closet."

Paul placed his fork on the table and crossed his arms over his chest. "I have one. We've been ignoring the elephant at the table, haven't addressed the past, and I agree we need to clear the air so we can move forward."

She didn't realize how hard she was squeezing her hands together until Justin nudged into the tight knot, pried her fingers apart, and took her left hand in his.

"And I'm not blaming you, but because of the way he automatically comes to your rescue, I need to ask," Paul said, indicating Justin's lap and their joined hands.

Justin shifted and leaned forward, looking as if he was about to explain, but Paul held up his hand, wanting to be heard.

"No, babe. It's not jealousy, and *I* don't have a problem with any of it," Paul said, his voice going softer as he swiped his palm down his face and rubbed his chin. "I don't understand why you broke up with such a great man, a man you clearly still have feelings for, and a man who still loves you. Why?"

Chapter Thirteen

Justin still loved her?

But he'd broken *her* heart. Bethany had been shattered, and she'd crawled into bed and hadn't been able to come out from beneath the covers for weeks.

Even after all that, she was sitting with him, as a friend, because she was a sucker for putting herself in the position to be hurt again. And considering she'd done exactly that, the night had taken a turn directly toward pain and disappointment.

"It wasn't like that," she said, trying unsuccessfully to retrieve her hand from Justin's hold.

"It was," Paul said, his gaze narrowing on her, and all the neighboring diners fading from her awareness. "I met him months after your breakup, and I saw what it had done to him to be thrown away because he didn't meet your daddy's socio-economic criteria."

Tears blurred her vision and the knot in her throat restricted her breathing, but Justin's warm hold grew stronger and she managed not to break down.

"It was a long time ago," Justin said, gripping her hand hard and gaining her attention. "We were kids. We're not any longer." He squeezed harder, making her look into his eyes and find fierce determination. "That relationship was doomed from the start, but we're not at the mercy of others any more. None of it's an issue for either of us. Okay?"

He was a bad liar, and she knew it was as much an issue for him as it was for her.

"We've agreed on something new," he said. "Something better."

In spite of suggesting they put things behind them, Justin hadn't defended her or explained the truth. The friendship card was because he believed it was the only way for them to be in each other's lives since he'd found someone else to love. Paul was an amazing man who had just proven he was willing to tackle the hard stuff for Justin's sake, but no one had ever compared to Justin for her. No one even came close.

"Our bond isn't one dimensional. We're woven into each other, heart and soul," Justin said, his dark gaze seeing past her shield. "The past doesn't negate our future, and our relationship will only get stronger. I'm willing to buck convention. Make it work. You're so worth it to me."

Justin's words went far to make her feel cherished and special, even if the circumstances of their so-called new relationship were peculiar. Then Paul's words register. Not the emotion or concern in his words. The actual meaning of the words.

"I didn't break up with him. Justin ended our relationship."

"I did not," Justin said. He released her hand and angled his seat away. "You know better than that."

"No, Justin. She doesn't," Paul said, moving closer to her and placing an arm around the back of her chair. With a finger on her chin, he turned her to look at him. "Did you read his emails?"

"No." What they were saying negated everything she'd known about the worst time of her life. He didn't end their relationship? Somehow, she managed to overcome the tremors raking her chest and breathe.

"Did you receive the package we sent you?"

"No," she whispered, unable to verbalize what she needed to know, but from the looks on their faces, both men knew.

"When you didn't reply to my calls or emails, I figured the best thing to do was give you time to accept my decision. I had no choice but to walk away from that scholarship."

"It was a full ride," she said. "It was a way for us to be together for four years. On our own. The way we'd wanted. The way we'd planned."

"There were conditions," Justin continued. "I had to do what I did. And when I did, I was confident you'd have agreed with me. I didn't think—"

"She *really* doesn't know," Paul repeated, rubbing his hand up and down her forearm. "Justin never walked away from you, *koukla*. He walked away from what your father thought should happen for you."

Pressing her fist in the center of her chest, she thought back to the very moment. Justin had dropped the bombshell on her with her father still in her dorm room. He'd said he couldn't do it. It wasn't fair to sign away their lives at such a young age. He was transferring and enrolling in a state university. She was being left behind. Alone.

"Your father was okay with me and you being together during undergrad," Justin said, meeting her gaze. "He wanted us together so nobody else would take advantage of his little girl. Right before I came to your room and told you I was leaving, I'd met with him, at his insistence, at the Union. At first, I figured it had to do with more overbearing guidance for his girl. But I was so naïve."

"It actually did," Paul said, caressing her shoulder. His voice was low and gentle. His touch strong and reassuring. With him at her side, she was confident she could listen to what was being said, no matter how much it hurt.

"I kept the contract he wanted me to sign. A fucking legal document put an expiration date on us. I mailed you a copy the following year," Justin said. "Paul was there. He was with me. I wasn't sure you would ever open the envelope, but I had to try."

"I never received a package from you," she said to Justin. "I deleted the voice mails and emails without listening to them or reading them. I was hurt and angry. I didn't want to ever see you again. I felt betrayed beyond belief."

"That makes sense," Paul said, the voice of reason. He cupped the side of her head and placed a kiss on her hair. "Listen to him, baby. He never betrayed you. Let him make it better."

She took a deep breath and closed her eyes, and for the first time in years, she believed she could be freed from the hurt of that betrayal.

"Right off the bat, your father promised me an internship for the first semester of my senior year. The internship would have been in the London office, and it was his way to initiate the beginning of the end for us," Justin explained. "I was supposed to return the final semester, start to distance myself and act like a dick to you by insisting we see other people, and finally call it off after I had secured a job with a company of your father's choosing. He would privately pay a year's salary as a signing bonus if I managed to convince you to continue with grad school before I called us off."

No. He couldn't have been so ruthless. Her father was opinionated and controlling, but he couldn't be so manipulative as to intentionally cause her pain.

"He said it was in your best interest, and if I cared about you, I'd agree," Justin said, the muscle ticking in his jaw the only sign of his distress. "I told him I didn't need his fucking money, and I would take care of my woman and my education on my own. That is why I couldn't sign away our lives. We didn't need to be rich, sweetheart. We needed to be us."

"I know," she said, wiping at the moisture on her cheeks. "And I didn't give you a chance to explain. I only heard you weren't going to be with me. I'm sorry."

"You don't need to apologize. I left that meeting with your father, and instead of coming straight to you, I went to my room and packed my bags. By the time I got to you, he was with you. Knowing how calculating he is, I assumed he'd told you about the internship and the job offer and was putting a spin on my response. I never thought you didn't know. I assumed that you knew. And instead of getting into a physical altercation with your father, I walked away, with every intention of discussing how you would also transfer with me once we were alone."

She wished he'd have explained then and there. She'd have left with him.

"I didn't want to make a decision about your education for you. He was still paying your bills. It had to be your choice to tell him to go fuck off and come with me, or to get your education, and then tell him to fuck off."

She sucked in a ragged breath, and bit down on her lip to keep it from trembling. She'd hated Justin for hurting her, but he hadn't meant to. And there was such a fine line between love and hate.

"We're okay now, *koukla mou*." Paul smoothed her hair and kissed the side of her head again. "You both know the truth, and the truth is what matters."

"That day changed my whole life," she said, pissed that the sniffles were audible and she had to hold her hand near her nose to cover them. "I lost my best friend, chose a different major than I truly wanted, and even transferred schools."

"I'm proud of you though," Justin said, leaning forward and insisting she listen. "You've done well for yourself, Bethy. Not only are you successful, but you're well respected in your field."

Justin pointed to Paul, who was looking at her with nothing but adoration and care. She didn't understand his complete acceptance, but she was grateful for it.

"Trust me." Justin brought his chair even closer to hers, and beneath the table, he fit his legs on either side of hers and placed his big hands on the sides of her knees. "Paul checked you out and scrutinized every deal you've ever made before we arrived. The only thing he didn't mention was your last name."

"You researched me?"

"Yes, he did. I did, too, this afternoon. And I wish I would have made the connection with Luxury Homes and done so earlier," Justin said. "But there's a reason for everything, Bethy. Always a reason." He wiped at the tears that wouldn't stop clouding her vision. "If I would have known it was you, I would have reached out to you. Then maybe you wouldn't have come. Maybe we wouldn't be together right now."

She shook her head. "I would have come."

"Don't cry then. No more tears." He stood and opened his arms to her. "The past is the past. It's behind us. Come here, Bethy."

It was with Paul's hand on her back that she managed to stand and move into Justin's embrace. Suddenly aware of the other diners, she hid her face in his chest.

* * *

She'd believed he'd walked away. Just left her. No wonder she hadn't wanted to speak with him. Justin did his best to soothe her and lay the conversation to rest. Tucking her trembling body against his, he motioned for Paul to settle up, and led her from the restaurant.

"Come on, sweetheart. We need some privacy."

She fell into step beside him, and he was able to shield her from the others as he guided her out into the quiet.

"I should have taken you with me and explained later," he said once they had crossed to the other side of the street and stood in the shadow of an overgrown bougainvillea. "I never thought to throw us away, and I'd never treat you in such a careless manner."

"That's why it hurt so much," she admitted, looking up at him. "But everything happens for a reason. That day happened for a reason." Throwing his words back at him, she smiled and leaned in to touch her lips to the underside of his jaw. "We are both where we're supposed to be."

As she spoke, she transformed from hurt to confident. Justin wanted her strong. He kept quiet.

"You're with Paul. And he loves you. You love him."

This time she waited for him to speak. He didn't want to hurt her, and she hadn't asked as much as stated.

"Very much."

"I can see why. He's good for you." She stepped away, steady on her feet, not needing him any longer, and back in control. "He's wonderful."

Justin wasn't willing to let her go. He placed a hand on her hip and held on. "Does my relationship with Paul mean you don't want me in your life?"

Shaking her head, she looked away and released her breath, before meeting his gaze again. "No, J. I want you in my life. I want to be in yours."

"Thank you," he said, lowering his head and touching his mouth to hers. "We'll make this work."

The signals in his mind crossed, and instead of moving away like a friend should, he moved closer.

She lifted her arms and ran her fingers through his hair, pressing her warm body against his, from thighs to chest, and moaning from deep inside her core when his erection pushed against her softness.

Inhaling sharply, her lips parted, and he felt her tongue wet them.

"Bethy?"

"Yeah?"

One. Just one taste, he thought. *Just a kiss.*

"Push me away, sweetheart."

"No," she whispered into his mouth.

And then he was kissing her, taking all she offered as he slipped past her lips, swept through her mouth, and asked for more with hungry nibbles as he grazed on the sweet offering.

One kiss wasn't enough.

He tangled his fingers in her hair and lifted it off her neck, angling her face to meet her gaze, but her eyes were closed as her tongue licked over her lower lip, and he lowered his head and took it into his mouth, unable to get enough of her. He held her tight, needing to get closer, and with one arm curved protectively around her back, he walked her backward until he pressed her against the wall, and she was stretched up on her toes. Lost in the sweetest little sounds she made, he deepened the kiss.

She closed her lips on his tongue and sucked it into her own mouth, and it was his turn to groan. She held him to her, as they shared breath, heat, and each other.

Lights appeared. A car honked. And Justin's logic returned.

He'd lost it. Taken. Demanded. Did her wrong. Placing his hands on her hips, he turned her so he could see her face in the light and make sure she was okay.

"I'm sorry, Bethy," he said as he steadied her and stepped back. Her lips were full and swollen, but she wasn't scratched by any of the hanging branches. "I'm sorry. I shouldn't have done that to you."

"I liked it," she said, staring up at him with a bewildered look.

"So did I," Paul said, walking up behind her, stroking a hand down her arm, and pulling her back against his chest.

"It's not happening," Justin said, realizing Paul held her safe and stepping farther away. "It can't."

He'd gotten caught up in the emotions of the past. His body had remembered. It had been a mistake. A temporary lapse in judgment.

He saw her swallow, saw the way her chest quivered, and wanted to reach for her and pull her back into his embrace. But he didn't. Thankfully, Paul dropped his forearm across her chest and kissed the side of her head. She leaned into him.

"It's okay, baby. It's him, not you," Paul whispered against her hair.

She still didn't speak, but Justin saw the hurt in her eyes and knew he'd put it there. He'd lost control, given in to a desire he shouldn't have, but fuck him, if it didn't burn deep inside him. He wanted her, and all he needed was to know he could have her for good. This one kiss or temporary shit didn't work for him.

"Fix it," Paul demanded, annoyance flashing in his eyes, but his hand caressed her upper arm and he kissed from her hair, to her temple, and back to the top of her head. He held her tight, her back still to his chest, and cradled her close beneath his chin.

Justin acknowledged how good they looked together, and not only was she good for Paul, Paul was good for her, if only he'd hold her forever. She wasn't temporary.

All Justin needed was for Paul to give him a sign that their temporary-only understanding didn't apply to her. But Paul didn't. He stared at him, waiting for him to make it right with her.

Justin inhaled and ran his palm down his face. He returned to her and rested a hand on the side of her waist. Then he brushed his lips over her cheek and placed what he hoped passed as a platonic kiss on her soft skin, breathing in her scent, and recommitting it to memory.

"Bethy, my body goes into overdrive around you."

"I like the way this sounds," Paul said, extending his free arm and cupping Justin's shoulder.

"But it can't happen. No more hurt," he said in a low voice. He wouldn't ever hurt her again. "Forget that kiss. It wasn't appropriate."

"Appropriate?" She finally spoke, but her confusion was laced with anger. "You're mad, Justin Bentley. Nauseatingly mad. And if you kiss me like that ever again, get my panties hot and bothered, then drop me like it doesn't count, I'm going to twist your balls into a tight and tiny knot, and you're going to scream like a little girl."

Shocked by her announcement, Justin dropped his hand and pulled back.

"Fair enough," Paul said, laughing and pushing on Justin's shoulder. "But don't feel obligated to wear panties for our benefit. Now let's blow this joint."

Paul turned her around, stood between them, and draped an arm over each of their shoulders. He started walking.

"The car is the other way," Justin said.

"Yeah, but the best view of the windmills is this way," Paul said, urging them on. "Our first date together is ending on a sweet note. I'm taking you for ice cream."

"It's not a date," Bethany said, echoing Justin's thoughts.

"You two BFFs keep telling yourselves that," Paul said. "I say it's a date."

Bethany sighed and settled her arm around Paul's waist. "I warned you to stop being nice to me. But I will gladly take the ice cream. Truthfully, I'd do almost anything for some ice cream after dinner and that failed kiss."

"I hoped you'd say that," Paul teased, and Justin couldn't believe how they'd both let go of the drama and were chatting like old friends. "Prayed for it."

"But Paul," she continued, "no matter how good that ice cream is, I'm still going after Vaso's Dream. Even if you don't like it, I'm going to make this deal happen. It's a very fair price and it's what your uncle wants. So you getting me ice cream is not going to change my mind on acquiring the resort."

"I know, baby. I heard you."

Chapter Fourteen

Careful not to wake Paul, Justin turned on his side and looked out the window precisely as the morning light filtered through the sky.

Paul followed and wrapped his arm around Justin, throwing a leg over his and breathing softly against his neck.

Justin hugged the muscled arm to his chest and counted his blessings for Paul. He then closed his eyes and counted his blessings for Bethy. He sighed in guilty regret, because he was lying to both of them. He wanted more.

He wanted Bethany in his arms and Paul at his back. Or Bethany in Paul's arms and himself at Paul's back. Or Paul in Bethany's arms and himself at her back. Fuck. He didn't care on the order. He wanted them both in his bed. He didn't want a BFF in Bethany. He wanted a forever lover.

"What's wrong, babe?" Paul asked in a morning rasp.

"It wasn't a date," he said. "It wasn't."

Paul didn't reply. Instead he kissed up Justin's neck until he reached the sensitive spot below his ear. "Justin, do you know why I asked her about the breakup?"

"Why?" The mention of the breakup countered the effect of the kisses. His morning hard-on relaxed.

"Because the sexual tension was off the charts," Paul said, sliding his hand down Justin's chest and to his abdomen. "If she would have answered any other way, and her answer hadn't revealed how hurt she was as well, things would be different right now. If she didn't truly love you, I would have pushed for a fling. She'd have accepted. And she'd be here with us. You'd fill her mouth, as I'd feast on every inch of her lovely body."

Justin closed his eyes, playing the scenario in his mind, and, hello, morning wood was totally back.

"Fine. We're all physically compatible. But we can't."

"I know, babe. You were right. She's the real deal," Paul said. "We need to keep her heart safe, so we can't have her body. I understand. But that doesn't mean I can't fantasize about my new friend."

Justin did enough fantasizing, so it was only expected for Paul to do the same.

"I will make her scream my name as I sink into her, watch her ride you to heaven as I jack off, take those pretty tits into my mouth and suck until she comes, but only in my dreams," Paul said, playing his fingers through the fine line of hair below Justin's belly button. "I won't touch her. You won't touch her. We will not hurt her. She's too good."

"You do get it," Justin said, turning to hug him and pressing against his hard warmth. "But are you okay with having her in our life?"

"Of course I am. She's a dream."

"Then can I ask you one last thing?" Justin settled a thigh between Paul's and stroked his chest.

"As long as I get the same opportunity to ask you a question."

"That's fair," Justin said. He looked at the big, muscled man, seeing more than his powerful body. He saw his kind and caring heart. "Are you really going to make her fight you for the resort?"

"I am."

"Why?"

"I don't want her father to get his hands on this place. Not only would he destroy everything we stand for, but he doesn't deserve such beauty in his life. Look what he did to you and Bethany." Paul kissed him, taking his time and chasing away the remnants of negative thoughts. "I'm not letting him hurt either one of you again."

"It's Bethany who wants the resort, not her father. She told me." And he knew why, but he had said he wouldn't get involved. Wouldn't take sides.

"If you feel stuck in the middle and don't want to prepare the financial presentations, you don't have to," Paul said, offering to let him off the hook and make things easier for him. "I can do it."

"Nope," Justin said. "All I have to do is present numbers. I already said I'm not taking sides. I won't discuss what you want with her or what she wants with you. She mentioned that the acquisition of the resort was her idea to Kosta and made it public knowledge, so I don't think it's wrong to discuss it with you. She wouldn't hide that from you."

With his arms tight around Justin's back, he tapped a hand on the curve of his ass. "My turn. You ready?"

"Shoot."

"If you're so okay with this new BFF thing, and you don't love her—"

"I didn't say I don't love her," Justin interrupted. "Of course I love her. I may not be in love with her that way, but I love her. She'll always have a special place in my heart."

"At least you're admitting that much, but you're still in denial," Paul said.

"I'm not in denial."

"You don't kiss a friend the way you kissed her. You still want her."

Justin didn't reply. That was a normal physical reaction. He'd wanted to connect with her, to soothe away past pain, and fine, he was justifying his desire with bullshit.

"How are you going to feel when she walks into a room on some other man's arm? Or it's not your tongue down her throat making her moan so sweetly?"

Fuck! Paul knew him completely. "Not fair. This is still all so new."

"The woman has needs. She's not going to wait until you're ready to meet them or be okay with her getting them met elsewhere." He cupped Justin's ass and tilted his hips to grind his groin against him. "You got laid yesterday, but she didn't."

"Are you saying that I flaunted our sexual satisfaction in her face?"

"No. I'm saying you got laid yesterday afternoon, and you were ready to go again when we got home." He slid a finger through his ass cheeks and pressed it against his sore opening.

Justin trembled at his touch.

"I gave you what you needed. Took what I needed. You rode that wave of pleasure for a long time last night. And when you couldn't hold it, you came in my hand. The only way she came last night was with her own hand. How long do you think that's going to last?"

"I don't know."

"How are you going to feel when someone, not you or me, makes our beautiful and sexy friend come?"

* * *

Bethany quietly opened the shutters and marveled at nature's beauty spread before her. Across the crystal clear blue water, varying hues of pink, yellow, and blue haloed the island of Delos in the light. She inhaled the fresh scent of the island, mixed with the sweet perfume of the flowers, and she physically ached to sit at the little table outside her window and enjoy the morning sun's dance on the sea.

Peeking to the left, she noticed Justin and Paul's shutters latched, not closed, which meant they'd probably slept real well, snuggled together in their big bed, with the windows open and the sound of the sea serenading them. A pang of something—what she wasn't sure—hit her, and she blew out a long breath.

She'd slept with the windows closed and the air conditioner on, and she hadn't slept well. The night had proven long and difficult.

She kept telling herself they were friends, but the way they looked at her, spoke with her, and touched her didn't feel purely friendly. Oh, and of course there was that way Justin had kissed her. How was it put in romance novels? *He'd plundered her mouth and made her dizzy with need.*

Jerk.

It wasn't that he didn't care, but he cared too much. He thought she'd be hurt if they didn't take her into their loving little family. And maybe he had a point, because she was falling for them both, but she wasn't stupid. She knew the world didn't work like that. There was no real room for her in their relationship.

Their hearts were full, so she couldn't ask for that romance novel kind of love. She could dream about that stuff you read about in other kind of novels, the one you read in private, with no cover showing. Earth shattering, body rattling, kind of fun. Like Paul had said, they had something, they all wanted it, and it wasn't going away.

But instead of trusting her to know what she was getting into, Justin had decided for her. In a moment full of emotion and passion, he'd gotten her hopes up and then had changed his mind.

Jerk.

Still. She was screwed. She couldn't turn her back on them because she did care, more than she wanted to, but she could focus on her original goal rather than think about getting naked with two gorgeous, handsome, panty-melting men.

She'd come to Mykonos to assess the resort as a business venture and to familiarize herself with the lifestyle of the island. And she knew a few things about denying life desires by burying her head in work.

No more dreamgasms.

No more being stuck in the middle.

She had work to do.

"Get going, girl. Go and make your dream a reality." Long summers. Simple pleasures. All in the lap of luxury of the Cyclades. "Go make Mykonos your summer home."

Bethany grabbed her tote off the window seat, gently opened the door and stepped into the crisp air, inhaling deeply as she pulled the door closed behind her. Avoiding the temptation of looking in on them, she circled to the right and walked to the covered terrace where breakfast was being served.

Impossible to settle on only one item off the buffet, she requested a serving of *kopanisti*, the mouthwatering cheese thing from the night before, a toasted slice of country bread, and some plump olives.

"Rather traditional," a male voice sounded behind her. "You should add a sweet Greek coffee to the selection."

She turned and looked up at a grinning Christo, bright and cheery before seven in the morning.

"Should I order it for you?"

"Thank you. Yes." She laughed, thinking how wrong Paul had been about the timing where Christo was concerned. "Join me for breakfast?"

"Of course." He ordered two doubles and took the plate from her hands. He stopped in front of the fruit station, spoke with the attendant, then moved to the omelet station and did the same, handing a server her plate. "They'll bring everything to the VIP table. Let's go."

"VIP table?"

Clearly, Paul was wrong. Christo was not a morning grump. He smiled, and the smile reached his eyes, and chuckled. "Maybe I've christened it the VIP table because it's my favorite spot on the beach to enjoy Apollo's work. He did a good job of harnessing that chariot and positioning the sun in the sky. Agree?"

"Agree," she said, recalling the mythology lesson on the handsome Greek god. "It was like seeing a painting when I looked out my window."

"Tell me about it. Many beautiful things here." He winked and swept out his arm, shaking a finger. "Don't tell anyone about our secret location. Noise would spoil it."

"In that case, I'm honored to share your table." She fell in step beside him as he walked across the terrace.

He stopped to greet guests and ask about their stay. The guests knew him by name, and they repeatedly invited them to join them. With four of the six tables he'd introduced her to, he'd added how lucky he was going to be to have the smartest and most beautiful boss lady in all of Mykonos. He put a smile on everyone's face, including Bethany's.

"You know everybody staying at the resort," she said as they reached a staircase, which looked like nature had carved into the rocky cliff side. It led to the beach. He unlatched the gate across its landing and removed the red sign.

"Not everybody, but these are our early risers." Taking two steps down, he turned and offered her his hand. "Please. The path is a bit steep."

"The sign said to keep out. Danger."

He laughed, and shook his hand at her. "Come on, *koukla*. There's no danger. I wouldn't put you in danger."

So much like Paul, her breakfast accomplice had attitude. Polite, but cavalier, Christo's confidence and demeanor made her feel safe. She took his hand and stepped on to the path. He motioned for her to continue to where he stood, and then latched the gate behind them and replaced the sign at its original place.

"Hold my hand. The railing isn't the best," he said, moving ahead of her. "Step where I step and don't look down."

"You're kidding, right?"

"Maybe a little," he said, chuckling as he descended. "But you can't blame a man for some heroic drama. You'll agree the end result is worth it."

She held on to his hand, looked from the span of his broad shoulders, down his muscular back, perfectly toned ass, and to his feet, and stepped as he'd instructed. She counted thirty-three steps before he stopped, turned back, and flashed another smile.

A slightly older version of Paul, at most ten years, it was easy to see how he'd gained his lothario status. With his good looks and killer accent, women would willingly throw themselves at him for a night of physical pleasure. Because, holy smokes, the man had a body that was made for pleasure, and his dark gaze promised he delivered.

"Are you okay?" Christo asked, tapping his fingers on her hip.

"Yeah," she whispered. "I'm just taking in the view." She let her gaze travel over the sandy beach to the little alcove nestled in the curve of the cliff. On the sand, only a few feet from the water, there was a solitary table with one chair pulled up to it. Three more chairs were stacked behind it. "Is that the VIP seating?"

"It is," he said, tapping his hand on her waist. The man did a lot of finger waggling and tapping. "Lean on me and raise your foot. You should take off your shoes before walking on the beach, otherwise they'll ruin."

Damn, these Greek men were panty-melting charismatic, built sexy-as-hell, and rather touchy-feely—in a nice, real nice, way. How was a woman supposed to keep a clear mind in the presence of testosterone overload?

Bethany placed her right hand on his shoulder, bent her left leg toward her ass, pulled off her shoe, and handed it to him. She repeated the same for the other shoe, then thanked him and took them both back into her hand. "Your turn."

Laughing, he kicked off a pair of Timberland boat shoes and placed them on a boulder. He raised his brow and leaned his head to the side for her to do the same. She did, and he nodded, motioning for her to walk ahead of him.

"Are all Greeks as domineering as you?"

"Not all," he said, dropping his Ray-Ban's on to the bridge of his nose, but not before she glimpsed the smile in his eyes again. "But the Lallas men do have a reputation for getting their way."

"I've noticed."

Amused, he snorted and seemed to suck a laugh between his teeth, peculiar, but definitely amused. "I see you've been spending time with my little cousin."

"I'd say Paul is a little of a control freak," she admitted.

"That he is."

They walked the final distance in comfortable silence, and once they were seated she remembered her lack of coffee. "How are we going to get our breakfast down here?"

"There's a staircase for the guests and servers to use." He pointed just beyond the shrubbery bordering the path they'd taken, and she was surprised to see sturdy, wide, metallic stairs, complete with thick railing. "Don't be mad. My way down is authentic. That staircase is for tourists."

"I did say I wanted an authentic island experience," she said, recalling their conversation the previous night. "But it took us ten minutes to climb down. I don't know how much longer I can go without my morning coffee."

"Gianni is on his way," he said, he lifted his chin to the stairs. "You'll be in caffeine heaven very soon. He's bringing the double Greek plus a frappé chaser and lots of food. We'll sample the guests' favorites and try a few new things we've put on the menu. I'd appreciate your opinion."

She nodded, reaching for her coffee mug the second it was placed on the table and taking a long overdue, delicious sip. He hadn't exaggerated. The rich Greek coffee hit the spot. It had a creamy texture, but no milk, and enough sugar to make her happy, but not so much to diminish the taste. Grateful he'd insisted on a double rather than the small demitasse cup, she held the mug close, closed her eyes, inhaled the heady aroma, and sighed.

"Awesome. Perfect."

"*Telia,*" he repeated in Greek. "You also said you wanted to learn the language, *koukla.*"

And there it was again. *Koukla.*

Chapter Fifteen

Was Christo flirting by calling her *koukla*?

Bethany looked away, but was pleasantly distracted when she spotted the almond cookies. "*Amygdalota.*"

"*Bravo*. Pretty soon you'll be fluent in Greek food," he said, playfully tickling her arm.

She smoothed her fingers over her forehead, trying to understand what was happening. Christo was nice, friendly, and cool. Sure he carried more machismo than her male friends in the city, and he didn't have an issue with touching. Most Greeks she'd met seemed okay with touching—a lot, but he wasn't rude or presumptuous.

He certainly didn't give off the "I want to get you naked" vibe. Yet, he'd called her *koukla*—twice. Paul had called her *koukla*, but when Paul had said it, she'd wanted to climb into his arms and nuzzle his neck. Not so with the handsome and charming Christo.

"What's wrong, *koukla*?"

Make that three times. "What exactly does *koukla* mean?"

"It translates as doll, and it's very common when addressing a female we appreciate and like." He took a loud breath and concern marked his brow. "I apologize if I made you uncomfortable. It wasn't my intent."

He switched out his coffee with the frappé chaser. "Adorable little girls are *koukles*, sisters are *koukles*, girlfriends, moms, and even grandmothers are *koukles*. It's a term of endearment. I feel comfortable with you, and I think we can be good friends. Nothing…" He rolled his wrist as if searching for the right word. Frustrated, he shook his head.

"Say it in Greek," she suggested.

"Nothing…" He snapped his fingers searching for the right word.

"Nothing devilish, sly, or sexually motivated. I meant it a simple way. Like a hug."

She giggled so hard that the fresh squeezed orange juice sloshed all over her hand. "I'm not sure that a hug is much easier for someone like me to understand, but it's fine. I'm not offended. I like it that you call me *koukla*. It's nice."

"Then why did you have that stormy look in your eyes?"

Blotting a napkin on the mess, she went for casual and dismissive. "Not stormy, just puzzled. Paul said it, too."

"Ah, now I see. Did he tack a *mou* to the end?"

She nodded, and he laughed, saying something in Greek that sounded very entertaining. He didn't bother to elaborate in English.

"This is a conversation for friends who have known each other a very long time and share unconditional trust or bottles of vodka." When she didn't object, he took the napkin from her hand and handed her a fork. "We'll come back to it, if you like, after you try the *omeletta*. It's my favorite."

She gladly accepted the change of subject and cut into the omelet. She moaned as the scent of that special cheese released into the air. "I already know I'll like it. I think I'm addicted to this cheese."

Her taste buds agreed, and she gave him a thumbs-up. They tasted a little of each item on the plates, repeating thumbs up for favorites and making the okay sign for good and fresh. Nothing garnered a thumbs-down. They watched windsurfers take to the slick-as-oil water, catching the island's famed *meltemi* winds, sipped on their frappés, and spent fifteen minutes in comfortable silence.

"So, Christo Lallas. You're proving to be a complicated man."

She met his gaze, surprised with his patience. Something had taught the man that the best way to get an answer was silence. He waited for her to continue.

"By night, you're a pool-side bartender. Early in the morning, you're a food tester and guest greeter, and then work the front desk and handle the resort exodus. What exactly is your official title?"

"I'm my uncle's nephew," he replied with a matter of fact tone.

"And what do you do?"

"Anything he needs me to do." He leaned back in his chair and rubbed his stomach. "If it's a day like today, when ninety percent of our rooms turnover, I work the front desk. When a bartender calls out for a shift, I tend bar. But on an ordinary day, I make sure the staff is on their game and things run smooth. And as for checking on the restaurant, what sane man would complain about having meals cooked for him every morning? Much better than a piece of dry toast at home."

"So you manage all those departments?"

"I coordinate," he said, remaining very humble about all he did. "The departments run well on their own."

"You're a GM."

"If you want to label it," he conceded. "I oversee the resort's operation, but we are very lucky to have a fantastic staff. Each employee was handpicked by my uncle or my aunt. They are very devoted to him and use their talents to make him proud."

"I'm sorry about your aunt's passing."

"There seemed to be a lot of that going around these past few years," he said in a low voice. He drank the remainder of his frappé and piled the empty plates on the tray Gianni had left for them.

Realizing it was one of those moments silence encouraged sharing she waited for him to continue.

"Three years ago, my mother got very sick. She refused to come to Athens as her doctor had recommended, so I returned to the island full-time to help with caring for her. She lived her last year exactly as she'd wanted. It was full of great experiences and good memories, and it proved to me that there is no other place in the world I'd rather make my own family. Unfortunately, it will need to be without my parents around. Mama's heart grew tired and stopped beating."

"I'm sorry, Christo. She must have been very young."

"Not young, but not old. My parents tried for years to have children, and I was a late surprise. Mama was in her mid-forties when she had me, and since I have eight years on Paul, you can do the math. She was in her late seventies when she passed. My dad was ten years older than she was, so he was old when his broken heart said no more. He passed one year after her passing."

She covered his hand with hers and squeezed.

"*Thea* Vaso lost her battle a few months after my father went. I stepped in to help Kosta when he couldn't concentrate on the daily activities of the resort. And while Paul and other cousins and family come and visit and are great, in reality my uncle and I have only each other throughout the year. So when it comes to his resort, I get the job done."

"You live here with him?"

"No," he said, checking his phone. "We have time so I can show you my home and show you why I love this place. Want to go for a quick walk?"

She glanced at his phone and saw it was five minutes to eight. She leaned her head to the side and looked at him.

"It's fine. We don't need to be at the desk until nine," he said, making her laugh.

She stood and dropped her napkin to the table. "Shoes?"

"*Ochi*," he replied, standing beside her. He held out his hand and motioned for her to walk ahead of him. "We're heading in the opposite direction, on the other side of the cliff. It's low tide and the water is shallow. Your dress won't get wet." He chuckled and then stepped out of her reach, placing his hands before him in a protective stance. "That's if you hike it up a few inches and piss off the forces above."

She tried to land a playful smack, but he caught her wrist in mid-air.

"It's going to be fun having you around, *koukla*. You make me laugh."

"Ditto," she said, then stepped into him and hugged him. "I don't know the male version of *koukla* yet."

"*Ochi, koukla*. It doesn't translate the same," he said, adamantly shaking his head and hugging her tight. "However, I wasn't teasing about pissing off the forces above."

She looked over his shoulder and up at the terrace. Sure enough, two rigid forms were silhouetted in the sunlight; one with his arms crossed over his chest, the other with his hands in his pockets, and both with legs planted in a combative stance.

They'd understand and calm down when—

"No. Not going there," Bethany said, as the reality of her situation body slammed her. "BFFs have no say in who I spend my time with. Screw them."

He kissed the tip of her nose and burst out laughing. He laughed so hard that he released her and placed his hands on his knees and kept laughing.

"I'm serious," she said, her cheeks getting hot. "I could offer my naked body to them on a silver platter, but they just want to be friends."

"That's not what I saw last night."

"That's what it is. They have no interest in getting some of this." She ran her hands down her body for emphasis. "They're immune."

"And you?"

Only slightly embarrassed, she shrugged. "I'm not dead."

"*Malakes.*"

She'd heard that word repeatedly; it was very popular, very colorful, and she wasn't about to ask him to translate the exact meaning of one of the biggest curse words in his language. Jerks, fuckers, assholes, was probably close enough.

"It doesn't matter. They can't handle me anyway."

"I'm not convinced," he said, shaking his head and bending over laughing again. Holding a finger into the air, he caught his breath and grinned. "It would be interesting for sure. So, in the spirit of good fun, my lothario reputation, as Justin put it last night, is at your full disposal. Nothing will make a man, and his man, realize what they want than thinking a big, bad cousin is making moves on the woman of their dreams."

She wasn't the woman of their dreams.

"I think you have it wrong," she said.

"I don't think so. I know what I saw. My eyes don't lie." Christo placed his hands on her shoulder and turned her around. "Come on. Let me show you the beautiful home my parents built, and the gorgeous vineyard I made them sell because I was too young and too stupid to know better. It's the vineyard I'm going to buy back at the end of the summer. Even if I told them I was never going to be a winemaker."

"You're going to live on the island year-round, permanently?"

"I am," he said, nodding and leading her down the beach. "And here is the fair warning I must share with the probable Boss Lady, not my new friend."

"Go on," she urged, strangely comfortable with the man.

"If you do go ahead with the purchase of Vaso's Dream, we'll be neighbors. I won't be putting in an application for general manager, but I do have someone in mind, someone I've been working with to take my place and help my uncle once I start work on the vineyard."

"You're definitely leaving?"

"I am."

Disappointment filled her. Not only was she confident Christo was a good and loyal manager, but she had a feeling he'd be someone she could always lean on.

"That's too bad, Christo. You've done a great job for Kosta, and I don't doubt you'd be a great fit with Luxury Homes. I have a feeling I'll miss working together."

He grinned that panty-melting grin and she had no doubt he could get the staff to do his bidding with ease.

Lallas charm, she thought. They all had it.

"Now that we're friends, I will never abandon you if you need me," Christo said. "I can take care of all the boring stuff for your company the same way I do for my uncle, until you're set. I'll do what it takes to keep Vaso's Dream beautiful. But, Miss Sexy Boss Lady, if it happens, you and

I will be neighbors. We're going to need to work together and get along well so our lives are good."

"Duly noted, Mr. Lallas."

Chapter Sixteen

"She's on the beach," Paul said, looking down at his cousin's hideaway. "Christo is hugging her and spinning her like a doll."

"What?" Justin nudged him out of the way and looked over the railing. He growled, obviously annoyed, and reached for the latch on the gate. "Not liking this."

"Neither am I," Paul said, holding Justin back from opening the gate. "You can't go down there and force her to stop talking to the general manager of the place she intends to purchase. It may be business."

"Bullshit. She's in his arms. That's not business."

"We'll be screwed if we show up, and you know it. Want her to shut us out again?" Paul stepped back from the gate and watched the turmoil brewing in Justin's eyes, but at least he wasn't storming down to the beach. "Let's calm down and consider our options." He fisted his hands and stuffed them in his pockets. "We may not be able tell her who to see or what to do, but I can talk with Christo. We know he's the love them and leave them type. She's not for him. He won't go for her."

When Bethany vanished behind the gray of the rocks, Paul stepped back and sat at a table. Justin joined him, his reluctance obvious in the way the veins bulged on his neck. A waitress came over and asked if she could get them anything. He needed a huge amount of control to remain polite and order their coffees. He managed.

"What if she goes for him?" Justin asked.

"Fuck me! Don't say that." Paul managed until Justin pointed out the obvious. "No fucking way!"

"Well, it's possible." Justin dropped his head into his hands and massaged his scalp. "Your cousin is the island's infamous womanizer. He's fucking gorgeous. He snaps his fingers and women line up for a chance to be with him. His bedposts are completely marked up and there is no more room for new notches."

"I'll talk to him. Promise," Paul said.

"We're keeping her at a distance to keep her safe. You think Christo is safe?"

"He's reasonable. I'll talk to him," he repeated. Suddenly aware of the other diners having gone quiet, he told the waitress to make the coffees to go. "We can't really do this here. I have a lunch meeting with the Luxury rep, Bethany Michaels, not our girl, Bethy, in only a few hours. I need to keep my head on straight. We'll discuss it in the afternoon. In private."

* * *

Paul instructed the maintenance team to check the showerhead in Villa Calliope for a leak and the main light sensor in Villa Euterpe. He touched his hand to the freshly painted exterior of Villa Clio, and, confirming it was dry, he removed the WET PAINT sign. Taking advantage of the early departure of a group of guests from Denmark, he'd spent three hours whitewashing two of the smaller villas they'd vacated.

His nose was sunburned and his shoulders ached, but the work had allowed him to focus on something other than Bethany.

That's a lie.

He'd thought about her non-stop; every damn minute he'd been painting the villas he was thinking of her. And if he kept replaying his earlier thoughts, he didn't stand a chance of making it through the so-called tour.

He entwined his fingers and stretched his arms ahead of him until he felt the pressure in his back release, deciding to be angry with his cousin instead. The shithead had designs on a woman he shouldn't ever consider. If she had her way, she could be his boss one day soon. Then what would the suave Christo do? Bang her to keep the job?

Paul immediately regretted the absurd and rude thoughts about his older cousin. Over his pity party, he knew he had to get Christo alone and settle the issue of a Bethany fling. She wasn't fling material, and in spite of his reputation, Christo wasn't an ass and would never take advantage of a woman.

Feeling a little optimistic, he stepped beneath the shade of a pink bougainvillea tree, with flowers Justin said looked like a breath of fresh air, and opened the app to send him a video message. He tapped on Justin's name and hit record.

"Hey. Hope you're almost done up there. Miss you. Spent the past three hours painting with a hard-on, and searching for a solution to our problem. No worries. We got this. I'm on my way to pick her up and give her the grand tour. I'll keep her busy and preoccupied. You'll take over when I go see Christo. So finish up and be ready. We'll get through this. Love you."

He hit send, then added a text message:

I love you lots.

I love you more came Justin's reply, and immediately a notification that he'd watched the video again. He sent another text: *Take a detour and we'll fix the hard-on issue.*

Paul grinned. *Boner self-serviced in the shower.*

In that case, you owe me one.

Say when.

Sex was never a difficulty for them. The "when" was anytime the other wanted, and they both wanted often. No one got him the way Justin did. So many times Justin knew what he needed before he did. That gave him cause to consider how Bethany fit between them.

Very, very nicely.

He strolled into the reception ahead of schedule and right into an intimate scene of Christo leaning over Bethany's shoulder. Romeo stood at her back, so close Paul thought he saw her lean on his chest as he breathed her air. Christo worked the computer mouse, spoke in her ear, and pointed to a pile of brochures spread across the desk. They shared the space with no qualms, functioning like they'd worked together for years, and taking care of guests with an apparent effortlessness and efficiency that had him grinding his teeth.

She saw him and smiled. "Hey."

"Hey, yourself," he said, returning her smile and lifting his chin in greeting to Christo. He stepped to the side and watched as a young couple came to check in. She was a natural in the hospitality world. Competent and knowledgeable, she pointed out the highlights of the island to the couple.

"Now, don't overlook our own view. It's heavenly. Since your villa isn't ready yet, please be my guest for lunch on our terrace by the main pool."

"I love this Greek hospitality," the young blonde drawled in a Texas accent. "We saved and planned for a dream honeymoon since we got engaged. We decided on a small family wedding in the backyard to afford this trip. I think we did okay."

"More than okay," Bethany said, drawing two circles on the map. "Don't hesitate to ask us for recommendations. We enjoy the island as much as the tourists and we all have our favorite hotspots. If you like seafood, Paul will tell you how to get to *Kalos Psaras,* my preferred waterfront tavern. Then just walk a few streets down for the best stracciatella ever. And be very happy gelato has less calories than ice cream."

She said it with such authority, yet by her own admission the night before, it was the first stracciatella she'd ever tasted.

"Love seafood and ice cream. We're there." The pretty Texan accepted and studied the map, tracing a manicured fingernail from the resort to Little Venice.

"Mykonos has a rad rep for beach bars and parties," the new husband added. "Any nearby? Walking distance so we can make it back on our own?"

"Enigma is close," Christo said, stepping up behind Bethany. "The bus stops in front of the resort. Board on our side of the street, ride it to the next stop, and you can party all night long until the buses start running in the morning."

"Can we grab a taxi for cheap or walk back?"

"Both. It's a fifteen minute walk downhill," Christo said, snaking his arm around Bethany's middle and resting his cheek against her soft hair. "If you're there tomorrow, Bethany and I will be happy to give you a ride back."

"You're going to Enigma tomorrow?" Paul asked.

"Yeah," she replied. "Want to come?"

Yes, he wanted to come. What sane person wouldn't want to come with her looking at him with those big brown eyes smiling and those lush full lips moving? But first he wanted to peel Christo's fingers off her body.

"Maybe. I'll check with Justin and let you know," he said. "Cuz, can I have a word with you?"

"Wait," the blonde said, waving at him. "Can you please give us directions to the restaurant Bethany was talking about first?"

"Sure," Paul said, hiding his reluctance behind a forced smile, but fuck him if Christo didn't smirk as the woman handed Paul the map and settled beside him.

Clearly the couple had splurged on the honeymoon of their dreams and was on a budget, so Paul suggested the bus again. He was in the middle of pointing out the stop they were to get off at, when Christo whispered something to Bethany and kissed the side of her head. He lifted his chin to Paul and mouthed "later" in Greek. Then he walked out, walked out before Paul had the opportunity to speak with him.

"Where did he go?" Paul asked Bethany when the guests were gone.

"He said he had to meet with your uncle about something." She reached beneath the counter and slipped a coiled key bracelet on her wrist. "I'm ready to go if you are."

They said goodbye to the staff and headed out into the noonday sun.

"We'll start with the public areas. You've already seen the main resort pool and dining terrace. There are two more café-bars, much smaller, but well utilized."

"Where is the second bar? I've only seen the one Christo was working last night."

Fuck. She'd been with and knew Christo since last night. Not good.

He stuffed his hands in his pockets and casually kicked a pebble off the path. "I'm guessing you've been to the Wandering Rocks and not the Oracle, right?"

"Right," she said, wrinkling her nose. "But why is it named Wandering Rocks? It overlooks the water and is so adorable. No rocks around."

"A testament to my aunt's warped sense of humor and love for literature. Since Kosta had the main say in naming all the units after characters, and I'm using that loosely, in Greek mythology, she thought it would be fun to name a bar you couldn't get up from after something not exclusively Greek. It's named from James Joyce's *Ulysses'* Wandering Rocks, which are not in "Homer's Odyssey". She took it one step further and identified the two doors to the side as Scylla and Charybdis."

"Because no man has ever passed through the Wandering Rocks alive, it's safer to opt for the six-headed monster and the whirlpool." She tapped a finger to her temple and smiled in amusement. "That's way too much detail for me to have retained, but my teaching assistant was hot. I hung on his every word."

Amused with her candidness, he laughed. "Did you now?"

"Me and the rest of the class, which just happened to be all female students but one. Antonio was drool-worthy." She fanned her hand before her face for emphasis.

"Hate to take the romance out of it, but Scylla leads to a broom closet and Charybdis houses the main building's electrical panel."

"Darn," she said, snapping her fingers in exaggerated flare. "You sure know how to put out a girl's fire."

He laughed louder, liking the playful and flirty side of her. "If you have time and want a good read by the pool, you should ask Kosta to borrow a book from my aunt's collection. She loved all books, from romances, to biographies, to the classics taught in university literature classes. They're in Greek, French, and English. She even had kids' books. I loved the Pendragon series by…"

"D. J. MacHale," she finished. "I remember them."

Impressive. Besides being a knockout, she was also a book geek. He liked it.

"Where's the Oracle?"

And she had a good memory. He didn't miss that little tidbit about her. So much more to the woman than he could have imagined.

Explaining that the little café was tucked behind the Muses' villas and mostly used by the staff, they agreed to try it for lunch.

Bethany continued to impress him on every subject they discussed. She agreed with the eco-friendly measures he'd put into practice over the past decade, added a few ideas of her own, and charmed every staff member they encountered. He searched his brain for a reason to keep her at arm's length, but came up empty with each attempt. They had more in common than their love for Justin.

He liked her. He liked her a lot.

They were at the Oracle, eating lunch and reviewing the energy-saving measures in place, while discussing possible additions, when her focus returned to the bottom line.

"So do you think the septic system could handle the small dishwashers? Or is it better to continue with housekeeping exchanging the kitchenware each time the rooms are turned over? I'm speaking from a financial point of view. The initial investment would be substantial, but it should balance over a few years."

"We'd have to consult with a plumber for the resort system, and definitely bring in a hydrologist that is familiar with the town's watershed. I'm more curious about the effect it would have on the septic tanks and drainage field," Paul said, admiring how much she considered the overall functioning of the resort. Nothing was too small or too big for her beautiful mind.

"I'd have to look into it more to see if it's truly cost effective. Maybe the additional manpower is the easiest way to go." She picked up her phone and typed something into the notes section. "I need more research on this."

"Honestly, I'm not too concerned about the maintenance cost overtime. I'm more concerned about sanitizing properly at the present time," Paul said. "We only keep service for four in each unit, and switch it out when guests leave. There are no cooking facilities in the rooms, and guests seem to be okay with washing wine glasses and cheese plates. That's all the glasses and plates are used for."

"I know," she said, dipping a fried zucchini slice into the *taztziki* sauce. "I used my wine glass yesterday and had no problem washing it and letting it air dry."

She handed him one of the yummy little fish, an *aitherina,* and held out her hand, waiting for him to eat the head and tail.

"We'll need to address the kitchenettes. They typically contain more appliances and frills to be considered timeshare units."

"But if guests cook their own meals, it might have an adverse effect on local merchants," Paul said. "It will definitely change their experience."

Her phone buzzed, and she giggled as she read the text. She typed out a one-finger response, and laughed aloud at the reply. Rolling her eyes, she placed the phone face-down on the table with exaggerated flair and turned to him. The twinkle in her gaze matched the lyrical laughter.

And fuck, she had an amazing laugh.

It went right through him and tickled his insides, doing things to his body a business associate should never do. He adjusted his seat, leaned close, and ran a finger down the bridge of her nose.

"Your face lights up so pretty when you laugh. That must be an especially nice text to have such an effect."

"My silly sister," she replied, handing him another tiny fish. "She's bugging me for more pictures. She wants to see exactly how handsome you are."

So...she'd told her sister about him. And she thought he was handsome. Nice.

"Let's send her one," Paul said, edging his chair close and draping an arm over her shoulder. He reached for the phone and held it for her to enter the passcode.

She punched in a sequence of numbers, but held herself away from him.

He wouldn't have it.

Paul leaned his head on hers, hugged her tight, and pressed the button. He smiled, then kissed her temple, and snapped a second pic. "Send me copies, too."

Bethany selected the first shot and hit send.

"I want both," he said. "Send both to me."

A blush crept over her cheeks, but she selected both pictures and sent them to his contact. Nice. He'd also been saved in her contacts.

He squeezed her shoulder and lingered a bit longer on a second kiss, when the screen flashed three consecutive messages:

OMG! Nine-alarm.

Fake it.

Get out now!

Shaking her head, she flipped the phone facedown again and laughed. "She says you're hot."

"Nice to know." But what he really wanted to know was what exactly she should fake. And why her sister was telling her to get out. He didn't ask. Rather he bit the tail and head off an *aitherina* and handed it to her.

They alternated between speaking like business associates and friends with ease, making him question what else could be added in order to meet all the needs between them. The more tiny fish heads he bit off for her, the more probable a physical arrangement seemed. Because damn, if it wasn't a possibility, he was an ass for envisioning it.

"I need to say something, and you need to listen," Paul said, clearing his throat, determined to clear the air. "Last night, you were correct. You did wow me. You are perfect for Vaso's Dream and you would bring so much to this place."

"Thank you," she said. "Vaso's Dream is wonderful and I adore everything about it. And with a few tweaks here and there, that won't even be noticeable to the guests…"

She kept talking, and while he should've stopped her, he didn't. Paul watched her mouth move and listened to her voice, because he could watch her for hours. But he didn't consider changing his mind. No matter how much she belonged here, her father did not. Beaming, she held her hands between her bouncing knees, but no matter what the result, he had to let her know the whole truth.

"…they're actually no-brainers. A win-win situation for the environment, the local economy, and the profit—"

"Stop, baby." He placed a finger on her lips. "Please listen."

Her bright smiled dimmed, and he questioned whether it was wise to share any more. But he had to. The woman was already too important to him and he wouldn't lie. He had to let her choose if she still wanted him around. And he had to respect her choice.

"You're making this harder for me than it already is, and that's because you're so amazing. I don't want to hurt you," he said, placing a hand on her knee and stilling the movement.

Fuck, his own heart raced and his gut churned. He didn't want to hurt her.

"I heard everything you said. I agree with you, Bethany. Those are only a few of the reasons why you're perfect for this place. And while

I cannot make my uncle's decision, I will not support him in selling the resort to Luxury Homes."

"But you said we're perfect."

"*You* are perfect." Aware of how the conversations around them had dropped in volume, he stood and held out his hand. "Come on, baby. Please."

He held his breath, waiting for her to decide whether or not to trust him and place her hand in his. His chest ached. He didn't want her to turn away.

"Please. In private."

With a sheen of sadness in her eyes, she gave him her hand.

Chapter Seventeen

Releasing a long breath, Paul tucked Bethany's hand through the crook of his arm, closed her fingers on his forearm, and covered her trembling hand with his own. He quickly led her away, not taking a chance she'd change her mind and want to end the conversation.

"I feel ridiculous," she said.

Once they were alone on a shaded path, he stopped walking, and turned her to look at him. "Why would you even think any of this is ridiculous?"

She pulled her hand from his and walked to a cement bench, which marked where the path opened to a sea view. She sat and dropped her face into her hands.

"Because I should simply walk away from all of this. I'm not getting anywhere. You don't take me seriously on the resort matters."

"I take *you* very seriously," he insisted, squatting before her and peeling her hands off her face. "You, *koukla*, are not the problem. Luxury Homes is. Your father is. He did you and Justin wrong. I can't stomach the idea of him being anywhere near this place. And I won't let anyone hurt the people I love."

"And once again ridiculous." She worried her lip, and he touched a finger to her chin to make her stop. "Not only am I in a difficult professional position, but my personal situation, actually *our* personal relationship is truly bizarre. Don't you get that the mixed signals are too much to handle?"

He could see the yearning in her eyes and his heart longed to answer. There was nothing bizarre about their relationship; they simply hadn't acknowledged what it meant. It was time. He needed to bring everything into the open.

"You love Justin?" Paul asked.

"Of course," she said, holding his gaze. "And you love Justin."

It wasn't a question, but he knew she expected an answer.

"I do."

"Then what am I doing with the two of you? This," she flicked her hand between them, "this isn't good. I can't be a business nemesis and a BFF. And, I can't be a BFF and deny what I feel inside. I'm a bundle of contradictions. We're a bundle of contradictions."

He leaned back on his heels, fit his legs between her feet, and nodded as he gazed up at her beautiful face. He knew exactly how she felt.

She wanted to buy Vaso's Dream, she fit all the criteria of a great investor, but he didn't want the resort sold to her company. Personally, he wanted to pull her against him and kiss the breath from her. But, she was supposed to be a friend. And friends didn't deal with friends like that. They respected certain boundaries—boundaries that were more than blurred in their case.

"Forget the business nemesis. It's settled. I will not aid Kosta with this sale." That was the easy part of their dilemma. In all truth, Kosta didn't really want to sell, and if Paul and Justin could come to an agreement on their future, the issue of Kosta needing to be on property all the time would be settled.

"You can't negate everything I've done. No," she snipped. "I'm not backing off because you say so."

"Don't back off." One never told the competition what to do. Nor did one discuss the game plan. "I didn't want the resort sold even before your dad was a factor. Now, I definitely won't condone such a deal. I agreed to today because of you. Because I didn't want to disappoint the woman Justin loves and the woman I want to get to know."

"Our past has nothing to do with the deal," she pointed out, every bit the strong and competent businessperson she was. "I've collected all the information, and I've already made my decision. The rest was just icing on the cake. A way to present it to Luxury Homes and assure what I want happens."

"And we don't need to work on this together," Paul added. "We can compartmentalize the different relationships. You deal directly with Kosta and Christo where the resort is concerned. I'll back off."

A solitary tear slipped down her cheek.

"But we still need to talk." He caught it with his thumb and wiped it away, unwilling to let a business transaction come between them. "Tell me what you feel?"

She grasped his wrist, and even though he wanted to keep touching her, she managed to move his hand away. She closed her eyes, took a deep breath, held it for what seemed like an eternity, then released it slowly, as if fighting for peace.

"Talk to me. Tell me."

"Paul, you know how it is between us," she said. "You brought it up and said as much last night. We have chemistry." She shuddered as she spoke, but she stretched out her spine, sat straight, and didn't avoid the difficult part.

Respect for this beautiful woman filled his chest, gripping his heart. She was more than wonderful. Brave and honest, she'd placed it all out in the open, with no regard to her comfort or ego.

"We do," he said, once again not willing to lie. "Justin and I knew right away. I felt it from the first moment on the ferry. We have sexual chemistry. But we can't risk our friendship. You mean too much to us."

Okay, so he was speaking about risking her getting hurt, but it wasn't a lie just because he didn't specifically say so.

"We discussed it," he admitted. "We've agreed it's best to remain friends."

"What? *You discussed it? You agree*d?" Annoyance colored her chest and the hollow at the center of her throat pulsed. "No one decides for me."

She stood and glared down at him.

"Damn it, this is the new millennium. Women want and have sex often." She held her hands out and opened and closed them. "Newsflash, some of us even have the audacity to initiate it." And like the sexy little siren she was, she looked over his shoulder at two German tourists and smiled. When they acknowledged her, she wiggled her fingers. The Germans started toward them. "See?"

"Stop it." Paul stood and yanked down her hands. He scowled at the Germans, and they changed direction. "You're not being fair."

"You know what's not fair?" She linked her hands at the small of her back and paced the tiny clearing. "You and Justin have each other. You go home together. I go home alone. And that's not fair. Maybe I want to go home with someone, too. But I can't because you two are stuck to me like white on rice, reminding me of what I can't have."

"I thought you were here for work," he said, grasping at straws to defuse the situation.

"Yeah, I am. And I can't do that when you keep looking at me like you want to devour me, or keep touching me and setting my body on fire, or then one of you kisses me and rejects me. It's too hard."

He knew it to be the truth. He wouldn't be happy in her position. And he didn't want her unhappy.

"I won't spend every free minute with you and Justin." She kept pacing, ticking off the reasons on her fingers one at a time. "And since there is no reason for us to spend time alone on resort business, *you* need to let me be. I need time away. Time alone. Without you and Justin."

"No," he said, reaching for her wrist. "You can't do that. That's his biggest fear. He doesn't want to lose you again."

"You love him enough to do anything in order for him to be happy."

"I do. I would." But he was finding he'd do anything to keep her happy, too.

"You're lucky to have each other. And I mean that from the bottom of my heart." She held her fist close to her chest and took a deep breath. "And while I'm truly happy for you, I can't keep subjecting myself to the pain."

"No. That's not acceptable." He burned to take her in his arms, tell her how important she was to them, and make it all better. "No pain. No hurt."

"What hurts is not that you're happy, but that you're giving me mixed signals."

Her gaze swept over him and her plea for distance was apparent. He didn't want to see it. Didn't want to think that someone else could get close to her. Not while they were in constant contact and communication. Maybe if she weren't staying next door, maybe if he didn't see her at every turn, then maybe he'd be able to accept it.

He scrubbed his hand over his face and shook his head.

No. Not even then.

He didn't want anyone else with her.

"I know you're committed to each other, and I'm working on being okay with being friends. I'm open to a relationship with you. I may be crazy, but I want a real relationship with you."

Hell, would she be happier being friends with benefits?

"It hurts so much when neither one of you is willing to walk away or act on the sparks between us. We're in a heated state of limbo. We can't just ignore it and hope it goes away."

The friends with benefits idea was front and center. Acting on it meant no ignoring of the sparks. He agreed. He wanted it.

"It's because he can't lose you again." Swallowing his pride, he reached for the no-lying part he was committed to. "I don't want to lose you. Don't walk away, Bethy. Give us a chance, not to ignore this, but to figure things out."

"I'm not walking away. I need some breathing room." She removed his fingers from her wrist. "It's just that this is too hard."

"I understand," he said, relieved she wasn't turning her back on them, but not happy about the melancholy in her voice. "How can I make it better?"

"You can't," she said, moisture shining in her pretty eyes. "My body knows what it wants. It wants what it can't have."

He reached for her, curled his fingers around her nape, and held her to his chest. He buried his face in her hair and breathed in her scent.

"It may not make things better, but know that my body wants the same, *koukla mou*."

She stayed in his embrace, her hands bunched between them, as her breath evened out and her body relaxed.

"Okay. We're in agreement." She pushed back and placed a soft kiss on his jaw. "You allow me time to acclimate to this new friendship. Don't crowd me and give me space. Let me have a night of sleep. I give you my word that I won't run."

Feeling like he had no choice, he watched her walk away.

Let her go.

Chapter Eighteen

Numbers bled on the computer screen, and for the first time in his life, Justin had no clue what they meant. While boring for most people, financial reports were his passion. Yet he honestly couldn't bring himself to care at this point.

Where the fuck had she gone off to with Christo?

Why had she gone?

And most importantly, what had they done while they'd been there?

He adjusted the climate control setting to twenty-one degrees. He needed to chill the hell out and concentrate.

His part in what Kosta had asked of them was less than a two-hour job, and once he had the presentation ready, he could spend every one of her non-work related hours with her, making sure she didn't wander off like that again. He wouldn't give her the chance to even consider anything with Christo or anyone else.

"How are you going to feel when someone, not you or me, makes our beautiful and sexy friend come?"

Paul's question taunted him on a continuous mental audio loop. Christo bending his head to her face was the featured video.

He stood and paced the office, acknowledging the friends' arrangement couldn't last as it was. Not only was she beautiful and sexy, but she was also the most sensuous woman he'd ever known.

Bethany liked sex. Needed sex. She had a ravenous appetite for the sensual pleasures in life.

Be honest. You don't want her as a simple friend.

A knock at the door surprised him, and he turned to see Kosta enter. He held a plate of grilled octopus, and the delicious smell made Justin's stomach growl.

"How did you know we skipped breakfast?" Justin asked, trying with all his strength to recompose himself and not think about Bethany in their bed.

"I didn't," Kosta said, placing the *meze* on the desk. "The octopus compliments the ouzo. Not as nicely as sausage could, but it'll have to do."

He produced a miniature bottle of chilled Plomari Ouzo from one pocket and two shot glasses from the other.

"Good call," Justin said, positioning a chair for Kosta before walking around the desk and taking his own seat. "Thank you."

Aware that Kosta was eyeing him, Justin twisted off the cork and poured the ouzo, wondering why he'd come to visit. He'd never concerned himself with reports before. He'd trusted Justin to review them and simply signed off.

"Did you have a nice dinner?" Kosta asked, raising a glass to his mouth.

"As always," he answered, knowing the old coot wasn't referring to the meal. He reached for a fork and speared a piece of octopus.

"Then why does it look like you've been pulling on your hair and it feels like the North Pole in here?"

The man was up to something. And Justin was in no mood for vague games. "Why did you bring this here, when you've never lifted a dish in your life?"

"*Eh*, you know." Kosta hedged meeting his gaze and pretended to search for the perfect piece of octopus. "A little bird told me what happened on the terrace this morning," he said at last. "I was worried you kids had an argument. I don't want Bethany uncomfortable."

"She's not uncomfortable," Justin said, thinking of just how comfortable she'd looked in Christo's arms.

"And I don't want unnecessary problems between Paul and his cousin."

Yes. They'd been overheard. News travelled quickly amongst the staff. Most of the employees had been with Vaso's Dream for years, and they were more like family than staff, so everyone knew Kosta wanted "the boys" to get along.

"It'll be okay. Paul said he's going to speak with Christo and set things straight. Paul won't let anything hurt their relationship." Or hurt Bethany, he added silently. "They'll figure it out."

Kosta's gaze narrowed and he put down his fork, as if needing his hand free to speak. "And how do you feel?"

"About?"

"Bethany," Kosta said, tapping his hand on the wood between them, clearly impatient. "I have eyes. So I don't need to know what you feel. I want to know what you're going to do about it."

Justin released a long, slow breath. He really didn't have the patience this morning. How the hell was Justin supposed to tell Paul's uncle that they lusted after the same woman, but only one of them wanted to keep her?

"It's not appropriate to discuss—"

"First, I'm not questioning your commitment to my nephew."

"Didn't cross my mind. But I don't think our relationship with Bethany is anyone else's business. I won't discuss it," Justin said.

"I don't want details, my boy. I simply have concerns to air."

The man was honest and smart, and his commitment to his family's happiness could never be questioned, either. He'd obviously thought a lot about the situation.

Justin decided to hear him out. "Go on."

"The first time I met you, my boy, you were barely young men, but I knew you were supposed to be with my Paul. Sometimes you just know. I knew." Kosta rested his arm on the desk and leaned forward to look into Justin's eyes. "The first time I heard Bethany's voice, my heart told me there was something special about the girl."

"She is special," Justin agreed.

"I can't explain it, but somewhere deep inside I knew I had to get you together. The three of you." Kosta held up three fingers and pinched them together. "I'm sure, beyond any doubt, I did the right thing. The three of you need each other. Together, you are complete."

Justin almost choked on the ouzo. Shaking his head, he placed the glass on the table and stared at Kosta. Maybe the language barrier was misconstruing his words?

"No," Kosta said, pointing at Justin. "You understand what I'm saying."

"You can't know that," Justin said, reaching for his ouzo again. "You didn't even know we had a past with Bethany."

"I didn't know. I told you. It was a feeling in here." Kosta pointed to his chest. "Don't you think you could have prepared this financial presentation from New York and Christo could have played tour guide instead of Paul?"

Justin liked Kosta's thought process, even if he wasn't ready to admit it.

Kosta tapped his finger to his temple. "In my mind, I had to introduce you and let nature take its course. I did. Nature did. So why not?"

There were so many reasons he could think of. The logistics of a life together and how society would react were a legitimate concern. More for her than for them. They'd already dealt with society. Furthermore, he and Paul had family support. Justin doubted Bethany would have that.

"We can't reserve for a table for three on Friday nights. What will people think?"

Kosta threw up his hands, then smacked them on his thighs. "Who cares?"

"Her father will care. She cares what her father thinks. And Paul doesn't want anything long-term with her."

There. He'd said it. He'd summed it all up in one breath.

Drained and empty, torn between his own happiness and the happiness of the ones he loved, he was forced to accept the consolation prize of friendship.

"All those Facebook posts about only living once and reaching for your dream have much truth, my boy. You must be honest with yourself."

"I am being honest," Justin said, combing his fingers through his hair. "I can't risk either one of them being unhappy."

"So you will be unhappy?"

Shrugging, Justin picked up his glass and didn't bother to answer.

"You are right, my boy. A woman cares what the man in her life thinks. Your job and Paul's job is to be that man, or men, for Bethany. If she has your support, she won't need anyone else's. And if her father cares for her...well, he'll come around because she'll make him. *Bethany needs you to care.*"

Surprised by the insight, Justin rose and hugged the older man. "Thank you, Kosta. But we're not going to talk about this anymore."

"Okay. I respect that." Kosta backed off. "They should be done with business and having lunch. Should we join them?"

"No. I'm not in the mood to be their intermediary. Let them deal with each other."

"Brilliant!" Kosta patted him on the back. "Just brilliant!" He turned and walked toward the door, making funky clucking sounds of joy. "What a smart boy. You know them well."

Justin burst out laughing. "This is an unorthodox convo."

"It is what it is," Kosta replied.

The door swung open, and Paul barreled in.

"We need to talk." Paul lifted his chin at Justin, while clasping his uncle's arms and setting him aside. "Now."

"I'll see you boys later."

Radiating with tension, Paul looked over his shoulder and watched Kosta leave. He released a breath and sank into a chair. "Time's up, babe. The lady knows what she wants. It's up to us."

* * *

Not happy with her request, but understanding it, Justin reluctantly agreed to the time needed to acclimate to their new relationship. The rest of the world wasn't as easy in accepting "unique" or "different" relationships as the people on Mykonos were. The island had earned its hedonistic reputation because of its open-mindedness. New York, Athens, and any other realm they occupied were not the same. They had no choice but to give her the time she'd requested.

He somehow managed to do *City Wings* stuff, clearing the remainder of the day for whatever came their way.

But a simple coffee and an afternoon swim wasn't cutting it.

"Where the hell is she?" Justin asked, checking his phone for the tenth time.

"We agreed to give her the space she asked for. You fucking insisted on it," Paul said. "So we're sitting around like dicks, not doing what we want."

"We want her long-term, as a friend," Justin maintained, hoping he'd manage to convince himself he believed it, before he saw her with someone else. "If we're willing to do that, she'll be good with it. She won't avoid us, will she?"

"No idea," Paul said, pulling himself from the water and sitting on the ledge. "She should be here by now. I'm turning into a fucking prune waiting."

The second the words were out of his mouth, she strolled into the courtyard. "Hey. Looks like you're enjoying the afternoon."

"Join us," Justin blurted, then kicked himself in the ass. *Nice of you to respect her need for space, dickhead.*

"Maybe next time," she said, clearly forcing a smile. "I'm going to take a short nap and get ready for tonight. Later, dudes."

She gave them her back, wriggled her fingers over her shoulder, and walked into her room.

"Later, dudes?" Paul muttered. "Seriously? She's just going to strut off like that and leave us hanging? We should go after her and make sure she's with us tonight."

Maybe, but what would that say about them understanding her needs? Squat.

"Look, she may know what her body wants, but she's not the kind of person to hook up easily. She's probably tired from a full day of work on jet lag. Needs to rest."

"And what if she goes missing again?"

"She won't."

Those fucking words came back to bite him in the ass an hour later.

Bethany was nowhere to be seen.

Done with his freddo cappuccino, Justin reached for the one he'd ordered for Bethany, the one that remained untouched, and pushed the almond cookie around the plate. He looked back at her closed door. It wasn't opening.

"You sure she's still here?" Paul said, voicing Justin's worry. "She could have snuck out when we went in to change."

What were they? In high school?

Justin walked to her door and knocked.

Nothing.

Paul came over and shouldered him to the side. He tried the knob.

Nothing. It was locked. "Now what?"

"She said she needs space. We give it to her," his mouth said, but his mind disagreed—strongly.

Go after her, you asshole.

"It's only fair. She'll find us before dinner," he said aloud.

Or someone else will find her, and you'll be without her all night.

"Not with you on this one," Paul said, trying the shutters. Shutters were locked, too. "She was pissed, and justifiably so. Yet, she has no problem giving us some of our own medicine, smiling sweetly, and throwing that friend shit and *dudes* in our face."

Paul had a point. She did smile sweetly. *Later, dudes.* She'd corralled them deep in the friend zone and had vanished. Again.

"She's not that kid anymore, Justin. She's not waiting around or pulling petals off of daisies looking for love. Either we're there for her or someone else is."

"We're there," he said, wiping his palm down his face. "Yup, we're there," he repeated, unwilling to accept someone else being there for her.

* * *

But they had no idea where there was.

She didn't return to the room, so at ten o'clock they went for dinner on the terrace and scarfed down…Justin couldn't even remember what they'd eaten. He was once again disappointed when she wasn't in her room when he'd knocked on her door hours later, morning coffee in hand.

"I'm going to work," Paul announced, coming out of their room and finding him sitting at the little table, now positioned between the two suites. "You go to work. We'll get through to her."

* * *

Almost twenty-four hours of not seeing her had passed when she breezed into his office in a tiny pair of denim shorts and a painted-on white Mykonos tank top. "Hey, J. How's it going?"

He swallowed the lump in his throat, not sure if he should jump her right then and there and put an end to the cat and mouse game they were playing, or feel happy because she was clearly enjoying herself.

Fuck. She was acting the part of a cheery tourist.

"I see you found Paradise Beach," he said, letting his gaze drift to her breasts.

"Oh, yes. It was amazing," she gushed. "And Super Paradise was awesome. Got this shirt half price."

Probably because they only used half the material needed to make it, he thought.

"Nice," he said, forcing his voice to sound easy. "Paul and I were talking about dinner in town. What are you in the mood for?"

"Aw, thanks. But Christo invited me to join the staff supervisors at their weekly get-together. He says the casual nights have done wonders for them. We're meeting up and heading out in a few minutes."

He wasn't good with her going out in half a shirt with Christo.

Leaning forward, he pushed up on his knuckles, and rose from behind the desk to tell her so, but didn't get the chance. She leaned in, touched her lips to his cheek, and wiped all thoughts from his mind.

"Have fun tonight," she said, turning on her heels and walking toward the door. She fluttered her fingers over her shoulder. "Maybe we can do lunch tomorrow."

* * *

"Lunch tomorrow." Paul didn't bother to mask his annoyance and his golden eyes went dark. "We've been relegated to lunch now?"

They were back in their room, meeting before dinner as they'd planned, but they were alone. No Bethany to share the afternoon almond cookies with.

"By the time I'd recovered and went after her, she was out of sight. I heard the rev of a motorcycle, and then saw her on the back of the Ducati."

He'd also seen the way Christo had leaned back, rubbed his palm over her thigh, and spoke against her mouth—which just happened to reach over his shoulder. How could lips reach so fucking far?

She'd placed her hands on his hips, tossed her hair over her shoulder, and her long waves swept down her back as she laughed harder than he'd seen her do in ages. Then the damn lothario pulled out his best move, and the front wheel left the ground. Bethany pasted her breasts to his sculpted back and wrapped her arms around his chiseled chest, clearly enjoying the fucking ride.

"Fucking Christo picked her up on the Ducati," Paul said.

Christo better not be fucking.

"Did he pop his wheelie?"

Grudgingly, Justin nodded. The Ducati was Christo's definite chick magnet and his preferred mode of transportation to their beds.

"Look, she wasn't dolled up in a slinky dress or in her business clothes, so they're probably not going out for long. For Pete's sake, she was wearing cutoffs when she got on the bike. The night out can't mean much to her if she didn't take the time to get all dolled up," Justin said, trying to not only convince Paul, but himself.

"Cutoffs and a see-through tank top," Paul growled.

"I said white. Not see-through."

"Right. Like the clubs and bars in Paradise Beach don't have wet T-shirt contests." Shaking his head, Paul tossed his own shirt across the room and strolled toward the shower. "You're the one who said she's super competitive. She's going to win all those fucking contests." Then he stopped and turned to look at Justin. "I know where they're going."

"Where?" Justin asked, stripping out of his own clothes and walking toward the shower.

"Enigma. They were talking about it yesterday."

Justin shoved his partner into the shower and walked in behind him.

"Get in. Get out. No fucking around. We're done waiting. She wants benefits. We give her the damn benefits. You and I. No one else."

Chapter Nineteen

"You look gorgeous," Christo breathed against Bethany's ear. "Certain body parts of half the bar patrons are standing up and saluting."

She smacked his bicep, but couldn't keep from giggling. "I feel sorry for any woman you set your sights on. She won't stand a chance against that panty-melting grin."

"Spent years perfecting the technique," he teased, snaking his arm around her lower back. Pressing his chest to hers, he dipped her, and covered her body with his, as the dance ended.

Bethany liked him, really liked him, and so she didn't like the way her thoughts pulled her out of the moment with this great guy and kept veering to two stubborn-ass men that had her insides tied in knots. She also didn't like the idea of possibly leading Christo on, even if he was the mastermind of the dance scene and had insisted he knew where her heart was.

"Hate being a cock block," she said in his ear. The music was loud and the massive amount of voices in the air weren't conducive to a civilized conversation.

"Did you say cock block?" Christo asked, smirking and failing to control his laughter. He smoothed his large hands down her arms and pulled her into a tight hug. "You're too cute. I can totally understand why those *malakes* are overwhelmed."

"I'm serious. I feel bad," she said, but didn't take her hands off his muscled arms. "There are a lot of beautiful women here. You're single. I'm the cock block, because I'm standing in the way of you having a good time tonight."

"That's where you're wrong, *koukla*. I'm having a wonderful time." He smoothed a thick finger over the bridge of her nose and kissed the tip. "I'm enjoying getting to know you. You are a pleasure. Have a sister for me?"

"Ha! Sure do." Sheridan would drive the big Greek he-man insane. She spun to the rhythm of a catchy new song, sang *hey nah nah nah nah*, and tossed her hair over her shoulder as she threw him a playful kiss.

Christo pretended to catch the kiss in mid-air, place it inside his shirt, close to his heart, and then danced up behind her, fitting his groin to her ass and flattening his large palms over her the top of her pelvic bone.

"They're here, aren't they?" she asked, feeling the tingles move up her spine.

"They sure are," he confirmed, smoothing her hair off her shoulder and nuzzling her neck. "I suggest you blush prettily, *koukla*."

"Done, *kouklo*."

"No." He stopped dancing, turned her against his body and looked down at her. "You don't call me *kouklo*."

"Why?"

"It's too pretty. Don't like it."

"Okay, stud."

"Better," he said, fitting his thigh between hers and moving them to the rhythm.

* * *

"Fucking shit. They're grinding like there's no tomorrow. There. By the DJ," Justin said, making to walk past their selected table and to the dance area.

Paul reached for his arm and held him back. "Wait. Something is off."

"What?"

"Trust me, Justin. Let's sit down and order our drinks." Paul motioned for Justin to slide over the plush loveseat. "Think about it. Has Christo ever shown such blatant interest in a woman?"

"She's not a normal woman," Justin argued. "If he played it cool, someone else would swoop right in and steal her from under his nose."

"Bingo!" Paul pointed his index finger at his cousin. "He's keeping the other guys away. And he's trying to tell us something, and he's not being as 'almost-subtle' as he was yesterday."

Years of summertime "watch-and-learn how the ladies should be treated" instruction flashed through Paul's mind, and he was certain that his cousin wasn't moving in on his woman. Christo was keeping her safe while forcing Paul to come to his senses.

"It's one of Christo's lessons," he said

"His notorious Romeo lessons?" Justin asked, realization dawning on his face.

"Exactly." Paul stretched his arm over Justin's shoulders and played his fingers through the hair at his nape. "And it fucking worked. It got us worked up and worried."

"And it got us here," Justin said, nodding in agreement.

"Sit back and enjoy the show, babe. We'll never have a sweeter view of that dance floor. She sure looks good out there." He adjusted the room in his pants, placed his right foot on his left knee, and pulled Justin in for a kiss.

"I'm so freaking blessed you walked into that cafeteria all those years ago."

"Back at you," Justin said, brushing his lips over Paul's mouth. "Love you, Paul."

"Love you more."

They settled back on the seat and watched Bethany work the dance floor like she'd been dancing in Mykonos's hottest clubs for years. Her shorts rode up just right, showing a perfect amount of rounded ass cheek. The tank didn't allow for a bra, so her breasts bounced beautifully with the music, and as the night heated up, a slick sheen of perspiration coated her freshly tanned skin.

"She's so damn beautiful," Justin said, biting his lower lip. "It's not about being jealous of someone else having her anymore. I want her with *us*."

"I'm right here with you," Paul agreed. "She's safe. And she's having fun. Give her a few more dances and we'll go get her."

The Adele song "Send My Love to Your New Lover" played, and a shot girl sidled up to Paul, blocking his view of the way Bethany's curves carried the tune. Paul waved off the artificial DDD blonde, who didn't take *no* very well, but he managed to finally shift her to the side by slipping a five into her tip belt. He looked past her, once again connecting with Bethany swaying her hips and singing the chorus.

She looked straight through the crowd and into Justin's eyes.

Bethany wiped the back of her hand beneath her eyes, and he realized she wasn't wiping at sweat. She was crying.

"Go," Justin said, as Paul rose from his seat and raced to the dance floor. "I'm not letting go of anything."

Christo had already gathered her into his arms and was kissing the top of her head, when Paul reached her and closed his fingers around her wrist.

"Come over here. You don't get to send it. Give him your love yourself." Paul cupped her head, held her against his heart, feeling guilty for loving the way she fit to him as her body trembled.

Justin smoothed his knuckles down her cheek, and urged her to look at him.

"No tears, love. No more tears." Hauling her against him, he cupped her face, bent his head, and claimed her mouth, crushing her lips and thrusting his tongue past them, leaving no question on how much he truly wanted her. "Tears were the only reason I stayed away, love. The only reason. So no more tears. Please."

Paul looked at them, really looked at them, and everyone else faded away. His partner placed little kisses along the line of her lips, licking over every swollen bit, and finally sinking into her pretty mouth with tenderness only a true lover possessed. Tenderness Paul knew, and tenderness he wanted for Bethany.

Justin lifted his head and met Paul's gaze, communicating their agreed intent and desire. *If she wants our love, we're going to love her.*

He turned Bethany toward Paul, and Paul placed his hands over Justin's, their fingers spread and alternatingly stroked over the softness of her jaw as Justin slipped his hands down the side of her throat and moved to her shoulders.

Paul lowered his head, slowly sweeping his tongue over her lips, gently closing his mouth on hers, and pulling her quivering body into his embrace.

"Come home with us, baby. We have things to see to."

She nodded.

"Love, I'm trusting you to know what you want on this one." Justin brushed his thumb over her cheek and swept away the last tear. He tucked her against his side, his lips on her hair. "Because I want everything. And I want anything you want. Anything."

With those loaded words, Paul knew his partner had placed his heart on the line for all to see. Justin loved her. He'd do anything for her. Including risk his own heart.

Paul glanced at his cousin, who lifted his chin in understanding. They said goodbye in Greek, and Paul followed Justin and Bethany through the crowd.

Once outside, Paul lifted Bethany into his arms, cradled her against his chest, and carried her to the car.

"I can walk," she whispered. "I'm okay."

"I'm not," he admitted. "I need this."

Handing the keys to Justin, he gathered her close and folded his body into the back seat, fitting her in his lap, and instructing Justin not to force the gears since they were driving downhill.

"I got this," Justin replied, starting the car. "Take care of Bethy."

"Done," he said, smoothing back her hair and touching his lips to her forehead. "You see what you do to me, baby? I'm letting Justin drive just so I can keep touching and holding you."

She laughed and kissed the underside of his jaw. "Thank you. You're truly sweet and brave."

He'd never been called sweet, so he wasn't sure how accurate that was. And as Justin stepped on the gas and the car lurched, he wasn't so sure how brave he was either. He questioned his sanity over letting Justin drive. He chuckled and lowered his face between her breasts.

"Or maybe I need a lobotomy."

"It's less than a mile," she said, her voice soothing, and her fingers playing with the hair at his nape. "I kind of like where I am."

"Me, too, *koukla mou*." He sank his hands into her hair and pushed it off her beautiful face. "I'm sorry, but I'm not strong enough to keep our agreement and give you the space you asked for. Agreement or not."

"An agreement made without my input," Justin said from the front seat. "Sweetheart, we'll take anything you give us."

"We can't give you any more space. My body knows what it wants, Justin knows what he wants, so I really hope your body still wants the same."

"No more talk. Let him drive," she said, burrowing into him and confirming they were all on the same page.

* * *

Justin drove into a parking spot and pulled on the hand brake. He would take anything they gave, for as long as they were willing to give it, to have them together. But fuck, it sucked to be so out there, heart on the chopping block, body vibrating with need, and without one bit of control over his own fate.

He rubbed the heel of his hand in the center of his chest, hoping Bethany and Paul would come to the realization that they could make being together work beautifully if they only tried.

Fuck society. Fuck obstacles. He'd make it happen. He loved them.

"I want us on common and neutral ground," Justin admitted. "Just the three of us, and nothing else present."

"Sounds perfect to me," Paul said.

"Me too," Bethany added.

"Good, sweetheart." He raised his finger and waved it side to side, aching to touch her lip and prevent her from worrying it. She did that when she was nervous.

He didn't want her nervous, didn't want any doubt between them, but even Paul showed signs of defensiveness. Paul held her close, as if shielding her from any hurt Justin would cause, and that's when the complete picture materialized.

Justin, the one who had held out from the friends with benefits relationship, was the common denominator.

She and Paul had looked to him to make it okay. He'd held back, concerned about the asinine remarks some of the staff had made.

Had they outgrown each other?

Was she the beard in their relationship?

Maybe it was summer spice?

Were they not enough for each other anymore...

None of the fucking above.

Paul and Bethany needed to know that they were each more than enough on their own, but together, the three of them were so much more.

They'd both stepped back and waited on him. It was his move. He either accepted them or he didn't. No time frame. Nothing. Just them.

Only true love and caring allowed another person power over you. And they had so much power over him because he loved them. But fuck, they loved him too. Their love for him was the very reason for the protective wall they'd built around themselves.

They really loved him, so Justin possessed the power to actually wound them.

He never would. Never.

Actions speak louder than words, he thought, steeling his resolve and walking behind the car to meet them.

He was not one to shirk responsibility or shy away from a challenge, and this relationship was his greatest challenge; he was more than willing to carry the weight and take a risk.

He bent and kissed Bethany while Paul held her in his arms, and in the same breath lifted to Paul and kissed him.

"You two are my greatest desire," he said, running his palm over Paul's chest and bringing it to rest on Bethany's abdomen. "Will you give me tonight?"

Bethany sighed her acceptance. Paul nodded.

"Good. The only thing I ask is for each of you to walk into tonight on your own." He smoothed his hand over the side of Bethany's thigh, lingering where Paul's arm held her. "Please put her down. Each of us walks in on our own."

Paul gently placed Bethany's feet on the ground, keeping his hand on her lower back. She reached across him and squeezed his hand.

Justin smiled. "I like that. You're here for each other, and I'm here for you."

"We're here for you, too," Paul said.

"I know. But you gave me tonight. Good?"

"Okay," Bethany whispered, the spot at the base of her throat exposing how quickly her heart beat.

"Perfect," Paul said, the muscle ticking at his jaw giving away his excitement.

Justin had made the right decision, and seeing how they responded only reinforced his eagerness to build a physical gateway that would blow their minds and refute any objections.

"Let's go, loves. Walk on into our courtyard." He stepped aside and motioned for them to walk ahead of him. He thought aloud as he watched them. "Paul, you shared what you want to do for Bethany in your dreams. I want those dreams to become reality."

Justin thought he heard Paul groan, and seeing how Bethany leaned into him and curled her fingers around his bicep, he was sure he hadn't misheard.

"Bethany, a long time ago you whispered a hidden wish in my ear. That wish has starred in my dreams for years. Tonight it will also become reality."

She glanced over her shoulder at him, her cheeks flushed and her eyes big. But she bit her bottom lip as she nodded.

They entered the courtyard and walked to the closest door—Bethany's door. But he didn't want it to be her room, her hospitality, and him and Paul as visitors.

They all had themselves to offer.

Nothing more. Nothing less. *Common ground*, he kept repeating.

He held out his hand and asked for her key.

Bethany searched her pocket, produced the key, and handed it to him.

He unlocked the door, reached his arm inside, and turned off the exterior light.

"Give me a minute. I'll meet you by the chaise lounges. The far end of the pool. Place them together, and wait for me."

He opened the door to their room—and that was the problem, it was Paul and Justin's and not also Bethany's room. He tossed the key on the table and walked to the bathroom. He grabbed the clean bath towels, swiped the covers off the bed, and headed back to the lounges.

Stepping into the dark night, he glimpsed the shadows in the reflecting light of the stars, and his chest barely contained his happiness. Bethany stretched to meet Paul's kiss. His hands pulled her up his body and on to her toes. She wrapped her arms around his neck and melted into him. They met soft, gentle, and sensuous as all hell.

"Nice," Justin said to himself in a low tone. "So freaking nice."

He quickly made up the chaises by placing towels over the cushions, stripped out of his clothes, and entered the pool. Barely disturbing the water, he swam close to where they stood, watching Paul and Bethany tangled in each other's arms the whole time. "Damn, you could kiss."

"Damn, you look kissable," Paul echoed, a satisfied grin on his face.

"Then I suggest you lose the clothes and join me," Justin said.

Positioning himself at Bethany's back, Paul snaked his hands around her waist, and worked the button on her shorts. He lowered the zipper, slowly skimmed his hands inside the denim, and pushed the shorts down her legs. He left her in a thong and the tank. "I've been thinking of seeing you in this shirt, all wet, all night long. Mind going in dressed like this?"

Hearing Paul voice his desires, Justin wanted to cheer in victory. Paul had never been the bystander type, but he'd held back where Bethany had been concerned. Now he was actively in.

Bethany let out a soft breath and sat on the edge of the pool. But Justin smiled at the irony of the relief pictured on her pretty face. She didn't know how visual Paul was in his sexual preferences. He'd want her walking around in tiny little see-through outfits all the time.

Shit, she was beautiful.

Justin swam to Bethany's side, fit himself between her legs, and raised his chin to Paul, indicating he expected him to strip and then join him.

"Wouldn't do it any other way," Paul said, pulling his shirt over his head and tossing it aside. He stepped out of his pants, and then jumped in, feet first, right beside where Bethany sat. He reached for Justin and cupped his nape, pulling him in for a kiss. "I said you look kissable. Kiss me, Justin."

Chapter Twenty

This was it. It worked or it didn't. They came together or fell apart.

Justin skimmed his palm over Bethany's thigh to pull her into the water, cup her ass, fit her snug between Paul and himself, then leaned in and licked over Paul's bottom lip. Groaning, Paul captured his tongue, sucked it into his mouth, and Justin lost himself in the sensation.

Justin angled himself against Paul, sliding his length over Paul's girth and grinding close.

Bethany placed a hand on his shoulder and he felt her preparing to push away. The awareness immediately sobered his mind.

Paul must have sensed her intent, too.

"Sorry," she whispered.

"For what?" Paul said.

She moved her leg. "I was in the way."

"Never in the way," Justin said. He wrapped his arm around her waist and hauled her between them. "Are you happy here? With both of us?"

"Yes."

"Good. Because you fit perfectly." Paul was first to claim her lips; teeth nipping, tongue licking, until she moaned. He covered her mouth with his own, crushing her wet body against his, and sliding his finger along the strap of lace on her lower back.

"I want this. And Bethy, I'm more than happy with you here," Justin said. He was careful to be gentle with his touch, but he didn't hide how much he wanted her.

"We're both very happy and want this to be what we all want...together."

She let out a long breath and smiled. "I want."

"Then, baby, let me see you," Paul said, his eyes sparking with heat as he traced his fingers along the wet outline of her breasts over her shirt, and turned her to face Justin.

Guiding her head on to his shoulder, Paul supported her as Justin lifted her lower body in the water. With her legs on either side of his hips, Justin pressed his palm to the triangle of white lace, circled against her, feeling her heat spread on his skin.

Paul moved his hands to her right hip, tore at the lace, then did the same on the left hip, and exposed her trimmed, dark curls to their view.

"Everything about you is so beautiful." Steadying her against his chest, Paul slid his arm beneath her, bent to cup her breasts, and slowly gathered the wet material in his hands. He lifted the shirt, exposing all her incredible curves. "I've been dreaming of seeing you exquisitely naked."

Justin skimmed his hand up her belly and between her breasts, keeping a hand on her back to keep her high in the water. He spread his fingers over her throat, to her jaw, and used his thumb to part her lips.

As Justin supported her, Paul moved and lowered his head, kissing each breast and suckling their rosy tips.

A growl built deep in Justin's chest, and his cock ached with need. His balls were so taut, he didn't know if he'd last until he could be inside her, but Paul firmly cupped him, and Justin settled at his familiar touch.

"Better than I imagined," Paul said, nipping around the tight buds, then sucking them hard between his lips.

She arched her back, pushing her center against Paul's palm, and a sigh mingled with a groan as he slipped a hand between her legs and caressed her.

"Kiss me," she said, wriggling in Justin's hold, and reaching over her head to wrap her hands around his neck.

Justin turned her in his arms and sealed his mouth to hers. Tasting like sweet heaven, she swept past his lips, stroked over his tongue, and grinded herself on his erection.

Paul pressed up against her back, touching his lips to her shoulder, sliding his length along her slick heat, the head of his cock nudging Justin's balls as he moved. He cupped Justin's ass with his free hand and held them tight and comfortable in his arms.

"This is ecstasy," she breathed.

Justin couldn't agree more. He angled his hips and pushed up against her, loving how Paul felt coming at him from between her legs. Shivers raced through him as Bethany placed open-mouthed kisses across his jaw and down his neck, and he lifted his chin, searching for Paul's mouth. He was greedy and wanted it all, but fuck, they'd granted him the night.

Paul crushed his mouth to Justin's, thrust past his lips, and Justin sucked on the man he loved with all he had while holding the woman he loved against him. As need and desire built, he pulled back, biting his lower lip for control.

Why the fuck had he chosen the damn pool? The pool?

"Bethy, hold on to Paul and let me get some protection." He lifted her against Paul, her legs moving with ease around his waist, and placed her hands on his shoulders.

She pushed up and out of the water, presenting a dark nipple for Paul to suck, and Justin almost came from the mere sight of the water sluicing off her body on to Paul's face, as Paul's tongue flicked over her.

"I'm protected and healthy," she said, arching her back to offer Paul more.

Justin met Paul's gaze. It had been three years since they'd been with anyone else, and they were both tested annually.

"I'm healthy," Justin said, stilling his progression out of the pool.

"I'm healthy, too," Paul said, moving to her other breast. He licked at the lush flesh. "Are you certain you want it like that, baby?"

"Yes," she said, arching her back so his mouth was at her nipple again. "Please."

Paul parted his lips and sucked her in, walking her toward what Justin knew to be the shallow end of the pool with a seating bench.

Seriously, why had he chosen the damn pool?

The water made it difficult for what he'd originally planned, and both of them taking her for the first time in these conditions wouldn't be pleasurable for her.

But he was about to explode, and he couldn't wait much longer. In order to make it good for all of them, he needed to get creative. Fast.

He moved to the little seating area, and sat on the edge to where Paul was bringing her.

"Bethy, I want your mouth on me," he instructed.

Paul released her nipple and guided her toward Justin, placing her on her knees on the seating area. Her soft ass in the air, her full breasts brushing against Justin's thighs, she crawled up between his legs, with Paul at her side.

Sliding his hand down her ass, Justin recognized the moment Paul pushed his fingers into her warmth by the way her back curved and she moaned in pleasure.

"You're so wet, baby," Paul groaned. "So wet, and not from the water."

Justin reached between her legs, and circled his thumb on the tight little bundle of nerves at the top. With a welcoming touch, Paul guided Justin's fingers into her warmth and groaned as she ground down and her muscles gripped them.

Paul closed his other hand on Justin's cock.

"Fuck." Justin growled, thrusting his hips into Paul's touch.

Paul held him firmly in his grasp, smoothed Bethany's hair away from her face, and instructed her to watch. He eased his long body beside her, kept an arm curled over her back, and continued to drive her need with his fingers while he pumped Justin.

Her eyes were dark with yearning, as Paul worked Justin and her in sync. Her tongue swept over her lip, and Justin groaned. Bethany bent her head, closed her kiss-swollen lips around Justin, and sucked him into her mouth. She moved her hand over Paul's and they stroked in tandem.

"Let me," she said, licking beneath the rim of his head, and dipping her tongue into the weeping slit at the top.

Paul met her tongue, and for a brief moment, Justin thought he'd lose the fight on his control and spill his release. He sucked in some air, as she took him deep in her mouth, and Paul cupped his balls. Groaning, he covered Paul's hand with his own, tangled the fingers of his other in her hair, and stilled her bobbing.

"Stop," Justin growled. "Not like this. I'm not ready. I want you trembling with need before I come."

He released Paul's hand, and loosened his hold on her hair. They both stared at him, Bethany with a perplexed gaze, and Paul with eagerness to make it so.

"My night. My call," Justin said, looking from one to the other. "You're going to come all over Paul. Paul and I are going to come inside you. And we're all going to come together." He guided her mouth back to his cock. "Slow, loves. Gentle."

Paul shook his head and grinned in ecstasy. He moved behind Bethany, positioned her knees farther apart, and slid into her.

"So good. So good together." He curled over her body, meeting Justin's gaze. "I'm not going to last long."

Justin was having a hard time concentrating on anything but the feel of his cock stroking over her tongue and nudging the back of her throat. He rolled her nipples between his thumbs and fingers, pinching tenderly as she increased the suction.

She was close to the edge.

Her body went tense and her mouth lax, as she forced herself to breathe.

Paul's thrusts grew harder and faster, pushing her up Justin's thighs, so he held her close and watched as the flush of her orgasm spread in a pretty pink blush on her skin and Paul emptied into her with a guttural groan.

He collapsed over her spent body, which lay deliciously loose on Justin.

His mind rejoiced and his heart swelled at the knowledge that Paul and Bethany had found their pleasure together. So unlike other sexual experiences, this one didn't have him needing his own orgasm to be satisfied.

Justin released a long breath and closed his eyes.

He was honestly happy, but still hard.

He felt the laughter build in his chest, but held it back. One hand smoothed over Bethany's cheek, the other curled around Paul's nape, and he inhaled deep. A few breaths later, and she'd recovered and her tongue eased over his aching head, while Paul's hand stroked his balls.

He may have been happy, but he wasn't stupid.

He didn't stop them.

Paul cupped and stroked, Bethany licked and sucked, and Justin was in heaven.

He thrust up and past her lips, feeling his release leave Paul's hand and slide down her throat.

Together…they all lay spent in the water.

Damn fucking pool.

Next time, they were making love on a bed.

Together.

Chapter Twenty-One

"Bethy."

Dream, she wanted to sleep and dream.

"Bethany, don't fall asleep, baby. Not yet."

If she scooted up Justin's body, she could rest her head on his shoulder and drift off on a dreamgasm.

"Come on, Bethy. Let me help you up, and I'll take you to bed."

Nope. She was good. Warm bodies, hard bodies, and the soft breeze made for the perfect dreamgasm, oh, and those bodies...did she already think that?

"Come on, sweetheart. Don't give in to it."

Why not? She was exhausted. She deserved the peace. No, she deserved the tingles.

"I'll take her," Paul said, squatting beside them and pulling her into his arms. "I love carrying her. And we need to get her to bed."

Bed?

She fought to open her eyes, and when she met Paul's gaze, she couldn't look away. Those eyes, those freaking telling eyes, not normal brown, but amber with gold flecks twisted her insides in a very nice way. They glinted with wicked promise, but somehow offered security.

"My bed?" Bethany asked a little hesitant.

"My bed," he replied. "It's bigger."

Yes, she was glad they'd showed up at the club. And yes, she could spend hours between these men. It was definitely Justin's intoxicating scent and the promise imbedded in Paul's eyes that had her lady parts awake again and ready for more action. How could she want them again after what had just happened?

"Fuck me." Paul's brow furrowed as he tucked her against his chest and he let out a long breath.

"Put me down. You don't need to carry me," she said, squirming in his hold. "I'll walk. It's okay."

"Like I said, I like having you in my arms," he said, raising her high, as if he was doing one of those arm exercise routines, and nuzzling his nose on the side of her breast. "But baby, you can't keep looking at me like that and expect to get any sleep. You're killing me."

"She has a way of doing that," Justin said, chuckling as he placed a towel over her and patted her dry. He touched his lips to her forehead, then leaned across and brushed his mouth over Paul's. "Let me get you a towel, and then we'll be good to go."

He stepped to the chaise lounges, returned seconds later, wiped a towel down Paul's legs, then draped it across his back. She loved the way they cared for each other. Loved the way they cared for her.

"All set," Justin announced, tossing the bed covers over his shoulder and striding ahead of them butt-ass-naked, doing nothing to calm her excitement as he held the door open.

Paul deposited her in the center of the mattress, crowding in beside her and tucking her against his chest. "Comfortable?"

"Very," she said, skimming her palms over his muscles. She brushed her mouth over a flat nipple. "Couldn't be better." A soft breath escaped her, and he grinned.

"Good," Justin said, sliding in behind her and sending more shivers down her spine as he fit the covers over them and kissed her shoulder. "Goodnight, loves."

Pressing his groin to her ass, he wrapped an arm around her, and settled his hand between her legs. "Sweet dreams."

Her heart skipped a beat and she held her breath. But this time it wasn't from excitement or anticipation. It was pure and simple disappointment.

"You can't do this again," she said, shoving back from Paul and pushing on Justin's hand.

She sat up. The covers fell away.

"You can't give me a glimpse at what it could be and then stop." Wriggling the length between them, she climbed from the bed.

"Get back in bed," Justin said, holding the sheet for her.

"No. I don't want to sleep. That's not what I agreed to." She really hadn't. He'd said her whispered fantasy would come true. "You, Justin, you're messing with me."

Okay. Maybe he wasn't deliberately messing with her, but he was avoiding what he knew she wanted.

She'd come this far. She might as well go for broke.

She'd never before been presented with a possibility of her body between two men, and now he was screwing with her. Stopping before she'd had the full experience.

Justin reached for her, smoothed his palm over her calf, and whispered again for her to come back to bed.

"Stop avoiding the real the issue with the testosterone smokescreen. We have one night to do this," she said, taking a step back. "And if you don't want everything I want, or if you can't handle it, then you don't get to touch me anymore."

"Three nights," Paul corrected, sitting on the edge of the bed and motioning for her to walk back to him. "We thought it would be nice to leave something for tomorrow. Something for you to come back for."

"Didn't we already discuss how I feel about you thinking for me?" She turned on Paul, frustrated and burning up from within. "I get a say on what I want."

"Every say," Justin responded.

"Well, in that case, I want a night of everything," she admitted. "I want to know exactly what it's like to have two men—"

"Men you want and trust?" Justin asked, his dark eyes full of need.

"Yes, J." She glimpsed the flash of vulnerability in his gaze, and softened her tone. This was just as difficult for him as it was for her. He'd been hurt once, too. He was taking the same chance she was by reaching for something they'd once considered unattainable. "I never would have been in the pool with you or standing naked asking for this one night if I didn't want or trust you."

"Three nights," Paul repeated. "Including tonight, we have three nights to share before reality shines its fucking bright light on us. Three nights of ecstasy before we need to be friends, friends forever," Paul said, standing and walking behind her. He snaked an arm around her hip and slid his hand between her thighs. "No reason for you to turn away from us. None. And we will not settle for one night. We want all three nights."

"Okay," she murmured, moist heat pulsing with desire.

"Just making it clear. We are not willing to give up your friendship after three nights of pleasure," Justin added, fitting a hand over her hip.

"I didn't plan on giving up on our friendship," she whispered.

"That's all I need to know. And since we're all together on this, and I haven't had enough yet, we're taking this back to bed," Justin said.

Somehow, she'd found it in her to insist on what she wanted.

Justin and Paul had come to stand with her, and the hands alternating between rubbing her back and stroking the need between her legs made everything better.

Strong fingers massaged the base of her scalp and swept her hair from her face. With a finger beneath her chin, Justin turned her to face him, and she closed her eyes, leaned against him, and when she felt his breath on her mouth, she ran her tongue over her lips.

"I want everything," she said. "Don't stop. Please."

"Fuck. You really are killing me. You can't be this sexy, all while being so sweet in your appeal." Deep and guttural, his voice rolled through her body.

She opened her eyes and looked into Justin and Paul's faces, both mere inches from hers. Paul's hand smoothed her hair back, and his breath caused her lips to part. She leaned close, and stroked her tongue over his bottom lip.

"Nothing sweet or innocent, Paul. I know what I want."

She trusted them to make it right.

Bethany allowed herself to fall into their hands.

Paul slid a calloused palm over her hip and around to her backside. He lowered his butt to the mattress, then kissed over her belly. "I'm so damn good without sleep."

Justin placed his hands on her shoulders, tapped his knee into the back of hers, and bent her so she crawled over Paul and on to the bed.

"I'm going to make you beg for more with each time you come."

"Me, too. Promise."

"I'll hold you to it," she said, excitement fluttering out of control in her belly.

"Yes." Paul slid under her, placed his hands beneath her arms, pulled her up his body, and settled her thighs at his shoulders. Raising his face to meet her, he groaned with appreciation as he swept his tongue through her aching center, and she rounded her hips in response.

Justin moved to her back, pulled her head against his shoulder, and sucked the softness of her earlobe between his lips.

With each stroke of their tongues, she fell a little more.

Justin and Paul did make her beg, and her thighs trembled as her climax hit and she came undone in Justin's arms while straddling Paul.

Every bit of her fantasy materialized at their hands, hands that guided and positioned her body between theirs. But reality proved better than fantasy. She burned with the need to have them both.

"I need," she cried.

Justin pushed into her, groaning his pleasure.

"That's a beautiful view," Paul said, feathering his thumb over her nipple and reaching between her legs to cup Justin's balls. "I could watch you all night."

"No, love. You're doing much more that watching," Justin said. "It's time."

Justin curved over her back, guiding her head down on Paul, rocking into her as her climax built and her body ached for release.

"Patience, baby," Paul said, reaching across the bed and retrieving a bottle from the nightstand drawer.

Justin slowed his thrusts, and positioned her higher on Paul, still pumping into her as Paul nudged at the sensitive bundle and made her legs quiver.

"Bethy," Justin said, withdrawing from her body. "We're going to take you together." His hands remained, spread her soft flesh, and he slid a cool, lubricated finger between her ass cheeks.

"Your body is ready, baby. So ready. So pretty," Paul rasped, while he circled his thumb at the tip of her mound and more desire rippled through her body.

"Let pleasure take over," Justin said, positioning himself but not pushing in.

She looked into Paul's eyes, waiting for more.

"It's all you, baby," he soothed, his thumb smoothing over her, the tingling matching the stretch. "Take me slow."

Justin held her hips, strong and reassuring as she lowered herself on to Paul.

"Move back on Justin when you're ready for both of us," Paul continued, still holding her gaze as her heart pounded in her chest. He lifted his hips, and moved deep within her.

She closed her eyes, reached behind her, and nodded.

Pushing back, her body trembled as Justin inched into her. He stilled. Paul claimed her mouth, nipping on her lips, until she sucked hard on his tongue. His taste had her craving more, and as she rounded her hips, and her breath grew ragged, Justin's hand slid over her back and he pushed in another inch.

Slow and gentle, until she was stretched with an incredible fullness, which had every cell in her body spinning out of control, they filled her and made the whispered fantasy come true.

"Breathe, love, just breathe," Justin said against her ear, guiding her body down on Paul.

As she inhaled, Paul wrapped his arms around her and pushed his hand over her lower back. He suckled her breast, and nipped on the hard tip, his teeth a temporary distraction from the sting in her backside as Justin seated himself deep with her.

"Let go, baby. We've got you now."

She blew out a breath, and buried her face in Paul's neck.

Justin withdrew, and Paul thrust. She was full and stretched, unable to think of anything but the blissful sensations they inflicted on her. They set a magical rhythm, strumming over every one of her nerves, and driving her higher with each stroke.

She wasn't sure how long they moved in and out of her body, but when they growled they were coming, she let loose, her spirit soared, and her body shattered in orgasmic ecstasy as they emptied themselves inside her, filling and completing her with their passion.

She was theirs.

Heart, body, and soul.

Theirs.

* * *

"I like watching her sleep. She makes the cutest little moans," Paul whispered to Justin. "Her hands reach and touch, and well—it's just nice."

There were lots of hands. Hers, Justin's and his. And it was more than nice.

"There's no way I can sleep now," Paul said, carefully tracing her face and lips, craving more physical contact, but not wanting to wake her. "How are we going to sate this need in only three nights?"

"We don't have to keep it to three nights," Justin said in a low voice.

"But that's all she wants," Paul said. "This is a fantasy for her, an adventure, and not a way of living. She won't accept us, Justin. She comes from a traditional upbringing, with societal restrictions shaping her choices."

"You don't give her enough credit," Justin said, bending to brush his lips on her forehead. "You don't give any of us enough credit."

That wasn't true, Paul thought, as Justin left the room again. He could sense how right they were together, but he was a pragmatist. Once they returned to the outside world, the staunch businesswoman wouldn't give of herself so freely, the city boy wouldn't be able slow down and just live in the moment, and he would still want a home full of children.

How did one explain to a child that it not only had two dads, but three parents?

"This is the last of it," Justin said, shaking Paul from his thoughts.

He placed her clothes in the nightstand drawer, switched off the lamp, and reached for Paul. He bent and kissed him.

"Don't think so hard in the middle of the night," he said, kneading the tension in his shoulders. "Put your head down and close your eyes. You'll sleep."

"I'm waiting for you. I sleep better with you in bed."

"I have to lock up next door. And then I'm done. You need to be up earlier than I do, in less than two hours, so try to sleep."

As usual, Justin was right. It was after four. "Okay, babe. Climb in on her other side so I don't wake either of you when I leave."

"You won't," Justin said with a soft chuckle. "Bethy sleeps like the dead. Much deeper than I do."

"I feel like I'm at a disadvantage," Paul admitted, surprised that the disadvantage didn't bother him. "You know so much about her. I'm just learning."

"Then you'll also need to let go for once and just trust me," Justin said.

"Justin?"

"Yeah, love."

"Is it wrong that I want her again?" Paul pulled back the sheet and presented his traitorous hard-on. "I can't erase the image of her lips around you, knowing how hard you come, and how much she must have worked to take you. I want that, too. I want to wake her and make it happen."

"And that's where you're at a disadvantage," Justin said, not bothering to silence his laughter. "Having known her longer, I *know* Bethy would love to wake up for you."

He walked away laughing and sporting a new erection.

He walked back to find Bethany kneeling on the bed, Paul's hands on the back of her head, as he held Justin's gaze and slid past her lips.

"Perfect, just perfect," Justin said, lust and wonder in his dark eyes. He stepped up behind Bethany, took hold of her hips, and thrust forward.

Chapter Twenty-Two

Paul stared out the window at the colors of the sunrise painting the sky. From where he lay, he could barely see the sea, but he refused to move away from Justin and Bethany. Nothing so carnal had ever felt so good. When they'd collapsed in a sated heap, she'd surprised him by asking that he never hold back from what he wanted.

"We have three nights," she'd said. "I never thought I'd know such total abandon. I want as much of you as you're willing to give. I'll take all of you. I'll give you my all."

She'd brushed her lips over his, then had snuggled against Justin and slept.

Paul hadn't slept, and he wasn't sure how long he'd watched them sleeping so soundly, their breathing soft and their intertwined bodies relaxed, but he finally forced himself out of bed.

Typing out a quick text, he asked Christo to wait for him at the villa. They needed to talk in private. When his cousin's reply flashed on the screen, indicating he was putting on the coffee and Paul should bring a loaf of fresh bread, Paul went to shower.

Five minutes later, dressed in a pair of jeans and a white tee, he bent over Justin and Bethany, touched his lips to each of their shoulders, and left to meet his cousin.

* * *

"I'm surprised you're up so early," Paul said, embracing the other man in greeting. "Who are you and what have you done with my cousin?"

"Good one," Christo said, leading them to the veranda and a table set with butter, olives, and cheese. "Got the bread?"

"Right here." He placed the paper-wrapped loaf on the table, pinched off the corner, and handed it to Christo.

"I owe you." Christo stuck a piece of cheese into the crispy bread, then popped it in his mouth. He held up a finger, disappeared into the kitchen, and returned with two mugs of Greek coffee. "Made you a triple, and it looks like you need it. Now you owe me, little guy. You look like shit."

Laughing at the little guy reference, Paul clasped his cousin's shoulder in a show of appreciation. Accepting the mug, he moved to the table. "And not just for the *triplo*."

"Yeah, you're welcome," Christo teased. "That's just how it is with little cousins. Our looking out is never done."

"I think I may owe you even more before the day is through."

"What's up? Why the serious tone? And why are you here without Justin?"

"Justin and Bethany are at the resort, sleeping in," Paul said, confirming what he knew his cousin had already guessed. "You knew we were watching that morning on the beach. Had a good time riling us up, eh?"

"It must have worked." Christo shrugged, chuckling while he sipped on his own dose of caffeine. "Actually, since Bethany is in bed with your man at this very moment, it definitely worked."

"Fuck off. I'm not here to thank you." Paul knew his cousin well. True, he'd been irked by the amorous antics at the front desk, but when the envy had cleared and his cousin's message had come through, he had figured out what Christo had been up to. He'd gotten over himself at the club, and while he was grateful for his concern, he didn't need to express it verbally. He knew. "How much did Bethany share with you?"

"The basics," Christo said, his brow furrowing in concern. "She and Justin have a past. They had a difficult breakup during their studies at university. You met her for the first time on the ferry ride over. And you claimed you had no interest in anything other than being friends, while you acted like a Neanderthal." Sucking the meat off an olive, he waggled his dark brow. "Do I have it right so far?"

"Yes," Paul said, engaging Christo in a fork fight for the same piece of cheese. "Did she tell you about her father?"

"No. But I've done my research on Edward Michaels." Christo placed his fork on the edge of the plate and crossed his arms. "He's a shrewd businessman, and also a very successful one. I didn't get any red flags on the deal."

Neither had Paul, before the connection had been made. "There's more to it. The man is a dick and will trample anyone that gets in his way.

Trust me when I say the likes of him aren't right for Vaso's Dream."

"Bethany's demeanor and work ethic are. She's the one representing Luxury Homes. She's right. I doubt her father will have much to do with it personally."

"I'm going to strongly, very strongly, recommend *Theo* doesn't accept his offer."

"You sure this isn't about you and not Luxury Homes?" Christo asked. "You don't want the resort sold. Could that be your problem with Michaels?"

"No." Paul shook his head, taking a deep breath as heat filled his head. "The dick tried to buy Justin."

Christo's laughter didn't surprise him. They both knew no one could buy Justin.

"When Justin told him to go fuck himself, Michaels crushed his own daughter to put an end to things. Things between Justin and Bethany were left unsaid, and both of them were devastated. You never saw the Justin I first met. He wasn't pretty. It took him a long time to get himself together and get over her."

"But he never really got over her," Christo said, not one to stand on political correctness and sugarcoat the situation for Paul's benefit. "You're worried he wants to go back to her? Worried you're not enough for him anymore?"

"No. Not like that and not in the traditional sense. Justin and I are solid. We don't take each other for granted and what we have is the real thing."

Paul trusted what he and Justin had, and they both knew never to take it for granted. What he didn't trust was his own sense of belonging with Bethany. There was an undeniable pull between them, but he wasn't used to falling for anyone so quickly. And he was falling for Bethany. Or maybe, if he considered his need to keep claiming her, he had already fallen. What did that say about him?

"The woman is beyond beautiful, super smart, and honestly sweet, but considering the time frame, only a physical draw makes any sense," Paul spoke aloud.

"I see," Christo said, sipping more coffee. "So while your relationship with Justin is not threatened by her, her resurfacing throws a wrench into your neatly made plans."

"Yes. I think that's why initially Justin came up with the friends crap," Paul said.

Christo laughed again.

"I know. I fucking know. I said it was crap," Paul admitted. "Even a blind man could see the sparks. Thankfully, she's more realistic about the situation than he is, and brave little Bethany called it like it was. Either we stayed away and gave her a chance to acclimate to the friends' relationship, or we stepped up and made good at dealing with the physical fire."

"She did call it," Christo said, respect evident in his voice. "Wow."

"Yes, wow. Bethany all but suggested being friends with benefits was better than ignoring the sexual tension."

"And that's why she's with Justin in your bed at this moment?"

"Even if it would have been better for her, we couldn't step away."

"Then everything has worked out," Christo said, patting Paul's shoulder. "And since this friends with benefits thing never lasts, I suggest you get your ass back in that bed and enjoy it before she finds a benefits man that offers her more than friendship."

Paul didn't like that, but he wasn't taking the bait. He let the dig roll off his shoulders in order to bring up the real reason for his visit.

"That's partly why I'm here. I'm not sure where this is going, but I don't want to undermine it before it starts," Paul admitted.

"I'm not getting how I have anything to do with your sex life—"

"I don't need your help in my sex life. Thank you very much," Paul said, sinking his fingers into his hair in frustration. "I want your help with the business dilemma."

To his credit, Christo didn't crack another joke. He waited for Paul to continue.

"Kosta has offered you the resort. Won't you reconsider?" Paul asked.

"I won't," Christo said, sadness crossing his face. "I get where you're going with this, and I wish I could help you out, but I can't. I need to move forward and piece my own life back together. I may have messed up in the past, but I'm lucky enough to have the chance to fix things. I'll continue to help with the resort for the season, but come September, I'm out. I won't have the time."

"Not what I wanted to hear, but I understand." Nodding, Paul searched his mind for options. The resort couldn't fall into the hands of a shady conglomerate, no matter how perfect its representative was. "It's a family-built operation. A large corporation would ruin it."

"He's offered it to you, too," Christo pointed out. "If you decide to take it, you know you can count on me if you need me. I can't assume all responsibility, but I can help. We're family. We stand together."

"Thank you. But, it's impossible. We have *City Wings* to consider. And taking on such a big endeavor is guaranteed to change our lives. Justin isn't really into white picket fences and a peaceful seaside. He thrives on the city life and the challenge of building things from the ground up. We're not ready to settle down yet."

"Doesn't Bethany change that though?"

"I don't think so," Paul said, finishing his coffee. "When *Theo* requested we come and help with the sale, I broached the subject with Justin and suggested long-distance management, with being hands on for the season. He made it clear he didn't want to be tied to the island every summer. He said *City Wings* still needs us and we can't change our life like that."

"I'm not convinced he would say the same thing if you asked him today," Christo noted. "What ever happened to that exit strategy you two had to avoid burnout?"

"We're not there yet," Paul insisted.

They let the conversation drop, and the two men who could have been twins born at different times, looked out at the sea and the resort below them. Such close family bonds were difficult to find, and Paul knew that having family like Christo at his side was a bonus few men ever knew.

"You'll do great with the vineyard. You'll get things back on track."

"It means a lot to hear you say that," Christo said, clearing his throat as he leaned his elbows on his knees and looked straight into Paul's eyes. "Pavlaki"—he used the version of his name that he'd used when they were children—"you know that above anything else in the world, we're cousins—brothers, in fact. Even if Luxury Homes buys the resort, you always have a place on the island. My home is your home."

He knew. He didn't doubt it for a minute. He placed a hand on Christo's shoulder and smiled. "Thank you."

"No thanks needed between us."

"I have a lot of work to do before her father arrives. I'm not sure how, but I need to make Kosta see the benefit of keeping this place. I'll approach Justin again on our options."

Paul was back to thinking about managing from afar and giving his uncle the free time he wanted, but with Christo stepping back, it would be even more difficult.

He was even more concerned about crushing Bethany's spirit. She didn't deserve to be lumped into the same category as her father. And while he'd been honest with her about his feelings on the sale, he didn't want her to think he was undermining her efforts.

Distance. Space.

He was the one in need of it when it came to dealing with Luxury Homes.

"Will you step in for me with Bethany?"

"I tried, but you shoved me out of the way last night," Christo teased.

"Funny," Paul said.

"And then there's Justin. Don't think I'd be any good in that department."

"Shut it," Paul said, rubbing his chin for patience. "Get serious."

"Fine. I'm here."

"Will you work with Bethany and take care of being the resort liaison while I do my homework on Michaels and try to figure out an alternative to the sale?" Paul asked.

"Consider it done," Christo replied.

"Thank you." Confident with Christo at his side, he stood. "I'm taking them into Chora for lunch. Want to join us?"

"Maybe you should order room service while they're still speaking to you."

And with that jab, Paul arranged for Christo to review any remaining items with the Luxury Homes representative on the following day, leaving him one day to just enjoy being with Justin and Bethany.

He made his exit.

Bethany and Justin were speaking to him. He wasn't staying away. First, he was going back to Justin to see if last night had changed his point of view on the resort.

* * *

Paul knocked, strode into their makeshift office, and stared in shock.

Rather than the desk being littered with legal pads and empty coffee cups, it was spit-polish clean. No yellow papers, no empty glasses, only a single folder and a dark laptop in the corner. Justin's backpack was stuffed with files and on the chair.

"What the fuck, Justin? Why you packing?"

"I'm cleaning up. Preparing for the *City Wings* teleconference," Justin replied, handing him the leather bound presentation folder. "You have everything Kosta requested for Michaels. I'm done. I'm out of this."

"You need to review it with him," Paul said, trying to ignore the obvious compulsive actions that pointed to Justin's mind working on overdrive. And fuck him, but it definitely looked like he'd been packing.

"You can do it just fine. There's nothing out of the ordinary in there. Everything's good."

"No," Paul insisted. "We'll do it together after we get back from lunch."

"Think I'm going to pass on lunch."

Paul tossed the folder on the spotless surface, then rounded the table and drew Justin into his arms. He touched his mouth to Justin's pulsing temple and sucked in a long breath of air for strength.

Before him stood a flashback image of freshman Justin—a troubled man. Paul didn't get it. Didn't know why Justin was so wound up and distressed after the spectacular night they'd shared.

"Come on, babe. What's up?" He drew back and searched Justin's face for a hint of what was going on, but the hollow look in his eyes gave nothing away. Dull and devoid of any emotion, Justin held back. Frustrated, Paul squeezed his arms.

He really couldn't understand why.

"Talk to me, Justin. Don't shut me out. I know something is bothering you, and it's giving me a bad feeling. You're not angry with me, are you?"

"No. I'm not angry with you." Even with the reassurance, Justin remained indifferent to Paul's concern. The stoic man didn't offer any explanation.

Paul had to try. He had to find a way to reach him.

Justin rarely pulled away.

Something big had happened to do this. It wasn't about *City Wings* or being absent from work. The staff was more than capable of dealing with the everyday stuff.

"You tired, babe?" Paul asked, curling his fingers around the side of Justin's neck and stroking his thumb over the dark stubble on his jaw.

Justin shook his head. "I'm good. I have work to do." He gave Paul a weak smile, then shoved out of his arms. "You see Christo?"

"Yeah. He's onboard. Even though everything has been covered, he's agreed to finish up with her tomorrow."

"She's not going to take it well. She has her heart set on this place, and she won't appreciate you looking into her father's past business dealings."

"It's not about her," he said, opening the folder and skimming the report. It was about her asshole father. He wasn't getting the resort. "Like you said, it's business. She's an effective businessperson, so she'll get that. Our place doesn't fit the Luxury Homes profile, and they'll inevitably alter it to do so. I'm not willing to let that happen. Vaso's Dream won't be changed for the worse. It won't lose its charm and appeal."

Justin gazed at him, and the atmosphere around them grew heavy as his eyes went dark and completely shut him out. Not only did Paul not know how to deal with it, but the concern was mixing with anger.

Anger toward Edward Michaels.

And anger toward Justin for pushing him away.

The distancing was something he thought was behind them, way behind them.

"I won't let him hurt you again."

"I don't give a flying fuck about Michaels," Justin said. "She wants the resort. You don't want to give it to her. And I have work to do. It's not all resort shit, you know. We have a business to run."

"This attitude has nothing to do with business and it has nothing to do with the resort. It's definitely not about Bethany and I wanting different things for it, either," Paul said, not willing to let it go. He leaned on the table and crossed his arms over his chest. "Talk to me, Justin. What's going on?"

Justin flipped up his laptop cover and pressed the on button. "Nothing. *City Wings* is coasting on pure momentum and it's going to crash if no one is there to see to all the bullshit. I don't have time to deal with fucking drama."

"Vaso's Dream is fucking drama? Dickhead Michaels is fucking drama?" Anger roiled in his gut and Paul stared at his typically level-headed partner. "You're looking for a fight. What the hell has gotten into you?"

"Nothing. I said I have work to do," Justin said, turning away and looking at the screen. "You find a way to deal with it."

"And Bethany? What about her? You going to turn away from her, too?"

"No." Justin gave a slight shake of his head. "We said two more nights. I'll see it through; after all, I'm not an asshole that thinks being with the two of you is a hardship. Don't put words in my mouth, Paul. Give me space. I have work to do."

Fuck. Space. What was it with everyone demanding space?

"Fine. I'm taking her to lunch in town. You coming?"

"No," Justin said, not bothering to look up. "I'll catch up with you after the teleconference."

"Fine," he repeated. "Suit yourself. I'm going to show her the island, and enjoy every minute she'll spend with me. You can stay by yourself and sulk over whatever has crawled up your ass and died."

Having had enough of the attitude, Paul grabbed the report folder and walked away. If Justin wanted to act like a dick over nothing in specific, then he'd let him. Today was about more than the two of them. Today involved Bethany, and he would make it an amazing day for the woman. He wasn't giving her a reason to regret what they'd shared. And neither would Justin.

"Get your head straight before you go anywhere near her. I'm not going to let you fuck with her because you have a stick up your ass."

Chapter Twenty-Three

Paul walked over the grounds, forced morning hellos to staff and guests, and longed for the solitude of their room. He had to step back and get a better perspective on the situation. He needed to figure out how to deal with the undertow of emotions Justin was caught in, and he needed to find a way to appease the yearning he had to see Bethany.

He ached to hold her and make sure she was okay. Ached to see her bright smile.

Actually, Paul ached to be held by her.

He unlocked the door, tossed the key on the table, and released a breath at the scene before him.

Bethany was in bed. Still sleeping.

Well she'd been sleeping before he'd woken her by loudly cursing when he stepped into the room.

"What's wrong?" She sat up and pulled the sheet up her chest. "What happened?"

He swiped his palm over his face and looked away from her full pink lips, which spoke of all they'd shared in the night. She should look wonderfully fucked, not worried. He couldn't stand the angst in her eyes.

"Sorry I woke you. It's nothing. Work stuff." He repeated Justin's excuse, feeling like a total fool for doing so.

She deserved better than that lame explanation.

But hell if the woman didn't strip him of all his defenses.

He turned his back to her and opened the refrigerator door, searching for anything so he wouldn't have to meet her gaze and let her read his own concerns.

Warm, comforting arms snaked around him, and her head lowered on to his shoulder. Fuck. He needed her. Wanted her to make him good.

He wanted her comfort.

"Whatever it is, you'll make it okay. Don't let it ruin our day."

Our day…he had to admit he liked that. He returned the bottle of juice to the shelf and turned to wrap her in his embrace. He cupped the back of her head, held her against his chest, and rested his cheek against her hair.

"You're right, baby. Nothing is worth wasting our day together." With his finger beneath her chin, he tilted her face up to his, calm washing over him as she looked up. "And you're the one making it okay. Thanks."

She flashed him a brilliant smile, and he wanted to come clean. He wanted to just be with her.

"Here's a quick summary so we can move on. Justin is pissed with me. You're going to be pissed with me soon. And I can't blame either one of you."

"It's okay. We'll make it okay." Caressing his back, she placed a series of soft kisses on his chest. "What is going to make me pissed?"

"The resort sale. We're on different ends."

"I already know that. It's not news," she said, kissing up his neck. "So, next." She flicked her hand. "Justin? Why is he pissed?"

"I'm not sure. Pissed is the wrong word. He's upset," Paul admitted, realizing she could probably figure out Justin just as well as he could. He lifted her and positioned her so she stood on his feet, close, real close, as he wanted her. He slid his hands to the small of her back and steadied her, feeling her warmth pressed against him. "He claims it has to do with *City Wings* being on its own, but I don't think so. When he's anxious, he throws himself into work and doesn't come up for air."

Holding her against him, he walked them to the window seat. She sat, curled up between his legs, making the view so much better because she was sharing it with him. They listened to the wind, which had picked up significantly since the morning, and looked out at the whitecaps on the blue waves.

"He always did," she said, after a few minutes, smoothing a finger over his forearm and soothing away the agitation he'd felt when he'd entered the room. "It comes from his dad being so complacent and leaving his mom in such a bad state when he died."

"He told me it had been real rough for them."

"More than rough," Bethany said. "We were only in tenth grade, but J had to grow up real fast. At first, it wasn't obvious, but once their measly savings were gone, they worked so hard just to stay in their apartment. Both Justin and Leslie."

While they'd discussed what had happened, Justin never harped on his father's shortcomings as a provider for his family. Paul knew his mother had worked two jobs until Justin had bought her a townhome and insisted on paying the mortgage and maintenance.

"His mom finally cut back to just one job three years ago," Paul said. "She gave up waiting tables and is now working as a receptionist for one of the legal firms whose offices she used to clean."

"It's about time. Leslie was great at anything she did, but Joe was so laid back, so she did everything. She deserves a normal workday. Deserves some Leslie time."

"How Joe was with his family wasn't right. She shouldn't have had to toe the line on her own," Paul said.

"Joe wasn't a bad man. He loved his family. But he didn't think anything past the rent and supermarket money was necessary. That's why he let his life insurance lapse without even telling her. They used the money Justin was saving for a car to pay for his funeral."

"That, I didn't know." Paul suddenly felt guilty for all the driving jokes. "I wouldn't have bugged him about being such a bad driver if I had."

"I'm sure that's why he never mentioned it," she said. Bringing her knees to her chest, she turned on the seat, snug between his legs, with her back to the window, and looked at him. "He's not one for pity."

"I know." As the wind tousled her hair and they eased into casual conversation, he opened up about what had happened in the office. "I lost my temper, but I shouldn't have. Something other than work and the resort is bothering him. I didn't know what to do."

"That's why you're upset?"

"Yes. He won't let me help."

"He's so freaking determined to give more of himself than he receives," she said. "He's definitely working himself up over something. And it could be the resort or your company. But he won't ask for help. He's stubborn like that."

"Maybe he'll ask you." Sliding his fingers through her long hair, he looked into her eyes. "He's confided in you in the past. Maybe he'll talk with you."

"Ha!" Bethany huffed. "Wishful thinking. And if you're referring to the time after his dad's heart attack, it was more like he just let me be there. He didn't ask."

"I'm sure he wanted and needed *you*."

"Perhaps, but his verbal communication was minimal. The only reason I know about him paying for the funeral is because I went with him to the bank and was there when he closed out the savings account. He never said why, but he withdrew all forty-one hundred dollars, and never spoke about buying a car again. It was a simple service."

It must have been. Paul knew his own grandfather's casket had cost way more than double that. And his Justin had to go through it as a kid. "It's a good thing you were with him."

"We were best friends by then. I couldn't let him go through it alone." She shook her head and gave a little chuckle. "Even Leslie let me in. She actually let me make finger sandwiches for people who came to pay their respects. Never before or after did she allow anyone in her kitchen."

"Typical Leslie," Paul said, feeling his connection with Bethany solidify over their love for Justin. "And you were still a baby, but you were there for them."

"That's what you do for people you love."

So true. While they'd never faced the same difficulties, he'd do anything for his family. Anything.

"Trust him," she said in a low voice. "He'll either figure it out or come to you. He trusts you."

Paul shook his head and rested his cheek against her hair. He inhaled the sweet scent of Bethany mixed with the fresh sea air, and restless optimism moved through him.

"Did you and Justin meet in school?"

"Nooooo," she said, enunciating the "o" for a good five seconds. She chuckled again and her body shook with amusement. "He was in public school. I went to a stuffy, all-girl private school. I bumped into him one time when he was helping Leslie clean my dad's office. And teenage girls can be rather crafty. From that day on, I tried my hardest to be the last one out of the pool at swim practice so it would be real late and one of the moms would drop me off at my dad's office instead of at home. It was easier for her when it was late."

"So, prepubescent Bethany had her eyes set on little Justin early."

"Sure did," she admitted with a big smile. "But there was nothing little about Justin. He was the biggest part of my life. Everything about him made my day." She held her hands out and formed a heart with her fingers. "I was so head over heels for him. But it took J a few years to notice me as anything more than a buddy…except maybe a cleaning assistant. And he was hard to work for."

"I could see that," he said, snuggling her close and kissing her shoulder. "What a stupid, ignorant guy he was for taking so long."

"He's still a cleaning tyrant?"

"Totally," he replied, laughing. The day before the cleaning lady came each week, Justin made him pick up all his clothes and put the bathroom toiletries in order, while he tidied the kitchen.

"I'm glad you're here," he said, repeating it in his mind, because damn, he was so happy she was still there and he'd look like a fool to keep telling her. He gazed into her big, bright eyes and shook his head. "I'm not crazy about the circumstances that brought us together, and I'm worried you'll hate me for it, but I'm so happy you're in my life now."

She feathered her thumb over his brow, gave him a genuine smile, and brushed her mouth over his. "Paul, that's how things work sometimes. It's not always moonlight and roses."

He kept his mouth to hers, slipping past her lips, and tasting her sweet breath. "Can I have another kiss before you change your mind about how things work sometimes?"

"As many as you want," she said, parting her lips and spreading her fingers over his back. "And when you do piss me off, do it with kindness."

He chuckled, wondering how with a simple request, she touched deep inside him. He leaned in and claimed a kiss before raising his head and looking into the warm, melted, milk chocolate-colored eyes that he couldn't get enough of.

The physical connection was undeniable. What baffled him most was how he felt he knew her…really knew her…and adored everything that was his Bethany.

Fuck. *His* Bethany? Where did that come from?

"Whoa. What's up?" She'd clearly felt his body tense at the thought, because she moved left to right, peering into his eyes. "What are you thinking?"

"You may not like what I'm thinking," he teased, tracing the swell of her breast through the sheet.

"Try me," she whispered.

"I'm thinking I want to carry you to bed, taste every inch of this sweet body, and then lose myself inside your warmth until you cry out my name," he said, lifting her into his arms. His lips grazed along her jaw, her throat, and over her collarbone.

Running his palms over her thighs, he wrapped her legs around his waist and cupped her bottom. He wanted more of her, so much more.

"That sounds like a good plan," she breathed, sweeping her tongue over his neck and blowing on the wet trail.

His pulse raced and his breath quickened.

"Baby, at some point, you and I need to really discuss what is happening between Vaso's Dream and Luxury Homes. Knowing you won't appreciate what I have to say, I admit to feeling guilt, so I leave the timing of that discussion up to you."

Passion glazed, but aware, her eyes looked into his. "About me or about my dad?"

"Your father," he replied, honestly.

"He and business have no place here, in this room, or between us," she said, settling her warmth against his erection. "We'll talk later. Not here."

"Are you sure, Bethany?"

"Take me to bed, Paul."

He didn't need to hear it again. He just needed her.

Bethany warmed his heart and soothed his spirit. Her essence filled him and made him believe anything was doable. With Bethany at their side, they were whole. It was impossible to understand how it was possible to need someone in only a few days. He didn't bother to figure it out. Paul let go and lost himself in *his Bethany*.

For as long as she'd have it, she was his, and he had it all. Everything.

Bethany and Justin were everything.

He sealed his lips to hers and carried her to bed, following her down to the mattress, putting only enough distance between them to pull the sheet away. He kissed her long and hard, reveling in the feel of her fingers in his hair as he opened his heart and soul to the woman with a magical touch.

Determined to make her want him as much as he wanted her, he made good on his word.

* * *

Bethany trembled with need as he looked into her eyes and silently asked for more than a physical connection. They already had more, and the simple fact that he asked touched her. As Paul took her mouth, she surrendered to what she had in her heart for the man. Love. Without any hesitation, she accepted her total and complete love for two men, two men who also loved each other.

Her skin tingled beneath Paul's touch as he slowly traced every inch of her body, and made slow tender love to her with his mouth. His tongue followed hands, down her neck, over her breasts, and to the straining peak of her left breast. His thumb feathered over her right nipple, as she arched her back and offered him all of herself.

"This isn't what I expected," he rasped.

"What did you expect?"

"Not you, *koukla mou*. Certainly not you." He closed his mouth on her other breast and spoke as he suckled achingly on her and trailed his hand over her belly. "Nothing could have prepared me for you. I never thought I could feel for two people the way I feel for you and Justin."

"Me, too," she admitted, closing her eyes as his touch validated her feelings.

"It's real," he breathed, bracing his weight on his elbows and meeting her gaze. "What we have is very real, Bethy. I want you every bit as much as I want him. And I'd want you regardless of your connection to Justin. It's difficult to wrap my mind around the intensity of these emotions."

"I feel the same. I even feel guilty."

"Why, baby? Why guilty?"

She took a deep breath and tried to organize her thoughts, finding the task more difficult as he slid his fingers through her heat and circled his thumb around the sensitive bundle of nerves at the top.

Moaning, she lifted to him. "Some women never experience what we have...never...and I have it, twice over, with both of you. It doesn't seem fair."

"Fairness has nothing to do with it." A slow grin spread over his handsome face and his amber-colored eyes twinkled. "We're blessed."

Paul's hair brushed over her skin as he lowered his head and his mouth joined his fingers. All thoughts of guilt fled her mind.

Drowning in a sea of sensations, he was her life vest and anchor. With each passionate stroke of his tongue over her core, the pressure built deep inside her and had her floating just a little more.

Patient and tender, Paul coaxed tremors from her body, and when he slid a finger inside her and swept over her sweet spot, her breath shuddered and she bucked against him.

"Give me everything, Bethy." He cupped her ass and lifted her to him, fitting his mouth on her warmth and sucking her between his lips. With a soft nip of his teeth, he groaned in appreciation. "Come for me. Come now."

Her orgasm splintered from her body and a bright, blissful energy wrapped around her as she shouted his name in release.

"That's what I needed to hear." He rose above her, claimed her mouth, and buried himself inside her pulsing heat with a growl. His movements sure and strong, no longer tender and gently, drove her higher, kept her hovering in sensual overload. He stole her breath and filled her soul with each thrust. And he didn't let her come down from the ecstasy, but built on the simmering effects of her first orgasm.

"It's too much," she cried, wrapping her legs around his waist and rising to meet his every thrust. She inhaled deep, moaned loud, and closed her mouth on his shoulder to keep from floating away.

"Again," he commanded, closing his arms around her. "Take me with you, love."

He sank deeper inside, ground against her, and claimed her mouth as a second climax exploded and colored her world. Paul called her name as he came, pushing deeper than she thought was possible and emptied himself while crushing her against his pounding chest.

Time stopped in his arms. He held her until their breathing evened and her strength returned. She caressed his back and kissed up his neck.

Resurfacing, he shifted down her body and laid his head on her belly, drawing tiny circles with his fingers on her chest.

"For a man who doesn't need, I need you, Bethany. You soothe my heart." He touched his mouth to the underside of her breast, breathed in. "You smell so good. I can stay here forever."

"Stay," she said.

"I want to take you on a proper date. I want to share the island with you. Show you the sights."

"It'd make me happy," she said, picturing the date in her mind. "It'd make me real happy."

"And maybe…just maybe, you'll understand," he said, looking up at her and smoothing his thumb along her jaw. "Don't hate me, Bethany—"

She placed a finger across his lips. "I don't want to hear it. Not now."

"Okay," he said.

She tangled her fingers in his hair and held him against her chest. She closed her eyes and carried the beauty of their joining into her dreams.

Chapter Twenty-Four

Remorse over the way he'd acted with Paul kept Justin from the room for hours, but the pull of a quiet air-conditioned space, complete with a comfortable bed, was too strong to dodge any longer.

Suck it up, man, you're a self-absorbed asshole, and maybe you don't deserve to be tucked between two people you're so in love with, but fuck it, you're selfish enough to go for it.

He went for it.

Entering the suite, he found them tangled in his sheets.

Paul was wrapped around Bethany, or Bethany was wrapped around Paul, both obviously sated.

Transfixed, he stood there and just watched them sleep. He rubbed a hand over his face and shook his head, thoughts ping-ponging between logic and desire.

Be cold and survive.

Stay, and possibly have his heart ripped from his chest.

Misery. Isolation.

Happiness. Completion.

The dilemma didn't last long. In spite of Paul saying Justin was the stronger one, he knew better. Giving in to his want, he went to Paul's side.

Justin skimmed his hand up Paul's naked thigh, and then shook him awake.

"You going to sleep the day away or take us to lunch?"

"Lunch," Paul said, tugging on his hand and bringing him close. "What time is it?"

"Almost one," he said, settling at Paul's side.

"Feeling better?"

"Yes. Much better."

Justin flattened his palm on Paul's chest and looked at the man that had been his rock for years. No malice or hurtful intent to be seen. Just the man he loved, who happened to fit perfectly with the woman he loved.

They fit. Pure and simple. It wasn't their fault. It just was.

"What happened with your conference call?"

"Rescheduled," Justin said. "I didn't want to miss lunch. The two of you are more important than a conference call."

Paul grinned, crooked his finger, and motioned for him to lean down.

"I'm sorry." Justin bent. "And thank you," he added, starting with a light kiss at one corner of Paul's mouth, and then the other corner. With a groan, Paul tangled his fingers in his hair, stilled his head, and took his mouth in a passionate, wet, and all-consuming kiss.

"Holy smokes, that's hot," Bethany breathed in a sleepy voice. She turned on her side and propped her head on her elbow. "You're beautiful. I can stay like this for hours and just watch."

"No, sweetheart." Justin stretched up and cupped her nape. He urged her to slide toward them. "Come here. I want more than your eyes on me."

Three tongues mingled, their mouths met, and one kiss blended into the other, with no beginning and no end. They stayed connected, mouths, arms, legs, for way too short a time.

One word played in Justin's mind:

Mine.

And that terrified him. Because while Paul and Bethy were both cut from the same cloth and they fit, he wasn't and didn't. He was different. He worked hard for everything he had, but was it enough for them? Was he worthy of them being his?

Paul was the first to pull away.

"If we don't stop right now, we'll never get to lunch," he said, smacking a pretty little ass that hadn't moved fast enough. "Shower. Now. Both of you."

"Like that's going to get us out of here any quicker," Justin said, offering Bethany a hand, and hauling her against his side.

"No sexy time," Paul said. "Wash. Rinse. Get out. Get dressed."

Bethany stepped away, wove her fingers together, and stretched her arms ahead of her. Shrugging, she looked around the room. "Doesn't take me long to get ready. I'll be back in less than fifteen minutes."

Justin caught her wrist as she started for the door. "Where are you going?"

"Next door to shower and dress," she replied.

"Not if you want to dress in your own clothes," Paul said.

"We moved your stuff in here last night. No need for two rooms, sweetheart."

Her hand fluttered to her neck in a nervous gesture, but she nodded, turned for the bathroom, and strutted that heart-shaped ass for their pleasure. "Thanks."

"I'm shocked you're not arguing, but I like it." Justin motioned for Paul to stay behind. "Give her a minute."

She glanced over her shoulder and stuck her tongue out like a typical brat. She wiggled her fingers over her head.

Justin laughed and waited for her to enter the bathroom. He wanted her to discover her toiletries, and honestly, he wanted her to feel at home. Once the shower water sounded, he moved to the table. Paul joined him.

"She's come into our room, meaning originally our space, but now she needs to know it's also her space. She has to realize she's not a visitor or a novelty in this room. She belongs here."

"That's good thinking," Paul said. "When I tried to speak with her about the resort sale, she said not here. Like she didn't want it brought into this area."

"Her whole life she's compartmentalized places and people. I don't want to be limited to one of her compartments any more. She'll need to accept us. Period."

A distressed look crossed Paul's face. "I only sort of told her how I feel about Luxury Homes. Not sure how it'll play out in the end."

"Period means period," Justin said. "Period," he repeated more for himself than anything else. "It'll work out."

"Is that what had crawled up your ass earlier?" Paul reached for a bottle of water and unscrewed the cap, studying him over the rim as he drank. "Had your own worries about those compartments?"

He shrugged.

"Bethany says you throw yourself into work because of how things were after your dad's heart attack. You know I'll always take care of Leslie, regardless of the circumstances. You'll never find yourself in the same situation again. Your mom will never need you like that again. You have me. I have you, Justin. We don't ever hide our worries from each other."

"Bethany knows me too well, but I love you both anyway." Justin heard the water stop running and decided to change the subject. "Your turn. I'll go last."

Bethany dressed while Paul showered. She followed Justin into the bathroom while he showered, did her hair, and spoke to him about how Sheridan had been hounding her for more pictures. They moved around each other in a comfortable pattern, and when all three were ready they headed for lunch.

"What's on the menu?" Justin asked.

"Our girl here says she has a grave need for souvenir shopping, and I'm thinking about a catamaran sail for the sunset. We got a late start. And we need to fit it all into today because she has things to do with Christo tomorrow, so what about—"

"Gyros," Bethany interjected. "Please."

"Pork?" Justin asked, hiding a smirk while feigning offense.

"Please," she repeated, clasping her hands together and shaking them in the air. "They're super delish and like Greek fast food."

"The lady has spoken. You can have the vegetarian pita," Paul said to Justin, shifting into third gear and turning for town.

Muttering about being outnumbered, he leaned back in his seat. He grinned as he looked out the window. Eventually, he told them he was in for dinner, but not the cruise. The conference call had been rescheduled for nine o'clock, local time.

"At least you'll be done by the time we get back," Bethany said.

"Or maybe, since you're the fucking boss, you can reschedule it again?" Paul asked. "Come on, Justin. How often do we get to experience Bethany's first Mykonos sunset on the water?"

"I'll see. But you can definitely count on another late night swim," he said, reaching through the headrest and tickling her neck, knowing full well this arrangement was turning into more than a bedroom threesome.

Now to wait for the two of them to admit it.

* * *

"Table for three," Paul said to the hostess. With his hand in the small of her back, he guided Bethany ahead of him, bent his arm behind his back, and reached for Justin's hand.

Thinking they looked like they were on a field trip, Justin chuckled, and the morning's apprehension vanished. *This is how it's meant to be.*

They walked through the canopied area and sat at a table with an unobstructed view of the port.

"This place has been here since I could remember," Paul said, as they sat. "And Mr. No Meat can attest to having the best zucchini fritters of his life at this very table."

"He's right," Justin agreed. "The fritters look like meatballs, but they're so much better. You'll love them, Bethy."

Paul ordered and the table was soon covered with a variety of *mezedakia* and two pork gyro wraps. Like he had the first night, Paul described each dish as he offered Bethany a taste.

Justin dragged a French fry through the yogurt dip and brought it to her lips. "This one happens to be light on the garlic, but some places make *tzatziki* strong enough to keep away the vampires for days. So tread carefully, sweetheart."

"As long as we all eat *tzatziki,* we'll be fine," she said, licking the sauce off his finger with a sexy sigh. She shook her head and threw up her hands. "Okay. I confess. I had *gyros and tzatziki* in Athens. I fell in love with them at first whiff."

Justin glanced at Paul, who was watching her with a grin on his face.

"So you fell in love in Athens?" Paul tapped her nose and laughed.

She nodded and winked.

Hopefully, she'd be falling in love in Mykonos, too.

"To us," Justin said, raising his glass and looking between them. "Thanks for being you. I love you both."

* * *

"I'm going to gain twenty pounds if you keep feeding me like this," Bethany said, wiping the drop of honey at the side of her lips.

Truth was, the cheese pie was delicious and she couldn't stop eating it. If Justin took it away as he teased, she'd let him have it. She leaned her chin on his shoulder for a second bite. He didn't disappoint. He lifted the pastry, wrapped in paper, to her lips, then turned his face for a quick kiss.

"Told you. Honey and cheese keep this woman happy," he said to Paul, grinning as she grabbed his hand and took a third bite.

"Nineteen of the twenty pounds are well worth it," she said, chewing slowly and savoring the sweet and salty mix.

"What's the one pound that's not?" Paul asked.

"The protein bars I brought with me from the States." She guided Paul's hand up, and sipped on the frappé. "They're not worth the calories."

The men's laughter was pure joy to her ears. She'd never felt as happy as she did roaming the twisting, little paths the locals called streets. Lined with endless souvenir shops, the whitewashed streets, which looked like the locals had hand painted the white around each gray slab, were only for pedestrian use. However, scooters, and even the occasional motorcycle, seemed to be included in the traffic.

Done with the cheese pie, she linked her fingers with Paul's, and was following him up some stairs when she was literally goosed.

"Hey!"

She turned to find Justin chortling, his hands up beside his head. "Wasn't me."

Paul chuckled and pointed to the left. "Meet Petros, *koukla*."

There he stood. The mascot of the island, a grand pelican, stared at them, waiting for her acknowledgment. Bending her knees, she held out her hand.

"Hi, baby," she cooed. "You're a handsome fellow."

"He's not looking for sweet talk." Justin placed the meager remains of the pastry in her palm, and Petros inhaled the crumbs with a grateful nod. He nudged her thigh, waited for her to finish petting him between his wings, then strode off to greet the tourists.

"He's adorable," she said, watching him go.

"He's a legend," Paul added. "I think it was in the fifties when a fisherman found an injured pelican and nursed him back to health. When he tried releasing him, the pelican wouldn't leave. So the islanders adopted him and named him Petros. But in the late eighties, he passed away and the whole island mourned his loss."

"Oh," she said, holding her hand to her chest. "That must have been tough."

"My family says it was really sad," Paul said, taking her hand and continuing up the stairs. "Jackie O. delivered another pelican to the island. She was named Irene. And I think a German zoo also donated a pelican and there was a third one that also required nursing back to health. So there was Irene, Nikolas, and the honorary Petros. I'm not sure, but I heard that one of them passed away recently."

"They just wander the streets?" Worried about the beautiful bird, she glanced over her shoulder, and saw a young boy playing with the pelican. "How do they survive?"

"As you can see, the tourists love them. The islanders take care of them," Paul explained. "Other than all of them being called Petros, and possibly offending them with gender confusion, because Petros is a male name, there's no issue." He flashed a big grin and pulled her into one of the shops. "Go on, *koukla*, pick out those T-shirts you wanted for Sheridan."

Paul and Justin didn't forget a single thing of what she'd asked for, and she was grateful they paid her such close attention. She went up on her toes and placed a kiss on Paul's cheek. Then she ducked into the air-conditioned store and shopped.

* * *

They were in store number bazillion, or so it seemed, and Paul wouldn't choose to be anywhere but with them. He actually didn't mind the shopping…when it put such a smile on her face.

She scooted close to the display and leaned her head to the right as she examined yet another option for Justin's little house collection.

"This one?" Bethany asked, pointing to a ceramic church.

"Have that one," Justin said, balancing the bags full of souvenirs in his arms, and moving down the aisle to a display on the backside of the wall.

"Which one doesn't he have?" She leaned her body on Paul's arm, fit her hand in his, and laughed. "I've shown him the most adorable little plaques, and so far, he has them all."

With his biceps snug against her warmth, Paul could stay and consider all the little ceramic homes, one at a time, inspecting each piece for the smallest detail in order to keep her pressed against him. Inhaling the floral scent of her shampoo, he brushed his lips over her hair. "Get comfortable. We'll be here for a good half an hour before he settles on one."

She twirled into his chest and smiled up at him, making his whole body hum with delight. He grinned at the memory of advising Kat and Charlie to find men who made their bodies hum. Damn, but he had that two times over in his man and woman.

Unconventional? Yes. But better than anything else he'd ever known.

"I'm a lucky man," he said, lowering his face and sealing her lips with his, stroking through her mouth, and enjoying the hum in every damn cell of his body.

"Not that I mind," she said, nipping on his lower lip, "but why do you think that?"

Pressing the proof of how lucky he felt against her belly, he traced her lips with wet butterfly kisses, touched his forehead to hers, and stayed there. "Like I said earlier, I never expected this."

She looked at him with questions in her eyes, but didn't persist in making him fess up. She accepted and didn't place conditions on it. No wonder Justin wanted her forever.

Bethany, on any level, made things better.

Considering how best to express what he felt without appearing like a total sap, he smoothed her silky waves over her shoulder, and trailed a hand down her back.

"I dreaded this trip," he started, opting for honesty. "You already know I never wanted Kosta to sell Vaso's Dream. I've always pictured myself here for long summers with Justin and our children. It just about killed me to board the plane in New York knowing it could be the last time I'd be coming to what I always knew to be my Greek home. I love this place."

"As long as I'm here, you can always come home," she said sincerely. "Consider it a fringe benefit of the resort being sold to me."

Coming home to her suddenly sounded plausible, good even, but with Edward Michaels in the picture, it wouldn't be possible.

"It wouldn't be yours. It's Luxury Homes, an international corporation owned by your father."

The dark pupils of her eyes widened and her nostrils flared, as her teeth scraped over her lower lip, and recognition dawned in her beautiful eyes. She knew that anything having to do with Michaels wasn't going to be like coming home for him or Justin. She understood. And like him, she was torn.

She turned around, and silently shook her head. There was nothing to say. They both knew it. Her gaze scanned the display of little island homes, but she kept her back pressed against his chest. Thankfully, she didn't walk away.

"You're going to tell Kosta not to go through with the deal," she said.

"I already have." He hesitated, sliding his palms down her arms and soothing the bumps on her skin. "I said as much before I even knew you had any connection to Luxury Homes. But, now that I know, and now that there's more important things to consider than what I want with the resort, I'm stepping away from the details of a potential sale."

"We all want different things," she said in a low whisper, curving her shoulders forward and crossing her arms.

Alarmed she'd come to her senses and would leave him, he held her in his embrace, felt her tremble, and wanted to kick his own ass for upsetting her. When she exhaled and her shoulders relaxed, he rested his chin on her head.

They did want different things.

"That may be true, baby. But we also have something inexplicable here…"

"Something special. Something unique," Justin said, rounding the corner and coming to stand before them.

Clearly he'd been listening. He cupped her chin and swept his thumb across her cheeks, probably wiping at tears she'd chosen to hide from Paul.

He had managed to spoil their afternoon with damn business.

"We're not having this discussion in a souvenir shop," Justin said.

Recognizing the protection in Justin's gaze, Paul nodded in agreement.

They couldn't define their personal relationship, couldn't discuss the intricacies of the resort sale, nor could they find a solution to the unexpected situation they were in amongst a crowd of tourists.

The three of them were more than good together. And Paul knew he was in, all in, and he wasn't willing to get out. The no long-term physical agreement had to go. He wanted more than temporary. He wanted a real chance at a true relationship with Bethany and Justin. He wanted everything.

"Justin is right. This conversation is important and deserves to be had in private," Paul said, reaching up and covering Justin's hand. "Can we table it until we get back to the room?"

A line of pretty white teeth scraped over her lower lip, a sign he'd come to recognize as her being nervous, so he bent and swept his tongue over her lips. "Even if I don't agree, I can't sabotage you. I've arranged for Christo to work with you from this point on, and I'm going to look for an alternative to this sale. Something that will work for all of us. Promise."

She sighed and nodded, turning her face up to Justin's.

Justin bent his head and brushed a kiss on her mouth.

She smiled. Then Justin squeezed Paul's shoulder in unspoken understanding and motioned for them to head outside.

In what Paul considered an incredible act of trust, Justin left her tucked against Paul as he led the way. Paul held her close, vowing not to disappoint either one of them.

"What about your little houses?" Bethany asked Justin's back, obviously still thinking of his wants rather than her own comfort.

"I'm good, love. I have all I need."

She glanced up at the display, and Paul didn't miss the irony of her gaze fixing on a white, circular *stefanothiki*, crafted in the image of an island church. She probably didn't know what it symbolized, but he did.

As the beautiful woman in his arms stared at the unique wedding crown case, he ached for one to house three crowns. Their crowns.

It was an arrangement the church would never honor.

"I'll find a way," he whispered against the side of her temple and touched his lips to her hair, wondering how he'd come to see them as a forever thing in such a short time. Honestly, he didn't know. He just knew the bond was undeniable and it had to be. "Together, we'll find a way."

Chapter Twenty-Five

Bethany rested her head against Paul's shoulder as they walked back to where they'd parked the car. "You're not going to let him drive home because you think you hurt my feelings?"

"No, *koukla mou*. I'm not looking for such a danger-infused adrenaline rush to soothe my conscience. I'd rather get us back in one piece."

"Good," she said, tugging on his arm and stopping at a storefront. "Look." She pointed at the window display. "It's a painting of the resort from Christo's view point. Like the artist was drawing from his terrace."

She moved closer and traced a finger over the glass. "And there's our pool. The rays of the sun are reflected in the water."

Their pool…yes, it was now their pool.

"The artist of this specific piece is a local gentleman that knows every nook and cranny on the island. George's work is sold in many of the town's shops."

"Beautiful," she said. "And you must admit that the view point from the villa would inspire any artist. It's heavenly."

"You're right," Paul said. "It does inspire. And once upon a time there had been an artist on Christo's terrace. She was one of the few women he's let into his life. Marie was a young British girl that had him signing up for language lessons."

"What happened?"

"It didn't work out," Paul said, recalling how difficult the summer's events had been on his cousin. "It's his story to tell though."

They had enough to discuss.

"I say we head up to the pool and relax before our sunset sail," he suggested.

* * *

Justin watched Bethany dive into the water, and shook his head at her always-smooth entry.

"You know she swam in high school. She was great at it. Made the all-star and all-academic state teams."

"Something more I'm learning now," Paul said.

Justin glanced at him, and saw the yearning behind the Ray Ban lenses. "You've fallen for her."

"Hook, line, and sinker," Paul admitted, rubbing his hand over his abdomen.

"She's definitely fall-worthy," Justin said, swinging his legs to the side of the chaise and facing Paul, feeling only a little smug. "I was counting on it."

Paul looked at him over the top of his sunglasses. "Counting on it?"

While his body was angled toward Paul, Justin watched Bethany's fierce arm strokes cut through the water like she was swimming for time trials.

"She's working out her thoughts in her own way," he said in a low voice. "Bethy is trying to find her balance."

"Back to what you were counting on," Paul redirected.

"It's simple," Justin said, leaning his elbows on his knees and looking at Paul. "While you're new to each other, I know you both. So, yes, I have a real advantage over you when it comes to knowing how Bethany is perfect for us."

Paul chuckled and his chest heaved. "You played us?"

"Nope. I know you. I know her. I know me. And I know that I love you both. And there was never a doubt that we'd end up together if given the chance." He leaned close and grinned. "You chose to give each other a chance. I stayed out of it until the decision had been made. So once that was done, you were bound to love each other, too. It was inevitable. Even Kosta knows."

"*Theo* Kosta?"

"Yes," Justin said, chuckling as the memory of the older man coming into the office and demanding to know what he was going to do flashed in his mind. "You can say Kosta played us. Played matchmaker. He got us here in order to introduce us and *let nature take its course*."

"That sounds like something he would say," Paul agreed, sitting up and placing his legs beside Justin's. "But how are we supposed to deal with this? What are we supposed to do?"

Justin shrugged, but was never surer of anything in his life than he was about what he wanted with Bethany and Paul. "Love, I'm in. I want this."

"You're willing to change our lives? Leave your carefree bachelorhood behind?"

He laughed and scrubbed a hand down his face. "Don't fool yourself. There's no bachelorhood. We may both be men, but we've been together and committed to each other for years. Bachelorhood has no commitment."

They'd been lucky enough to have worked together, and live a life that was free of any responsibilities other than to themselves, but they definitely had each other to consider.

"Okay, so we know my family is good with us, your mother will love it, but what about Bethany's family? Will they give her a difficult time?"

"Absolutely," Justin said. "But I knew that coming into this. I don't give jackshit what Michaels wants or thinks. I just care about her."

"What happened to her mother?" Paul asked.

"Not sure," Justin said. "She left when Sheridan was six months old. They don't keep in touch with her. I don't believe she'll be an issue. The woman is nowhere to be found."

"And Bethany?"

That was the real question. He stood and walked to the deep end of the pool. "We'll need to work on that one, Paul. Give her a little more time. If she has the support of the men who love her, she won't care about anyone else's."

"That's another one of Kosta's ideas, right?"

"Yup." Justin pushed off the edge and dove into the water just past where Bethany swam. Holding his breath, he turned and wrapped his arms around her legs, bringing her under and against his body. He sealed her mouth in a kiss and didn't stop until all oxygen was depleted.

With her hands around his waist, she kicked her feet and they came to the surface.

"Silly man. What if you ran out of air down there?"

"It would have been worth spending my last breath on your mouth."

She laughed, placed her hands on his shoulders, and dunked him.

When he came up and shook out the water from his hair, drops flying in all directions, she wrapped her legs around his waist and lowered her head.

"You make me totally crazy, J. You always have."

He took her mouth, kissing her until his world spun. "I missed you."

"I missed you, too."

Smoothing the wayward strands of hair that had escaped her ponytail, he cupped the back of her head and pulled her close, vowing never to miss her again. He wasn't letting go.

"Are you feeling okay?" Justin asked.

She nodded against his neck, and a content sigh drifted from her lips. "I'm fine. I think I understand why he's so against Luxury Homes, but that doesn't make me want to step away. I love this place. Even more so now that I've been here. I'm going to find a way to make this happen."

"That's what he said." Justin lifted his head and looked into her face. "Maybe we can come up with something all together. The three of us."

"The three of us?"

He rested his forehead to hers and smiled. "Yes. The three of us. I like the way that sounds."

And he did. It would be the three of them, together, making each other happy for years to come.

"Paul and I need to speak with you. Run things by you before anything else is done. You up to it?"

She nodded and brushed her lips over his. "I'm up to it."

Grinning, Justin set his hands on her waist and turned her toward the stairs.

Paul was gone.

His towel and flip-flops were there, but he was not.

"I don't know where he went," he said, feeling her sag against him.

* * *

"What do you mean he's here?" Paul asked, hurrying beside Christo to Kosta's office. "He wasn't due until the day after tomorrow."

"I know," Christo said, holding the door open for Paul to enter ahead of him. "We don't even have a vacant room for him."

"Put him in Bethany's room. We moved her stuff out already."

Christo walked behind the desk and leaned his hands on it. "Seriously? Think he'll like the neighbors?"

"You can put the three of us up while the dickbag is here," Paul spat. "We don't need to remain on the property."

The farther away the better. He'd be civil for Bethany and his uncle's sake, but he didn't need to be neighborly or accommodating. Michaels was not getting the resort.

"So now it's the three of you?"

"Yes. It's the three of us," he said, eager to make it known and permanent. "It's going to be the three of us from now on."

"I see," Christo said, lowering on to the desk chair. "*The three of you* have discussed this and are all in agreement?"

"We haven't talked about it yet." Paul blew out a breath and shook his head. "We haven't had the chance. Michaels showed too early."

"His jet landed an hour ago," Christo said. "I tried calling you, *the three of you*, but got voice mail. I sent a car to collect him. He should be here in the next ten minutes."

"We're not selling to him," Paul said, hating the fact that Edward Michaels would be tainting the resort with his negative energy, even temporarily.

"I gathered as much," Christo said, picking up the phone and instructing housekeeping to ready Bethany's room for a new guest. VIP.

"Fuck the VIP," Paul growled. "He's lucky we're giving him a room."

"If it's really *the three of you* from now on, I suggest you find a way to deal with how you act toward the father of the woman you love," Christo cautioned. "You don't want to put her in the position to choose between you. It's going to tear her apart."

"I told you what he did to her and Justin. He's a bastard."

"He may be a bastard, but he's her father."

Paul didn't want him anywhere near Justin or Bethany. Father or not, he wouldn't give Michaels the opportunity to hurt them again.

"Where is *Theo*?"

"I also sent a car to collect him from the *kafeneion*."

"We'll get this straightened out between us first and I'll speak with Bethany and Justin. Then—"

"Doubtful we'll have time," Christo said, lifting his chin and indicating the man in the three-piece suit strutting through the terrace, a briefcase swinging by his thigh. "Looks like it's showtime."

Fuck. Not only hadn't Paul had the chance to discuss things with Bethany and Justin, he hadn't had the opportunity to run his plan by his uncle. His hands were tied. He had to be cordial to the bastard.

"Mr. Lallas?"

"Yes," both Paul and Christo replied and stood, drawing a confused look from Michaels and an associate.

"I'm Christo Lallas, General Manager of Vaso's Dream. This is my cousin, Paul." Christo offered his hand in greeting.

"Nice to meet you," Edward Michaels said, shaking their hands and introducing his assistant, Rachel. "I realize we've arrived ahead of schedule. I was hoping to meet with the owner, Constantine Lallas, and see if we could finalize the purchase a day or so early. Our representative has filed detailed accounts of the resort and we are looking forward to incorporating Vaso's Dream in our portfolio of properties. It is a charming getaway."

Over my dead body, Paul thought, fisting his hands at his sides and stepping back.

"Thank you," Christo said. "We pride ourselves in keeping the island charm while delivering the luxury our guests require." He gestured to an empty chair. "Please have a seat, Mr. Michaels."

"Our representative has done a detailed job of keeping us informed, so we are looking forward to assuming control as soon as would be preferable to the current ownership."

The representative is your daughter, you jerk. Bethany is so much more than your representative.

"Understood," Christo said. "However, as you can ascertain from the fact that you've caught us in swim trunks, we're not quite ready to discuss business at this point. My uncle is currently off property and will not be available until dinnertime."

Michaels checked his watch, and then looked between them.

"European summer dinnertime," Christo added, in a charismatic tone. "It's only seven and the sun hasn't set yet. Perhaps you and Rachel would like to enjoy something on our terrace while the staff prepares your rooms?"

"That's generous. We appreciate the hospitality, but if we are causing any inconvenience, we can make arrangements at a different location."

"No need," Christo said. "I have a party that is scheduled to depart in…" he made a show of checking the computer screen, "probably within the next half hour. Then housekeeping will need a bit of time to prepare the rooms. Please make yourselves comfortable at the restaurant and enjoy the glory of our sunset in the meantime. The concierge will see that your luggage is delivered to your suites."

Shit, his cousin was laying it on thick, but it worked for Paul. It gave him the opportunity to inform Justin and Bethany what happened.

"Thank you. That sounds very nice," Michaels said, extending his hand to Christo. "Please let your uncle know we're here and would like to meet with him at his earliest convenience."

"Will do," Christo said, coming around the desk and motioning for the restaurant host to approach. "Saki, please show Mr. Michaels and Rachel to number fourteen. They're my guests for dinner, so make sure to tell Katerina to feed them well."

Paul grinned at the choice of table. Christo had placed them in a romantic and private spot, overlooking the water, in perfect view of the sunset, but limiting their view of the resort.

"By the way, do you know what room our acquisitions rep is in?" Michaels asked. "She's my daughter."

About time he remembered that little fact.

"I've been trying to reach Bethany since we left Croatia, but she hasn't answered my calls or texts. Her phone must not be getting good reception on the island."

Edward Michaels's gaze narrowed on Paul and searched his features. Paul felt like he was under a microscope. The way Michaels's eyes shut down made it clear he'd realized something new.

"Possibly," Christo said, walking back around the desk, fitting a pair of reading glasses on his nose, and once again pretending to look on the computer screen. He glanced at Paul.

"Cell signals are sometimes spotty," Paul added, giving credence to Christo's search on a computer that he knew wasn't powered on.

"I don't see her name here," Christo said, looking up. "However, my uncle has several rooms flagged for his guests. I'm assuming she's in one of those. I'll ask at reception and let you know what I learn. Would you like me to share your suite location with her if I see her?"

"Of course," her father said. "Do you know if she's with any of the staff?"

"I don't think so," Christo said, placing the glasses on the desk and coming around again. "I think she may have mentioned an island excursion for today, but I'm not sure. I haven't seen her this afternoon."

Nodding, Michaels thanked Christo, didn't address Paul, and followed the host behind the intricate lattice of jasmine.

Paul squeezed his cousin's shoulder in approval. "Good choice of table."

"Yeah, well, get your ass over to your room and then get them up to the villa. This isn't going to go well."

"Other than the obvious, why?"

"Because in addition to being her father and a cocky money man, Edward Michaels appears to be a sound businessman. He's also very perceptive. Seemed to be sizing you up in the end." Christo lifted his chin, indicating the newcomers. "Go get Bethany settled, and then speak with *Theo* before Michaels does. I'll run interference."

He glanced at Michaels's table. Rachel had already made use of the free Wi-Fi and was pointing something out to her boss.

Edward Michaels didn't look amused.

Chapter Twenty-Six

Justin sat at the kitchen table, listening to the water run as Bethany showered. He had just disconnected from the teleconference. He was finished with work ahead of schedule and they would all go out on the catamaran together.

There was a quick knock as the door swung open and Paul stepped in. "Hey. Where did you go?"

"To see my cousin. Why are you still working?" Paul asked, but didn't wait for an answer. Instead he walked to the en suite bath and looked in. "Hi, baby."

"Thank God you're back. I was worried Justin would have to drive us to the catamaran," Bethany called. "I'll be dressed and ready to go in five minutes."

"No need to dress for me. I like you the way you are," Paul said, disappearing into the bathroom.

Justin couldn't help but smile. He liked what he saw, and the image of his man and woman fooling around like that made his body take immediate notice. Undoubtedly, Paul had pulled Bethany into his arms and had greeted her properly.

Decision made. He was going to propose that Paul assume responsibility for the resort and the three of them make it their home base. He needed to work out the details of their time back in New York. He typed in a real estate search.

Did they buy or rent?

How would they break it to her family? Her father in specific. But even the annoyance of Michael's wasn't enough to make him focus.

All he could think about was what Bethany had admitted in the pool.

She'd told him she loved him. She'd fallen for Paul. And Paul had fallen for her. It was only a matter of clarifying what they were to each other to move ahead.

His cock kept interrupting his search, telling him to check out the action in the bathroom. He gave up trying to find suitable housing, leaned back in his seat, and waited for Paul to return.

"Get a little wet," he said, chuckling at the state of Paul's clothes when he finally returned.

"Well, you know, the showerhead isn't very precise in that bathroom."

Justin laughed and patted the seat beside him. "Come here, love. Sit and talk to me while Bethy gets ready."

"Can't. Our plans have changed. You need to get dressed and pack." Paul pointed to the towel wrapped around Justin's middle. "Bethany will be out in a second."

Justin was more than a little happy that Paul was eager to head out. Fuck, he was ecstatic. Paul was thinking about more than they'd discussed, and if the idea of spending more time together made him look so happy. Justin was all for it.

"We're staying at Christo's tonight. We need to get out of here quick," Paul said, and Justin realized that Paul wasn't excited. He was anxious.

"What happened? Tell me."

But Bethany walked out, wrapped in a towel, and he saw how distracted Paul was by her cute little butt swaying its sweet way to the nightstand for a pair of panties.

"Not yet," Paul said. "We need to talk all together."

"We can order room service," Bethany said. "I don't mind staying in."

"No. Get your things. We're not staying here. We're spending the night at Christo's villa," Paul repeated. "The three of us, as it should be, with no interruptions or concerns. Just the three of us."

"I can't think of a better way to spend the night." Justin smiled at Paul and walked over to Bethany, running his finger along the edge of her towel. "We can have breakfast in bed. Once again, the three of us."

"Please let Bethany dress," Paul said. "We seriously need to talk, and I can't think past the two of you in towels."

"Talk can be overrated. And I've got all morning for breakfast," Justin continued.

"I'm meeting Christo at eight," Bethany said.

"That would be nine," Paul and Justin said in unison.

She laughed and the whole room appeared to temporarily brighten. "Fine. Nine. I'll text him to let him know."

"I'll do it. You go get ready." Justin pulled off the towel as she attempted to walk away. "Paul is right. I can't think with you strutting around all naked."

She giggled and walked into the dressing area.

"It would be nine, if you were meeting him," Paul added. "I don't think you will be though," he called. "We have a lot to discuss." Paul stepped to Justin and placed his hands on his hips. "But fuck, no matter what shit happens, she feels right. How did we get so lucky with her?"

"I think it's a three-way charm," Justin said, sealing his mouth to Paul's and kissing him long and slow. "I love you, Paul."

"I love you more."

Justin turned and found Bethany standing in the doorway in only her panties.

"Sorry," she said, looking away, discomfort in her defensive stance. "I didn't mean to interrupt. I forgot my bra."

"No sorry needed," Justin said, extending his arm. "Please come here."

She didn't move, she simply stared, and a solitary tear slid down her cheek.

Paul went to her and pulled her into his embrace. "Don't ever, ever think you're interrupting anything. We don't hide from each other. Okay?"

He tipped her chin up and she nodded.

"But baby, we have a problem."

"I know," she whispered. "It's okay. I knew from the start."

"You don't know," Paul insisted, pressing his palm against the side of her neck, tangling his fingers into her hair, and looking into her eyes. "Your father is here." He turned to Justin. "I met with him in the office."

Justin's blood rushed through his veins and pounded in his head. Edward Michaels had once again superseded his plans.

"He's not sup...supposed to be he...here until the day after tom... tomorrow," Bethany, stammered.

"He's here," Paul said.

She pushed out of Paul's arms and scrambled to the armoire, before tossing clothes on to the bed. "I have to see him. Talk with him."

History wasn't going to repeat itself. No fucking way.

"No," Justin said, wrapping his fingers around her arm like a man in need of a life ring, and insisting she meet his gaze. "You will not see him until we've talked. I need you to hear me. Paul needs you to hear him. Your father will not fill your head with bullshit again. You'll hear us out. This is about us."

"It's okay." Trembling, she looked from him to Paul, and worried her lower lip. "I know," she said. "It's obvious. You don't need to explain."

"Good," Paul said, rubbing the back of his neck. "We're all in agreement."

"We are. We're good." Smoothing her hand over Justin's bicep, she gave a meek smile. "We thought we had more time, but now it's up."

"Nothing is up," Justin replied, his body going stiff at her wrong assumption. "Nothing." Realizing his hold was too strong, he loosened his grip and smoothed over her soft flesh. "Paul said we're heading to the villa to be alone. Your father doesn't get to see you until we've had our say."

"Where is he?"

"He's on the terrace having dinner with his assistant. They're making up your old room for him as we speak," Paul said, stepping up and twirling a strand of her hair in his fingers. "Rachel will be getting this room. We're leaving. Christo told him you're on an island excursion, so he's not expecting you to answer calls or meet with him tonight. Keep your phone off."

"We have one more night?" Bethany asked, moisture glittering in her eyes.

"We don't want one more night, sweetheart," Justin said.

"We want everything," Paul clarified.

* * *

"Please, *koukla mou*." Paul offered her his hand, squatting beside the car door and staring at her. "Give us a chance, Bethany. Please."

She placed her hand in his, but didn't move. Bethany didn't trust her legs to walk into the villa. She couldn't. She'd run from her life for one more night of fantasy…a fantasy her heart ached for and couldn't deny.

Paul leaned in, secured his arms beneath her knees, and lifted her like it was nothing for him to carry her in hold.

"Don't think so much," Justin said, as he came to them and touched his lips to her forehead. "We're going to make this happen. No one will stand in our way." He glanced up at Paul and nodded. "Door's open. I'll get our things."

Not willing to miss out on a single moment they had left together, she wrapped her arms around Paul's neck and rested her cheek against his chest. "Can we watch the sun set?"

"Anything you want," he said, carrying her inside the home and directly to the terrace. He kicked out a chair, and still cradling her, he sat. "We'll deal with your father in the morning. Let's celebrate tonight."

It was the last night of completion for her, so celebrating seemed a bit difficult.

"She didn't hear us, love," Justin said. "We may be talking together, but we're hearing different things." He placed a single wine glass on the table and poured from a carafe. "We're going to start from the beginning."

"You don't need to explain," she said, squirming to sit up. She'd known what she was getting into, and she didn't expect them to reciprocate her feelings and desires. It was naïve to think it possible for them to fall in love.

"Fuck," Paul said, squeezing her hip. "I'm so dense. I just realized why you've been quiet and sullen." Then he laughed, laughed loud, and playfully nibbled on her neck. "I'm such an ass. I thought you were worried about your father. Don't be. Trust me."

She looked into his amber-colored eyes for clarification. Gold specks danced in the brown, and she saw the twinkle of relief.

"What are we in agreement about?" She closed her eyes and braced for the truth.

"Look at me, Bethany," Justin said, caressing her hand. "I loved you years ago, but I fucked up and I lost you. I never thought I'd be able to love or let myself be loved again, until I met Paul. I love him, and I'm so damn lucky he loves me."

"I know," she said, biting her lip to keep it from trembling.

"But I love you more today than I did all those years ago," he continued, clasping her hand in his and bringing it to his mouth. He placed a kiss in the center of her palm and looked into her eyes. "I'm asking you to love me."

Sucking in a breath, she blinked to keep his face in focus. "You know I do. I've always loved you, J."

She not only loved him, she was *in love* with him.

"Baby, I never thought I'd fall for someone else the way I had for Justin. I was wrong. So very wrong." Paul closed his hand around both of hers and Justin's. "I have. I love you so deep it hurts to think I could wake up without you. So like Justin, I'm asking you to love me."

Bethany couldn't see past the blur of tears. "I do love you."

She was *in love* with two men.

"Then breathe," Justin said. "Just breathe, honey."

"You love me, too?" Paul asked, hugging her close and crushing that breath Justin had insisted she take. "You really love me? Not a convenient love by association? But like in love with me? Like I'm in love with you?"

"Of course I'm in love with you," she said, giggling as he rubbed his nose against hers. "I love you, Paul Lallas. I do." Running a fingertip along the stubble on his jaw, she smiled against his mouth and sealed her lips to his, pouring every feeling she'd held back into the man.

No longer worried that she could love only one man or concerned that only one man could love her.

"I love you, Justin Bentley," she said, resting her forehead against Paul's chin as she turned to look at the tall, dark, and handsome man who had held her heart for over a decade. "I've never stopped loving you."

Justin raised his arm high in the air, high-fived Paul as if he'd just won a prize, then scooped her into his arms, pressed her to his chest, and twirled her until she was dizzy with joy. He placed her on Paul's lap, wrapped his arms around both of them, and crushed his mouth to hers.

Laughing Paul held them both, and Justin looked up and reached to pull him close. Bethany's heart swelled as their lips met, tongues stroked, and sensual growls came to the surface.

"I may not deserve this much happiness, but I'm not a fool to let it slip from my hands." With a finger on her chin, Justin turned her face up to Paul's, and kissed them both. "I love you."

The "you"…well, it was in its plural form, and it was perfect.

"There's a reason for everything," she breathed against their lips. "Everything. All those years I'd thought Justin had done me wrong I'd loved him."

"There's a fine line between love and hate," Justin admitted.

"Wait. Hear me out," she insisted. "You said you thought you'd never find love again, yet you love Paul, and Paul loves you. It's because of what happened that we're all together now. We, I, have Paul, too. It's the three of us."

"I would have found you both," Paul said, straightening his back. "I'm not about to thank your father for that. I have a difficult time being in the same room as him after what he did to you."

Justin could identify. No longer the insecure college student, he wanted the opportunity to confront the man. But the look of despair in Bethany's eyes kept him levelheaded and focused. He had her.

"Don't worry, Bethy. We know he's your father, and we know you love him," Justin said, watching the hope bloom in her gaze. "We won't do anything stupid, but we will not let him or anyone else keep us apart. Do you hear me? You're ours and we're yours. That's what counts."

She sighed, and looked to Paul. He nodded.

Then her phone sounded from inside the house.

"Do not answer it," Paul said, tightening his hold on her hip.

"I want to. It's Sheridan. I texted her on the way up." She scrambled to her feet and ran for the phone. "Hello?"

Paul had stood up and was beside Justin, arms crossed, watching her through the door. She nodded and paced, but her expression was surprisingly tolerant.

"Are you sure?" Bethany asked, sounding just a little panicked.

Paul started for her, but Justin placed a hand on his arm.

"Sheridan is great. They're very close. And Bethy loves her so much. Actually, she even loves the dickhead. So, we cannot isolate her from either one. We need to find the right answer," he said in a low voice.

"Layover in Zurich...when....now? You're boarding?" Bethany asked. She turned and looked at them, then covering the microphone, she pointed to the ground. *Sheridan is coming*, she mouthed

"Okay, sis. No problem...I'm fine...Really." She rummaged through her laptop case and pulled out a business card. "Yes. It's still the same. He'll keep it on. I'm turning my phone off, so write down Paul's number, too. Just in case."

They walked to her and leaned in on either side. Justin held out his phone and snapped a picture.

"Sheridan, is your number still the same?" Justin asked.

"Yes," came from the phone.

"Don't power off yet," he called, and selected her contact. "I'm sending you a picture."

He typed:

Fly well, little sis. Send me flight info. We'll meet the plane. Love you, J.

He hit send, and sent both the picture of the three of them standing in Christo's living room and the text message. He also sent Paul Sheridan's contact info.

I love you, J. We'll keep Paul, too. He's hot. Now take care of my sis... or I'll have to kick your butt. xoxo

"I think we need more wine," Bethany said, then snaked her hands around Paul's waist and leaned into him. "Daddy already knows about you...both of you."

Chapter Twenty-Seven

"Good," Paul said. "That should make it easier on you when we meet with him."

Bethany inhaled and closed her eyes. *We meet with him?* She hadn't expected that and hadn't considered the outcome of such a meeting. It would be best to get him one on one and pave the way to such a meeting.

"I'm not sure—"

"It doesn't matter," Justin said, not waiting for her to complete her thought. "You're not going alone. Don't say it. Don't even think it."

"Edward Michaels is not going to tell you what he thinks he knows about us without Justin and I being at your side. That's just something you're going to have to get used to. We're not stepping away for anyone."

Her insides quivered, and while she should have been annoyed with the caveman attitude, she liked it.

"Sweetheart, look at me," Justin said, squeezing her hand and standing silently at her side until she looked up. "I know you love your father. And while we do not like the man, we will respect your wishes when it comes to any relationship you want with him."

"I'm not sure—"

"We're sure," Paul said. "We want you happy, so we're not going to make you choose. We'll find a way to deal with what we feel."

Justin led them back to the terrace, bypassed the chairs, and indicated a lounger. Justin straddled the seat, with his back against the cushion. She sat between his thighs, and Paul straddled the length of the seat facing her, placing her legs by his hips. Intertwining her fingers with Paul's, she leaned her back on Justin's chest and stared at the setting sun.

Justin reached for their glass and held it while Paul poured. They sat, passed the glass hand to hand, and sipped on the homemade wine, not speaking as the sun disappeared beneath the horizon.

"Am I supposed to feel upset, apprehensive, and nervous as crap?" Bethany finally asked, gaining puzzled looks from both men. Instead of bursting into tears, she burst out in laughter. "Call me crazy, but this feels real good right about now."

Downing the glass of the wine, Justin shook his head and smirked. "You, my love, are a real wonder."

"She certainly is," Paul said, laughing with her, caressing her thighs, and falling on to her. "If we didn't have Mr. Serious watching us, I'd show you exactly how good it could feel."

"Show me. Go for it," she said, cupping his jaw and planting a noisy kiss on his lips. "I swear, either I'm totally nuts, or the wine is really potent." Free and comfortable, she kissed Paul again, then turned her face up to Justin.

"It's called shock," Mr. Serious said. "Sweetheart, you're in shock."

She stopped laughing and let the thought sink in. Maybe it was shock? Not only was she in love with two men, but she actually believed she had a chance in hell of getting her father's blessing.

"Then what am I supposed to do?"

"Well, we missed the catamaran sailing, so we can stay here and harp on your father ruining our immediate plans, or we can enjoy a night out on the town and celebrate how much quicker we've realized what's meant to be," Paul said, standing and holding his arms out to them.

"Celebrate," Justin said, cupping her butt and lifting her off the seat. "Take us to that cute little Love Nest perched on the top of the hill that overlooks the port. I've wanted to go forever, but for one reason or the other, we've never been there."

"Bethany is that reason," Paul said, taking her hand and pulling her up to him. "*Tis Agapis H Folia* is meant to be our special place. The first place we eat as an official…"

"Ménage a trois?" she offered, searching for the right term. "Couple threesome? Triad? Affair? Relationship?"

"No, baby. The name of the place actually translates as Love Nest. And there's not a term good enough to define what we have. This is not a temporary physical tryst."

"We're in this together. Always," Justin added. "No definitions or restrictions on what we have. There's no giving up on us."

"What about other people?" Bethany asked, her chest going tight anticipating their response. "You said no restrictions. Did that mean no commitment—no exclusivity?"

A growl rose in Paul's throat. "Call me a selfish asshole, but I'm not good with that. I want it to be us. Only us." His gaze narrowed and fine lines formed on his forehead. "Fuck it. You may think I'm easy going and open to everything, but I'm not. I want my family to be my family. I want you for myself."

Her thoughts flitted back to the morning. She'd been alone with Paul, made love with Paul, and Justin hadn't been there. She'd awakened to Paul and Justin entangled in a passionate kiss, and she'd liked it. A lot. There'd been no jealousy or possessiveness. Then, she'd been with Justin in the pool, and there was no denying how good it felt to be wrapped around him, kissing him, loving him. If it wasn't for the conference call, she was sure they would have ended up doing more than showering together.

"Don't get that look, sweetheart. He's not referring to us." Justin glanced at Paul, and Paul shook his head. "What happens between the three of us, two of us, two of you, well, all that is…well, it just is. And, fuck, but I get hard at the thought of the two of you together. It's one of the few fantasies I could imagine while I'm working myself."

"I'm down with that," Paul said, flashing her a big grin. "I'm not putting a number requirement on what happens between us. Two. Three. I'm happy with that. I don't feel the need for anyone else. Justin and I have had the opportunity to discuss what we want from a family, so I believe he feels the same."

"I do," Justin agreed. "All I want and need is the two of you. But Bethany, do you want something different?"

They both looked at her, uncertainty and concern written all over their faces. The irony of the situation didn't escape them, so they felt the same guilt she'd had at the previous thoughts. Damn, she loved them. Loved the way they loved each other. And loved the way they loved her.

"No. You are what I want." They released synchronized breaths and the fist squeezing her chest also released. "I want you. Need only you." And then she couldn't hold back the tears. "Tears of happiness," she managed between sniffles. "You're everything I could ever want. Even more."

"You and Paul are my world, I will do everything in my power to deserve you." Justin's thumb feathered over her cheek.

She turned into his hand and placed a kiss in the center of his palm. "This is crazy, but I'm totally and completely in love with two men."

"Yup. It's great." Justin grinned and Paul laughed.

She took their hands and led them inside. "Where?"

"Upstairs," Paul said. "Second door on the left."

* * *

Tis Agapis H Folia was everything Justin had hoped for. They looked across at the illuminated windmills and the lights of the harbor glittering on the water, enjoying their first meal as an official...couple... threesome...team...*whatever*...the name didn't matter. They were them. Pure and simple. Together.

"I knew there was a reason I always preferred peanut butter and jelly as my afternoon snack. It's just like our initials say. Together we rule the world."

"Hey, I like that," Bethany said, a big smile warming his heart. "That's what we are. We're an official PB&J. That's us. Just us."

"PB&J? I think the two of you have had too much wine," Paul said, laughing and shaking his head. "But, hey, I'll stick."

"And then will you drive us home and take advantage of us?" Bethany cooed, sounding so cute and corny.

"Sweetheart, I think it's you who is going to take advantage of us."

She nodded in eager agreement, and once again they all laughed.

Paul raised his hand and cocked his head, a sober look settling on his handsome face. "I hate to put a damper on our night or stop the laughter, but we have some serious decisions to make."

"I may be the one obsessed with details, but he connects the dots on the whole picture." Justin smoothed his hand over Bethany's nape and urged her to relax. "Go on. We're listening, love."

"Being on the island, having the villa to ourselves, and enjoying time alone has the tendency to shield us from the daily challenges we'll encounter." He poured water, rather than wine, and drank the whole glass. He was clearly feeling the strain.

"Okay," Justin said, resting his forearm on the table, because the same concerns had played on a continuous loop in his mind since the moment Paul and he had realized that Bethany was not an option, but a necessity for them. "First, we need to agree on where to live."

"Where do you live in New York?" Bethany asked.

"We've been renting near the office," Paul said. "It's nice. Large enough for all of us, and we can—"

"I just bought a place on the Upper East Side," she said. "It's in need of a lot, and I mean a lot, of work, but it has three bedrooms and a killer view."

It was Justin's turn to stress, but clearly sensing his hesitation, Bethany placed a hand on his arm and squeezed.

"J, it's mine, not my dad's," she said in a low voice. "I know how you feel about accepting anything from anyone else, but it's part of me. Me—not a stranger. If we're doing this, we accept what we each bring into this relationship. I bought the coop knowing I wouldn't be able to fix it for a long, long time, but it's a sweet little piece of heaven for me. I want that little piece of heaven for us."

Justin met Paul's gaze. This trust thing had to go all ways for it to work. He nodded.

"Hold on, Bethy. We can find a place to live that will be that little piece of heaven and won't need a lot of work. Will that make you happy?"

"This place makes me happy," she said, and the bubbly smile, which reached all the way to her eyes, returned. "The view is magical."

"It needs work?" Paul asked.

"It does," she said, shrugging and fitting her hands beneath her thighs. She rocked side to side as she explained how the balcony was perfect, but the bathroom and kitchen nozzles needed a little extra wiggling to work properly.

"Renovations don't scare me," he said, clearly happy to see her so enthusiastic. "I will take care of the nozzles when we get back. We'll hire contractors as needed, and we'll make it beautiful. Your dream place."

"Our dream place," she corrected.

"Or we can find a place that doesn't need as much work," Justin said. "As long as we're together, I'm happy."

"Don't listen to him, *koukla mou*." Paul glanced at Justin and made a slicing gesture across his throat. "You should have seen the dump Justin made us live in until *City Wings* got off the ground. We're not leaving the housing decision to him. It's us, baby. You and me. Not him."

"Hey," Justin said, trying hard to find a compromise and defend himself at the same time.

"No hey," Paul said. "It's two to one, Justin. That's your compromise."

Fuck he was screwed. The man could read his mind.

After all the years together, after all the compromises Paul had made so Justin could contribute the same amount of money for their lifestyle, it was his turn to compromise. Taking a deep breath, he nodded, and draped his arm around Bethy's back.

"Our dream place," Justin said, touching his lips to her cheek. "Ours."

"Finally." She smiled, turned, and kissed him full on the mouth. "Thank you."

From the way she gushed happiness, one would think he'd bought her dream home. Paul just shook his head, beaming like a proud patriarch, because he also knew what it meant for Justin to agree. There was nothing simple about it, but fuck it was worth being subjected to hurt in order to have them. Anything was worth it.

"Cut it out," Justin groaned, staring at Paul, but holding Bethy against him.

She kissed his forehead, then his chin, kissed along his jaw, and returned to his mouth. "I love you, J. Love you so much."

"Now that we have a place to live, we need to discuss work, careers, objectives." Incredibly prepared and discerning, Paul always amazed with his attention to the big picture. "We're already accomplished and making our way in the business world. And we need to merge our lives, while no one sacrifices anything dear to his or her heart that can cause resentment. I know this kind of talk isn't romantic. I'm sorry if I'm killing the buzz. I promise a long, sexy getaway...location of your choice... when it's all settled."

"How about Santorini?" Bethany asked. "A cave house on the Caldera?"

"Done," Paul said. "Now let's deal with the boring stuff. I don't want any more surprises from the outside."

"You're right." Justin placed his hand palm up on the table and waited for Paul to smooth his own over it. He did, gripping his wrist in a show of understanding. "And we need to be in agreement on what we want before tomorrow. Details and all."

"Yes," Paul said. Nothing else was needed.

Bethany placed a smaller hand over both of theirs. "Let's get down to business."

The gold specks in the brown depths of Paul's eyes seemed to spark, as he cleared his throat and looked at Bethany. "Christo, Sheridan, and most likely Kosta by now, know about our relationship, but I'd like to suggest we tell anyone else that matters together."

"Specifically my father," Bethany said, straightening and pulling back her hand.

"Your father has separated us in the past." Justin knew the words hurt her, but he couldn't ignore the truth. Honest and forthcoming. They had to be. "Whether because of communication, timing, or intent, we were both hurt. I won't let that happen again."

"Neither will I," Paul said, still holding her gaze.

Bethany worried her lower lip, closed her eyes, and nodded. "Okay."

Paul exhaled and rose from his seat, reaching across the table and caressing her neck. He came beside her and lowered his head.

"Way to compromise, *koukla mou*," he whispered against her mouth. "I love you. Never doubt that, Bethany. I love you."

Her chest heaved and she closed the distance between them, caressing his cheek and touching her lips to his. "I love you, Paul."

Sliding his chair close, Paul sat beside them. "We are three, and there are three things to consider: Luxury Homes, *City Wings,* and Vaso's Dream."

"Luxury Homes is Bethany's domain," Justin said, hoping that Paul would present her with the opportunity to run Vaso's Dream. "She can deal with it as she sees fit. I have *City Wings.* Trust me?"

"Completely," Paul said, grinning at him. "And I'll see to Vaso's Dream."

"I guess that means you want me to walk away from the acquisition," Bethany said, sad, but acquiescent. "You are what matters most to me. I will."

"No walking away from what we want. You don't ever walk away," Justin said. "Kosta has offered the resort to Paul. Are you okay with spending our summers in Greece?"

"Yes," she breathed. "So okay."

Paul stood, dropped some bills on the table, and hurried them from the restaurant.

"You do know the waiter was just bringing out the main course, right?" Justin asked, chuckling as they walked, each with a hand at Bethany's elbows, her feet barely skimming the ground.

"My appetite is for something else," Paul replied.

Without any objection from Justin or Bethany, he took them home and showed them exactly what he was in the mood for. Hours later, he carried a platter of cheese, olives, sausage, and bread to their bed.

Chapter Twenty-Eight

Pavlaki, siko.
Siko, Pavlaki.

A beam of light crept into the room, and reflected off the glass featuring the predawn sky. Paul disentangled his leg from between Justin's thighs and smoothed his palm over Bethany's shoulder, then turned to look at the open door. Recognizing the broad figure illuminated in the light, calling for him to wake up, he raised his arm in acknowledgement.

Marveling at how deep they both slept, Paul grinned and left the bed. He reached into his duffel bag and felt for a pair of gym shorts, stepping into them before he walked down the stairs and into the kitchen. Christo had the *briki* on the portable gas burner, warming water for Greek coffee.

"I thought you weren't coming home tonight," Paul said, dropping into a chair.

"It's morning. Six o'clock. And we have a new problem."

"Ochi, pote problima." Paul looked at his cousin, conveying *their* situation was never a problem. "They're mine. Both mine. And I don't care what anyone thinks about it. No one will hurt my family."

"Michaels requested a private meeting. You, me, *Theo*, and him. His professional demeanor is gone." He scooped two heaping teaspoons of the dark powder into the water, added four of sugar, stirred, and stared at the mixture. "Family, eh?"

"Justin, Bethany, and I are together. Forever."

"Pavlaki, a fun, summer romance is one thing. Forever is different." Christo glanced at him. "There are major consequences with such an arrangement."

"There are major consequences without it. We've thought about it, and we're willing to deal with anything that comes our way."

"Where will you live?" Christo lifted the *briki* and poured the creamy coffee into two demitasse cups.

"I'm going to talk with *Theo* about his offer. We'll stay on Mykonos for the summer." It made sense. It gave them the opportunity to adjust and enjoy.

"What about your company?"

"Justin is figuring it out."

Christo placed the coffee on the table, wiped a palm down his face, and sat across from him. "Okay. So you have a plan for the immediate future and work, but how are you going to deal with society's judgment down the line? How are you going to deal with her father in half an hour?"

Paul had dealt with society's judgment for the past decade, and narrow-minded people didn't intimidate him. What happened inside his house was no one else's business.

"If it were up to me, I wouldn't care what her father thinks or does," Paul admitted. "But it's not, because she cares. So, we've agreed to tell him together and deal with him together. What matters is what we have, not what anyone else thinks."

"I think you're blinded by your love for them, and you believe what you're saying, but are you willing to subject them to the nasty bullshit in the world? Questions, sneers, gossip are just the tip of the iceberg." Blowing out a frustrated breath, Christo shook his head. "There's more to consider than her father. What if she gets pregnant? What will you do then? It's not like any church or court would recognize a marriage between the three of you. What will the child have to deal with?"

Swallowing the coffee like it was battery acid, Paul lowered his cup and met his cousin's gaze. Christo had a valid argument, but Paul wasn't about to give up. They'd figure it out when they'd get there. He couldn't walk away from them. "I know it was a quick fall, but I can't imagine a day without them. I can't."

"I have your back. Any way you need. They're now my family, too."

"Thank you," Paul said, knowing his cousin would do anything to keep his family safe from the ugliness of people's words.

"No thank you needed between us," Christo said, shaking his head. He stood and collected the coffee cups. "Let them sleep. Use my bathroom to wash up. Choose anything you want from the closet. And please pick a shirt to cover that hickey on your collarbone."

* * *

Paul had all of thirty seconds with his uncle before a knock sounded on the front door.

"I stand with you on anything you decide," Kosta said, tapping his finger over Paul's heart. "Trust yourself, my boy."

Christo swung open the kitchen door and indicated for them to join him and Edward Michaels in the sitting area. Inhaling deep, Paul walked toward the man who had caused so much pain to the people he loved.

"Edward Michaels, this is my uncle, Constantine Lallas." Christo made the introduction. "You've already met Paul."

Refusing Kosta's outstretched hand, Michaels nodded. "I'll make this quick. There's no reason to pretend this is anything other than a twisted and juvenile ploy."

The skin on the back of Paul's neck prickled. He crossed his arms and stared into the cold eyes of a man who embodied the ugliness Christo and he had discussed. Ugliness he wouldn't let near Bethany.

"It has come to my attention that Justin Bentley has a personal interest in Vaso's Dream and has been dangled as bait to lure my daughter to invest in the resort."

"Not so," Kosta said. "Bethany had no idea about Justin's connection."

Her father waved his hand in the air. "Regardless, Bentley has no place in my daughter's future."

Christo placed a steadying hand on Paul's shoulder. "You said together," he said in Greek, preventing Paul from lunging for the man. Paul shrugged off Christo's hold, but remained in place.

"I'm offering double the agreed-upon price for the resort to get his boyfriend out of my daughter's bed for good. Out of her——"

"Get him the fuck out of here before I tear his piece of shit heart out of his chest," Paul said, a primitive growl escaping his chest as he shoved his cousin toward the other man. "This conversation is over."

"Double," Michaels repeated, looking back over his shoulder as Christo pushed him toward the door. "She's my daughter. Not a plaything for two gay men who want a temporary woman. It took me a little while to make the connection, but I recognized you from the pictures on the internet. You're not only Bentley's business partner. You're his bed partner. And you don't even bother to hide it."

"Why would they hide it?" Kosta asked. "There is nothing to hide about making a life with people you love."

"She deserves more than you," Michaels spat. "She deserves the kind of life I raised her for. A life with proper etiquette and respect. You won't use her as your beard——"

"Don't go there," Christo warned. "Have more respect for your daughter."

Paul's gut tightened. Pressure pounded in his head and his eyes burned. Edward Michaels had the power to hurt Bethany again. He felt it. He wasn't exposing her to him again. Not personally. Not professionally. Not until he was certain she'd be safe from the venomous words and archaic beliefs.

"I will pay double," Michaels repeated, the veins at his temples pulsing. "Leave my girl to me. In time, she'll forget about this fiasco. She'll be happy with the resort. Fuck it. I don't care about the money. State your price."

"Vaso's Dream is not for sale to you," Kosta said, stepping in front of Paul and blocking the path to Michaels. "Christo will arrange for you to be delivered wherever the hell you choose to go. Take your money and your company, and get off my property, Michaels."

"It's a lot of money. More than you'll be able to spend in your—

"*Malaka!* You put a price on that beautiful girl's happiness," Kosta called, lunging forward, his fist so quick that Paul almost missed catching it in midair.

"Get him out of here. Now," Paul roared, lifting his chin to Christo, while holding his uncle back as Christo shoved Michaels out of the house. It took everything he had not to go after him, but he'd glimpsed more than the man's ego. He'd seen protective intent. There was more to this than what appeared on the surface.

He let him walk. For Bethany's sake.

When the door closed, and Christo had led him to a car, he turned to his uncle.

"The *malaka* is Bethany's father. Putting him in the hospital will only hurt her. We don't hurt the woman I love."

Kosta blinked and nodded. "Okay."

Deciding on how to keep his family happy wasn't difficult. Ready and willing, he met his uncle's gaze.

"Anything, *Theo*?"

"Anything," Kosta confirmed.

"Okay." Paul walked to the antique coat hanger and retrieved a set of keys hanging on a brass hook. "I'll be back."

* * *

Bethany stretched her arm over her head and past the pillows, but only found more pillows. Paul and Justin were not in bed. She was alone.

She reached for her phone and checked for texts. None.

Seeing it was almost ten o'clock she sighed. It had been ages since she'd slept so late. Years since she'd awoken so rested. She climbed from the bed, feeling sore muscles she'd never known she had, and smiled as she pushed her hands into the sleeves of Paul's shirt. She glanced back at her phone, then dropped it back in the shirt pocket.

Coffee first.

Shower later.

Practically skipping down the stairs, she smiled when Justin looked up at her. Flashing her a dark and sexy grin, he stretched out strong arms, which she gladly walked straight into. She curled on to his lap. She nuzzled against his neck and inhaled the unique scent of Justin she so loved. "Good morning."

"*Kalimera*," he said, sinking his fingers in her hair and tipping her face up to his. "Since we're going to spend the rest of the summer in Mykonos, we may as well start saying good morning in Greek."

"*Kalimera, kalimera, kalimera,*" she said, loving the way the syllables rolled off her tongue and sounded in her mind. Plus, she didn't miss his statement about spending the rest of the summer in Mykonos.

She brushed her lips over his jaw as she sang her happy song, enjoying the feel of rough stubble, and reveling in the dreamy bubble being near him had created.

"*Kalimera, Justin mou.*"

"*Kalimera,*" he repeated, dropping a kiss atop her hair. "The three of us in Greece...the three of us together...sounds pretty perfect to me."

"Do you really think we can do it? Will *City Wings* be okay without you there?" Hope and joy danced inside her, as her fingers moved through his dark hair. Maybe life had put responsibilities on her shoulders, but she'd do anything to experience more of what she had over the past few days. Anything.

"I may have to go back to settle some things, but I've been working on the nitty-gritty details for the past two hours, and I think it's very doable," he said, lifting his chin to the computer screen. "Have you thought how spending the summer here would affect your job with Luxury Homes?"

She shrugged, feeling irresponsible, but not one bit regretful. "I'm not married to it, J. It was a job, a job I really enjoyed, but you know it was a way to prove to my father that I'm a competent businessperson. Suddenly, that's not important enough for me to not live life. I'll find another job if my dad doesn't want to keep me on because I want to be with you. Nothing is as important as you and Paul."

"I like your priorities, sweetheart. In fact, I love them."

The way his eyes sparked and showed his appreciation released a slew of dancing butterflies in her belly. His mouth touched hers, his tongue swept over her lips, and time ceased to matter.

Sighing in contentment, she felt his smile. Only one person could add to her joy.

"Where's Paul?"

"Probably at the resort. He was already gone when I got up," Justin said, reaching for his phone and engaging the camera. "Let's give him an incentive to hurry back."

She leaned into Justin and puckered up.

"Love it," she said when it showed on the screen. "Can I send?"

He nodded, and she did.

"But it would be nice to hear his voice, too."

"Of course. Sure he'd love to hear you just as much, Bethy. Especially when the sexy cute and sweet sleep is in your voice." Justin pressed the contact on the screen, immediately placing the call on speaker. It went to voice mail.

Disappointed, she sank against him and pouted. "Not what I meant when I said it would be nice to hear his voice."

Justin called the Greek cell number, but again it went to voice mail on the first ring.

"Strange," he said, adjusting her in his lap and typing out a quick IM on his MacBook. "Both lines shouldn't be occupied."

No return message.

No call back.

"Let's give it a few minutes, and I'll try him again. Want some coffee?"

"Sure," she said, her mind flipping through all the potential scenarios Paul could be involved in, then skidding to a halt over family expectation. His family's expectation. "Do you think Kosta has a problem with me in your life?"

Justin surprised her by laughing. Shaking his head, he placed her feet on the ground and moved to the kitchen.

She followed close behind, pasting her chest to his back as he poured.

"Kosta has already admitted to playing matchmaker in order to introduce you to us. Trust me, he has no problem with you in our life. He adores you."

"It's hard to process everything that has happened this past week," she said, admitting that she never thought she could love two people at the same time.

Justin placed the mug on the counter, and turned to wrap his arms around her waist, helping her process exactly what she felt. Comfort. Belonging. Love.

"I knew I loved two people, beyond any measure, the moment we saw you on the ferry. I just didn't know what to do with it. I couldn't lose you again, so I had to find a way to make sure you didn't push us away."

"I mean the physical attraction was definitely there from the first moment. I'm not revisiting the love-hate-love I had for you for years, but when I saw you on the ferry, I totally freaked. I wasn't sure I could handle being near you again." She pressed her cheek to his chest and simply inhaled. Damn she loved his scent. She'd never get enough of it.

"That's what worried me. And while I knew Paul would love you, we had that agreement of no permanent additions in our life. Anyone other than us was only a sex partner."

"Did you do that often?" After all, they had lots of energy, were phenomenal lovers, and not shy about taking what they wanted.

"No." He feathered his fingers over her face. "Do you really want to know?"

"I don't want to invade your privacy," she said in a barely audible tone.

"Nothing is off base for you. So ask anything you want, anytime."

She didn't want to know, but she did. Truth was she'd always question why she was the exception to their temporary rule if she didn't ask. She nodded. "Yes, if you don't mind sharing."

"Twice to be exact," he said. "Once in school at one of those weekend-long parties and once a few years ago."

"You didn't like it?"

"The sex was good," he admitted. "But it was just sex. An experiment of sorts. The truth is we didn't need it. We agreed to remain open to future possibilities if either one of us wanted to try it again."

"Whose idea was it to try it again with me?"

With a big grin on his face, he touched a gentle finger to her mouth, and she realized she'd been nervously scraping her teeth over her lip.

He lowered his head and soothed the ache with a gentle swipe of his tongue. "Paul suggested it that first day on the ferry. I said hell no."

Perplexed, she searched his eyes. The chemistry with Justin had always been off the charts. Why wouldn't he have gone for bringing her into their bed, especially if Paul had been okay with it? Suggested it, even.

"You may have freaked, but so did I. I wasn't losing you again... not because of the temporary agreement or anything else. I didn't want you regretting anything new about us." He went on to explain the painful attempt at friendship, how each time he and Paul made love they'd end up discussing her, how seeing her with Christo or thinking she could end up with someone else had them climbing the walls, and how in the end he'd lied to himself about being okay with temporary if it meant he could be with them.

"I can't tell you when it happened for Paul, but I think it was way before last night. Your father's arrival last night had him admitting it aloud."

"Because it's scary, J. Being in love with two people at the same time is scary. It's not as easy as admitting I love you or you love me. Loving *you* was practically a given," she said.

"If you didn't hate me."

"Deep down, you knew I couldn't hate you. I knew you too well."

He brushed his lips on hers and she felt him smile again.

"I've loved you since forever. Loving Paul so much hit me out of the blue. I fell so hard and fast for him, I definitely lied, not to myself, to you, about wanting only one night of pleasure in order to be able to have you both."

"And I'm so glad you did, my brave, beautiful Bethy. So very glad." He wiped his thumb across her cheek and looked at her with such cherishment, it made her body tingle with need as she fought the sting of happiness building behind her eyes.

"That doesn't mean I love you any less, because I love you completely, J. I love him completely, too," she said, blinking back the tears and swallowing past the lump in her throat. "It's difficult to understand, so I'm not sure I'm even explaining it right."

"You don't have to explain, Bethy. I know." He placed the mug in her hand and led her back to the table. "I feel the same. I love you both, so I know."

"Don't misunderstand me, but I miss Paul. I just wish he was here. He should be with us for this talk."

"I know." Justin tried calling again, but both calls went directly to voice mail.

"If Paul's not here, it's his loss," Justin teased, skimming his finger down the bridge of her nose. "Now drink your coffee. As soon as you're done, we're heading for a shower. I want you very alert for that. Can't miss washing a single inch."

She giggled, sipped, and very much looked forward to their shower.

Chapter Twenty-Nine

Bethany and Justin's phones chimed with incoming text messages simultaneously.

"Might be Paul." Justin tucked the edge of the towel between her breasts, brushed his lips across her jaw, and then strolled into the bedroom to check the message:

On the veranda waiting for you.

"Christo is downstairs," he called, pulling on a pair of cargo shorts. "I'm going to see what he needs. Take your time."

If Christo was there instead of Paul, something was up. Not wanting to upset Bethany if his gut was wrong, he avoided returning to the bathroom, placed the damp towel on the doorknob, and went to meet Christo.

"Good morning."

"Good afternoon," Christo replied, rising and shaking Justin's hand.

Yes. Something was definitely up. Christo's aviators did nothing to hide the concern lines at the corner of his eyes. Fuck. A lot could have happened in a few hours.

"What's wrong?" Justin asked, guiding them toward the seating area farthest from the door. "Why are you waiting outside your own home? Where is Paul?"

"I'm waiting outside because seeing you in the buff once a day is more than enough. Especially when your ass has a way of hiding the prettiest view in the bed."

Okay, if Christo could crack a joke, whatever it was couldn't be that bad.

"I came up this morning and woke Paul. Took him for an exclusive meeting at Kosta's, at her father's request."

"Michaels wanted to see Paul?"

"The man has balls," Christo said, combing his fingers through his hair. "He specifically requested—no, more like demanded—to meet with *Theo*, Paul, and myself...alone. He walked in, and like the steamroller he is, went right to work. Then Paul kicked his ass out."

Christo smirked, shrugged his broad shoulders, and the anxiety lines changed to laugh lines.

Justin would have liked to have seen Edward Michaels hauled out. He only felt a little slighted at not having had the honor himself to toss him out, but he was damn proud to have Paul at his back. "Go on. Tell me."

Flashing that charming Lallas grin, Christo lifted his chin toward the door. "Hello, *koukla*. You're glowing like a woman in love."

Man, was that the truth or what? His Bethy totally outshined the sun.

"I am a woman in love."

Justin couldn't take his eyes off her sweet curves as she sashayed over the veranda, wrapped her arms around Christo, and he leaned down to accept a kiss on the cheek.

"Are all Greek men so observant?" she asked, coyly smiling at Justin.

"We've already covered the exceptional attributes of the Lallas clan," Christo reminded, tousling her wet hair like a big brother would.

In spite of his lothario reputation, a past tumultuous affair caused Christo to keep women, especially women friends, at a distance. Sex was one thing. A true relationship another. But Bethany had clearly gotten through. She'd obviously charmed the big, tough man, and he stood protective and loving at her side.

"I'm here for two reasons," Christo said, pulling a sealed envelope from his pocket and tapping it in his palm. "Want the story on what happened this morning or do you want to read this first?"

Justin stretched out his arm and she took his hand.

"What do you think?" Bethany asked, pressing against his side.

Not the way he wanted her pressed against him. She rarely deferred choices to others and generally grabbed the opportunity to make them herself. Asking him to decide meant she was worried. He curved his arm over her and tucked her closer.

"Let's hear what happened." He glanced down at her and touched a finger to her mouth. She released her lip and he nodded. "Better." He smiled. "It involves Paul."

Agreeing, Christo asked them to sit and relayed the events leading to him dropping off her father at a resort on the other side of the island, and then returning to Vaso's Dream.

"By the time I'd tracked Paul down and made my way to the airport, his plane was wheels up on the runway and on its way to Athens. I received this text while I was driving over," he said, showing them his phone:

Saw your car pull up as we took off. Won't be available for a few hours. Meeting Bethany's little sister in a few. Be in touch soon.

Justin retrieved his phone from his pocket and handed it to Bethany. "Call her."

But the phone chimed an incoming text before she finished dialing. He reached over her and tapped the screen.

We are landing @ seven. Vaso's Dream—our pool @ seven thirty. Love you both.

They read it at the same time, and she blew out the breath he'd been holding. Justin laughed at the coincidence, and taking the phone from her, he touched his lips to her temple. "We're good, sweetheart. Let it be."

Bethany's body trembled as she buried her face in his shoulder, and he realized she'd been more than worried about her father's interaction. She'd been worried Paul had changed his mind.

With a finger, he tilted her chin up so she could meet his gaze. Looking into the soulful dark eyes, he shook his head. "No. Never that. Trust."

She blinked and nodded. "I do. I really do."

Christo cleared his throat, pulling Justin's attention back to the envelope he held.

"Who's the letter from?"

"Her father." Christo handed it to Justin and tugged on her hair. "I'll go make us some frappé. *Entaxi*?"

"Yes. Thank you," Justin replied. "That would be great." With a hand in the small of her back he led her to a seat. "We'll read it together."

He'd never seen her so unsure. Never. This was weighing heavy on her, and he ached to carry her load. But this was something she needed to decide. He'd be there, support her, but she had to want it in her heart.

Shuffling along at his side, she waited for him to sit, and then lowered herself on to his lap. She nuzzled against his neck. "I'm not certain I want to open it."

He smoothed her hair down her back, waiting for her to make up her mind. But he had to be honest; if it were up to him, he'd rip it up and throw it away. He didn't care what Michaels had to say, didn't want him near her, and couldn't care less if they never heard from him again, but the asshole was her father. He mattered to her.

"Whatever you want, Bethy."

"Together," she whispered, smiling at him. "Together." She tore open the envelope, unfolded the sheet of paper and began to read:

> *My dear Bethany,*
>
> *Since I've asked Christos Lallas to deliver this to you, I'm assuming he's told you what happened at his uncle's house less than an hour ago. I realize you may be angry with me, but I did what is best for you.*
>
> *I love you and want only good things for you. This situation is not that. There are many things to consider, things you're not aware of, and things your young and optimistic heart can't see. Give me the chance to explain my reasoning and motivation in person.*
>
> *I have instructed Raul to be ready for takeoff at five. Let me know where and when you would like to meet before we leave. I'll be there. I'd really like you to bring your passport and return home with me.*
>
> *I do love you.*
> *Always,*
> *Your father*

"He loves me," she said, probably to herself, and leaned back on Justin's chest. "I know he does. But he's wrong. This is best for me. You are best for me."

Justin tried his hardest to remain seated, not stand, and swing her in his arms. But mentally, that was exactly what he did.

"Do you want us to meet with him?"

"It doesn't matter at this point," she said, sounding calm and decided. "Paul won't be back until seven, so obviously he can't make it by five. We agreed to tell him about our relationship together. Anything else can wait."

"Yes." He was back to monosyllabic answers and he didn't care one bit. Tangling his fingers in her hair, he held the back of her head and looked into her eyes. "Yes."

Christo returned with three tall glasses of the iced coffee. The relief on his face was evident in his broad grin. "I'm guessing you're okay with the letter."

"Shoot. I need to text him." Bethany jumped up and skipped away. "Tell him we'll see him in New York."

He was still her dad, and she still loved him. Justin would make do. "He said he did what he did because it was best for her. Wanted the opportunity to explain in person."

"He's a manipulative dick," Christo said, making Justin laugh. "But he clearly loves his daughter, and he's not wrong about the fact that this isn't an easy thing to deal with. You're going to come up against a lot of nastiness from the outside. People will talk and it won't be nice. But you only live once. I'd do the exact same thing in your shoes, my friend. No one will ever have the opportunity to speak negatively if I'm there. I'm with you."

"Thanks, Christo. I know. Appreciate it."

They drank their iced coffee in silence, both waiting for her to return, and going into action when she asked if their old room was available for them. Now that Rachel was gone, she wanted them to move back and for Sheridan to take the room next door—*not our room, but my old room.*

"I like the way you say our," Justin told her as they packed.

"Good," she cooed. "Because I like saying it."

* * *

Sheridan stepped out of the taxi, happy to be on solid ground after the wild ride from the airport to the center of Athens. She turned in a full circle, taking in the city's pulse.

"Ancient meets classic meets modern."

While Hadrian's Arch and the Temple of Olympian Zeus, built over five hundred years apart, had stolen her breath as the taxi had driven down the congested avenue, past well-known business awnings and eclectic hotels, it had been the National Gardens that had captivated her. A green oasis in a cement desert, the gardens promised hours of escape from the bustling traffic.

She stood in Syntagma Square, about the size of a short city block, which was lined with as many cafés as trees, and sat smack in the center of centuries of architecture. While on a typical day she'd lose herself in the marvel of the living museum, she itched to get to her sister.

"You're beautiful. You look just like her," Paul said, his tall, sexy, and very built form towering over her.

No wonder Bethany had thought of jumping his bones from day one.

"Except for the color of your hair and the few inches in height—"

"Hey, you're calling me short." Her whole life everyone had pointed out how Bethany had the height, taking her seriously, and Sheridan had the fun and bubbly personality, dismissing her opinions as flighty. "My height has nothing to do with anything."

"Okay," he drawled, raising his hands at his side in the universal gesture of surrender. "I was only commenting on how you resemble each other. Not on what a shortie you are."

"Hey!" She stuffed her hands in her jeans pockets and stretched tall... well, as tall as her five-foot-two height allowed. "I'm an inch shorter than the average American woman."

He raised a doubtful brow and grinned.

"Fine. Maybe two inches," she said, looking toward the top of the square to the Parliament building and the guards in funky white kilt-like skirts, standing perfectly still while an invasion of pigeons entertained tourists.

"The Presidential Guard is known as Evzones, and while they're part of the military, their duties are ceremonial," Paul explained. "Today, they guard the Tomb of the Unknown Soldier in front of the Parliament Building."

She recognized the building, knew it would take days to see all the monuments in Athens, and felt guilty for mentally scheduling a return trip when her sister was in such bad straights.

"First, Bethany is just fine," her sister's sexy new guy said, as if hearing her thoughts.

She looked up at him. And because of boring etiquette classes, Sheridan remembered to keep her mouth closed and not gawk. Hopefully her sunglasses did their job of hiding her admiration of that dizzying grin.

"I know you're not supposed to trust a man who says trust me, but trust me. She's fine. She's with Justin. And I wouldn't have left them if I thought otherwise." Paul placed his hand on her elbow and led her down the block.

She knew Justin, trusted him, and loved him, except for when she'd hated him for abandoning Bethany. She sighed and stopped walking.

"I appreciate you taking me under your wing for the day, but I need to go. I can find my way back to the airport and get to Mykonos. I don't want Bethy to deal with my dad alone."

"She won't deal with your dad alone."

Was he being arrogant or ignorant? Edward Michaels wasn't a man to be put off. He functioned on his own agenda and no one else's. He'd manage to get to Bethany.

"Trust me," he repeated. "Not only is Justin with her, but the three of us have agreed to be together when she talks to him about what happened.

With the resort no longer an issue, the only thing they'd be dealing with is personal."

Shaking her head, she crossed her arms, and stared at an artistic window display. "He can be very convincing. You don't know my father."

"I know Bethany," he said, once again flashing that grin and distracting her. "Please trust me on this. We'll only be a few minutes in the office. Maybe twenty."

Twenty wasn't a few. And twenty minutes could turn into two hours.

"I promise we'll be out in enough time to watch the changing of the guard."

"Why do I need to accompany you? Isn't it safe for me to wait at a café in the square?"

In truth she wouldn't mind getting out of the heat and into the air conditioning, but she didn't want to appear nosy about his business. She'd been dying to know what the all-important documents he *needed* to collect were all about, but he hadn't offered any information.

"It's safe," he said, shrugging those broad shoulders. "It would make me feel better if you stayed with me."

Charming caveman. Protective, overbearing, insistent, but charming.

Considering her phone was dead and she'd packed her charger in her luggage, she figured she'd deal with the air-conditioned space. But she hadn't needed to worry about appearing nosy, because Paul insisted she join him in the attorney's office, where he spoke rapid-fire Greek, tucked a massive dossier beneath his arm, shook the man's hand, and hustled her back out to the street.

It all took less than twenty minutes.

Plenty of time. They watched the changing of the guard.

"Do you like honey as much as Bethany does?" Paul asked, checking his watch as the guards took their stations.

"Yes." What did honey have to do with the time?

"Great. We'll grab some *loukoumades* on our way to our next stop. I need you happy and feeling good so you can help me out."

Okay. So maybe Charming Caveman was a bit eccentric.

"*Loukouwhats?*" She hurried to match his stride, but he didn't really slow until they lined up before a small café that seemed to be straight out of the early nineteen hundreds.

"*Loukoumades* are little balls of fried dough, infused with a honey-syrup, and loaded with nuts and cinnamon." They made it to the counter, and he ordered two iced coffees and a serving of the sweets.

"Frappé, light and sweet," he said, handing her the plastic cup. "Let's grab a table. We have fifteen minutes before the appointment."

"Paul, how am I supposed to help you if I don't understand the language and have no idea what you want me to do?"

"You'll help just fine." There was that grin again. "And what I want you to do is point, *koukla*. Be you and point."

Chapter Thirty

Bethany glanced at her phone for the umpteenth time in half an hour. "They're late. Should we check the flight status?"

"Five minutes late. And I did check. The plane landed on time."

She wanted to shout...loudly.

"I don't get how you can be so calm," she said. "He hasn't called or touched base since that text. Neither one is answering their phone. What if something happened? What if something went wrong?"

Justin shut down the laptop and walked to her. His large and sure hands untangled her arms from her body, and snaked around her waist. He fit his hips against her belly and lowered his head to the side of her neck, pressing his lips to the very spot that made her whole body tingle.

"Do I have to take you to bed and make you relax again?"

She laughed. "Is it such a hardship?"

"Nope." He slid his hands down her ass and to her thighs, lifted her against him, and settled her legs around his waist. "A man has to do what a man has to do."

"Stop," she said, feeling the butterflies in her tummy take flight. "Paul and Sheridan will be here any minute."

"Paul won't mind."

"My sister will," she said, squirming down his length. "Wine. Outside. In the open. Now."

"Yes, ma'am." He reached for a bottle and two glasses, motioning for her to bring two more glasses and the corkscrew. "As you wish."

Way too relaxed, he winked and walked out the door to their table. She followed, handed him the opener, and enjoyed watching the simple act of J uncorking a bottle of wine. She enjoyed it even more when he poured a single glass, took her hand, and strolled to a chaise lounge.

Sitting between his outstretched legs, his hand protectively draped over her, she inhaled the heavenly scent of the local wine and brought it to her lips for a sweet taste.

"Again, just one glass. Are you a true romantic, wanting your lips where mine have been, or are you just stingy with glasses?"

The taunt received exactly the response she'd aimed for.

Justin curled a hand at the back of her neck, looked into her eyes, and brushed his lips over hers. "Have you missed the lack of a dishwasher?" Then giving her no chance to respond, he claimed her mouth, swept past her lips, and showed her exactly why she didn't mind sharing a glass.

A second hand moved from her nape up through her hair. "Exactly what I like coming home to."

Her heart leapt with joy at the only thing that could have made the kiss better. With a soft touch to the side of her mouth, Paul was there, his tongue stroking over theirs, making everything perfect. Just perfect.

"Nice to know, but you've insisted to witnesses coming home with you," Christo's voice broke through the haze.

Aware of their audience, Bethany lifted her head, and found Kosta pretending to shield Sheridan's eyes, while Christo stood like a Greek god Mr. Clean, his shirt stretched to the max over his muscled chest, as he crossed his arms and looked down at them.

"Sheridan!" Her heart overflowed with happiness at the sight of her baby sister, and she pushed through the sea of testosterone to pull her into an embrace. "I'm so happy you're here."

"I'm here, sis. I couldn't let you go through this alone." Sheridan wrapped her arms so tight around Bethany, it was difficult to breathe. "I won't let dad's prehistoric beliefs make you miserable again. Never. Go for what you want, Bethy. Just go for it."

"I am," Bethany said, pulling back and meeting her sister's gaze. She smoothed back the beautiful golden waves of her hair and smiled. "I truly am. You don't need to fight my battles with Dad. He's gone." She glanced at Paul. "And since I doubt he'll be back any time soon, we'll see him in New York when the summer is over."

He gave her a knowing grin, and her heart swelled with love. She returned her attention to Sheridan.

"I'm happy you're here so you can experience this beautiful place. Not to mention meet the Lallas men, who have enchanted your big sister in the most magical way."

Sheridan rolled her eyes and giggled as she glanced from Paul, to Christo, to Kosta.

"You've already been exposed to their charms, eh?"

"Sure have," Sheridan said, and then turned into Justin's waiting arms. "And I've missed you, you big lug. I've missed you so much." She buried her face in his chest and balled her fists beside it. "I've missed my brother."

With a barely perceptible inhale, Justin hugged her close and dropped a kiss atop her head. "I've missed you more, missy."

Bethany's life was complete. She had all she could ask for, and she sent up silent gratitude as she smiled at the love standing around her.

"So what do you think of the Lallas compound?" Bethany asked, taking her sister's hand and guiding her toward the table.

Kosta had pulled up more chairs and had already poured the wine. He flashed that same grin his nephews had perfected, and motioned for everyone to sit.

"There has been a slight change in that, my children," he said, handing Paul a rolled canvas, and taking a seat.

"*Efharisto, Theo.*" Paul tapped his hand over his heart in gratitude. He looked from Bethany to Justin, managing to speak to them with his eyes. He loved them. Needed them. And there was no doubt. Paul unrolled the canvas and placed the painting from the souvenir shop on the table.

"Vaso's Dream," she said.

"And our pool," Paul added. He knelt between her chair and Justin's. "I love you. You are my present and my future. You are my everything."

She and Justin shared a past. Justin and Paul shared a past. But they all shared today, and she wanted nothing more than to share the future. It was the three of them, together, as one.

She glanced up at Justin, noticing Christo, Sheridan, and Kosta standing over his shoulder. Justin met her gaze, and grinned.

"Very true." Justin leaned down and brushed a kiss on Paul's lips, then leaned across and did the same to hers. "I love you, too. You're *my* everything."

Her vision blurred. She placed a hand on each of their cheeks. "I love you more."

"While the courts and church won't let us marry or recognize our union in official capacity, our families do." Paul reached for a thick folder. "You both know *Theo* offered me Vaso's Dream as my own, and I've accepted on the condition that you both accept it as our own. It may be untraditional, but I'm asking for your hearts forever with our joint ownership in the resort."

Bethany sucked on her lower lip. "A proposal for forever in the form of the resort?"

"Yes, baby. What's mine is yours and Justin's, forever."

"And what's mine is both of yours," she said, placing a hand in Paul's and turning her palm up for Justin to take.

Justin hadn't pulled away, but his body had gone stiff. His dark gaze narrowed and his nostrils flared, and she shuddered. She knew all too well what was going on in his mind since he didn't accept things from others.

He'd worked twice as much and refused to compromise on anything. She knew he'd invested every dime Paul had in *City Wings*, which meant he'd also put everything he had into the joint venture. Paul had said he'd made them live in a dump until they could afford better. Meaning he hadn't allowed Paul to pay for better.

Releasing a soft breath, she closed her eyes.

Trust, she thought.

"With this resort, I thee wed," Paul said, squeezing her hand.

She opened her eyes as Justin squeezed her other hand.

"With this resort, I thee wed," Justin said.

"With this resort, I thee wed," Bethany repeated, pulling both their hands to her chest as their mouths met in the center.

Applause drew her from the moment, and she smiled. "I never thought I could ever be so happy. I love you."

"I love you more," Justin and Paul said simultaneously, standing and pulling the three of them into a tight circle, their hands clasped together.

"Wait, wait," Sheridan exclaimed, pushing three red boxes into Christo's hands and shoving him forward. "I chose them. You do the honors."

Christo flashed that perfect Lallas grin and closed his fingers over Sheridan's hands, bringing them to his lips for a kiss. "My pleasure, *koukla mou*."

Christo opened the ring boxes and removed three Trinity de Cartier bands. He touched them ceremoniously to the top of their joined hands. "As witnesses, we wish you love and happiness always."

As traditional in the Greek Orthodox Church's wedding ceremony, Christo the symbolic witness and *koumbaro*, exchanged the rings three times between them, placed the wedding bands on their fingers, and joined their hands.

"Marriage is not before man, but before God and your hearts. I'm honored to witness this union. I love you, Cousins."

Christo kissed each of their cheeks in turn, swept his thumb over Bethany's cheeks, collecting the joyful moisture, and then stepped back. Kosta approached, and kissed them as well.

"Married in a pair of Levi's cutoffs," Sheridan said, shaking her head and kissing Bethany. "That's a Michaels first." She laughed and touched her lips to Paul and Justin's cheeks. "Take good care of my precious sister."

"The best," Paul said.

"Always," Justin added.

"Sign these papers and we'll leave you alone to watch your first sunset as husbands and wife," Kosta said, signing the documents, and then offering the pen to Justin.

Justin, Paul, and Bethany signed, Kosta kissed them again and placed the pen in her hands. "Your family pen, *koukla*."

She glanced down and recognized the Santos pen. She smiled. They'd thought of everything. "Thank you."

"Good. And now we're off," Christo said, draping an arm over Sheridan's shoulders. "How would you like to watch the sun set from the resort's VIP spot?"

"Hey, that's my little sister you have your paws on," Justin chided.

"She's not *my* little sister," Christo said, and led her off the terrace.

"I love you, children. Blessings of happiness and love for your family." And with a big smile on his face, Kosta left as well.

They stood, hands joined, the three of them together watching the sun set.

When the fiery orange globe ducked beneath the horizon, and indigo and gold glowed in the sky, Paul turned to them.

"I hear the sunset in Santorini is spectacular," Paul chided, because there was no place with grander reputation for its beautiful sunsets than the volcanic island. "Tomorrow we watch the sunset over the caldera, on our first honeymoon."

"First?" Those funky tingles wouldn't go away, and Bethany felt caught in a fairytale. She had her princes, had her castle, and was darn sure claiming her happily ever after. "Will there be more?"

"As many as we want," Paul said.

"I didn't know you were such a romantic, Paul, but you thought of everything and made this perfect. Thank you." Justin smiled, his dark gaze glinting with unconditional love. "Now, I think it's time I get to kiss my bride and groom."

"One more thing," Paul said, reaching into his pocket and retrieving a gold coin. "I have a very *non-romantic* request for the two of you."

Swept away by all that had happened, Bethany had no idea what a non-romantic request was, but was willing to grant them anything they asked.

Paul placed the coin in her hand, but looked at Justin, who looked just as hard back at Paul.

"Today, we are blessed that society accepts a child with a father and a mother, or two fathers or two mothers," Paul said.

Justin nodded, clearly higher on the comprehension scale than she was.

"We are one, together before all this splendor, forever and always," Justin said. "But unless our society changes, we, Paul and I, will put our children before our personal and legal pride."

"Yes. Thank you," he said, bringing Justin's hand to hers, and placing his over both. "On the day we learn you are pregnant, this coin will determine which one of us signs the marriage license as a husband and which one as the witness."

"But how will we know—"

"Bethy, no matter what a piece of paper says..." Justin began.

"We're a family," Paul finished. "I will love Justin's baby as much as I will love yours, as much as I will love mine. The matter of biology is nothing compared to what we have."

Could she really be so lucky to have such a beautiful marriage?

"The baby will be ours. The babies will be ours," Justin said, placing a finger on her chin and looking into her eyes.

"You're going to flip a coin to sign a paper?" Bethany asked, love for them growing with each second.

"It's as good a way as any," Paul said, and Justin agreed.

Scraping her teeth over her lower lip to keep from laughing at the absurd amount of happiness she felt, she stepped closer and looked up at them.

"I think it's time this bride gets to kiss her grooms."

"And this groom his bride and groom," Paul said.

Justin cupped her neck, and brought her mouth to his and Paul's.

"I love you more," he said. "Always."

Their mouths met, and they shared that love as husbands and wife.

Demi's Recipe for
Amygdalota *from Mykonos*

Please be aware that in my family's Greek cooking and baking, there is rarely an exact recipe. Much is done by 'eye' or 'feel' and not measurements. For example, in most of my mom's recipes, there isn't an amount for flour—you simply feel it when it's right. In that spirit, if you feel you need an extra few pinches of anything, go for it.

Ingredients:
- 2 lbs raw almonds
- 1 lb. sugar
- 5 eggs (use only 4 if Jumbo eggs)
- Rosewater
- Powdered sugar
- 1 stick butter for baking

Preparation:
- Grind almonds to a very fine consistency
- In a bowl, mix almond 'powder' and sugar really well
- Add eggs (I like to beat them before adding them into mixture)
- Add a few drops of rosewater (Seriously, just a few drops. It's potent.)
- Mix and knead until the dough goes soft, but keep in mind it should remain tight.
- Scoop a spoonful on to a well-buttered parchment-lined baking sheet—it is difficult to shape by hand, so just guide dough with spoon. (The island bakers shape the dough into peaks or crescent cookies. I also like to stick a whole skinny almond in the middle for decoration before baking.)
- Bake at 400° F until golden brown (15-18 minutes)
- Wait 30 minutes so you can handle the baked cookies and transfer them to baking racks to cool for approximately 3 hours.
- Prepare a short glass of water, with a few drops of rosewater (I really use it sparingly—others make it much stronger with 1 part rosewater, 3 parts water. Your preference.) Dunk the cookies into the water/rosewater solution.
- Sprinkle with powdered sugar (use a sifter for even distributions) and store in Tupperware-style container.

Amygdalota are best shared with friends and enjoyed with your favorite coffee.

PS: They look really pretty when arranged in cute cupcake liners and then sugared. If you keep them a few days in the fridge, sift some sugar on them before serving.

Enjoy!

If you enjoyed *One Week in Greece* be sure not to miss Demi Alex's

FOUR NIGHTS AT SEA

Four days on the water . . .
Four nights in his arms . . .

Charlene "Charlie" Stanton doubts her maiden voyage on a lusty singles cruise will direct her sails toward love. But an unexpected lothario just might change the tide in her favor . . .

Charlie boarded the Cozumel-bound Lovers' Sail cruise hoping for nothing more than writing an article that would make it into the pages of *City Wings*, a trendy travel magazine. Still recovering from a highly publicized divorce, love is the last thing on her mind—especially when she realizes she's mistakenly booked herself a spot on a kink cruise. That is until she meets Ford, an outsider just like her, and he whips her attitude into submission. Despite rules limiting their interaction, he shows her a world where pleasure is encouraged, and nothing is forbidden. And with Ford as her anchor, she begins to wonder if she can turn four nights of fantasy into more nights of reality when the trip is over . . .

Read on for a special excerpt!

A Lyrical e-book on sale now.

Chapter One

Charlie debated whether to kiss her boss or kick him in the balls. Paul was off his rocker with this one.

"That's right, ladies. This is your chance. We're going to feature the winning article in the Valentine's issue," Paul said, puffing out his mouth-watering chest and grinning haughtily. "The selected piece will join 'Aphrodisiac Foods from Around the World' and 'How to Say I Love You in Twenty Languages' in *City Wings'* Valentine's edition."

Holy shit! This was it. This was the chance Charlie had been waiting for. It was the break she needed.

"Our readers devour anything and everything having to do with international desires," he continued. "It's a way to escape the daily grind and dream of possibilities. Who would have thought New Yorkers were so romantic?"

Yes, Charlene—Charlie—Stanton wanted her writing to win. She wanted to publish a real feature, with her own byline, in one of the trendiest travel magazines for New Yorkers. No, she didn't want to compete against her friend and roommate, Kathryn Taylor, though. They'd worked together at *City Wings* for over two years, worked well together as copy writers and staff writers, and now Paul was pitting them against each other as feature writers. It was so messed up. A disastrous idea.

"Get out there. Do your research," Paul said, circling his hand above his head like he was a Texas rancher. "Lasso someone who makes your body hum, and write about the perfect place to find love, ladies."

"Seriously, Paul? Lasso someone who makes our bodies hum?" Kathryn rolled her eyes, then smacked her forehead with the back of her hand. "Wait. Hold on a minute. Wait . . . wait. I'm seeing a handsome man, in a far off and romantic place like Paris, sweeping me off my feet."

Paris. Kat had to go and mention Paris. Like, why? Did it really matter if Paris was the most romantic place on Earth if neither of them wanted to fly over and find out?

Charlie didn't travel well and wasn't in the mood for a trip to the doctor in order to get a prescription so she could get on a flight. Kathryn had to stop speaking about the perfect place to find love on the other side of the Atlantic. How did one argue the romance of Paris?

Wondering why she'd ever picked up the vape stick when she'd never even smoked, Charlie eached for her pink, sixty-dollar vaporizer, and twirled it in her fingers. She answered the silent question in her mind. The thing was a crutch. Something to keep her grounded when thoughts crowded her mind and she wanted to scream at the world. Screaming and throwing temper tantrums were not allowed in the grownup world. Puffing on vanilla-flavored vapor kept her mouth occupied. It kept her from engaging in unladylike behavior.

"I think we can take a small detour from the publication's travel angle on this," Charlie said. After all, living in New York did have its benefits when it came to an abundance of male prospects for the feature. "Why can't a woman find love in her neighborhood, and *then* sail off into a foreign and exotic land with the love of her life?"

"If it's done properly, I can see it working. However, any featured lovers must take off in the end for a foreign destination." Paul nodded, tapping his fingers on the table as he considered her argument.

Maybe, just maybe, Charlie could convince the sexy tyrant to see things her way? Hope spread in her chest and she leaned forward in her seat.

"There is a pragmatic benefit, too," Paul added. "If we concentrate on finding love locally, more of our readers will relate to the accessibility of that goal and can dream of escaping to a romantic place with their loves."

"Exactly," Charlie said, breathing with relief.

Paul encouraged her to continue, so Charlie barreled on. "The dating scene has evolved so much over the past few years. There's always the chance of meeting someone at a bar or a club. Online sites host a bunch of events in this city. And let's not forget the old-fashioned way of being introduced by common friends."

"Great options." Kathryn looked doubtful. Charlie and Kathryn had exhausted all those options, but neither had found Prince Charming at a neighborhood hangout. Her friend was even more disillusioned than she was. Kat didn't believe that love could last. Yet she was blabbering about far-off and exotic locations. Maybe because Kat loved to travel, and Paul was willing to tag along?

Charlie was screwed. For some perturbed reason, Kat angled for
Charlie to write about Paris. What was up with that? Wasn't she
just arguing Paris was perfect for finding love? And, why couldn't they
keep it in New York? Considering how many people lived and worked
in Manhattan, if you couldn't find love in the Big Apple, you couldn't
find it anywhere.

"How are those local options working for you?" Kat asked, snapping
her fingers before Charlie's eyes.

Kat continued on her Paris Romance 101 introduction, but if Charlie
was honest with herself, she had to admit she was just as disillusioned as
her friend with the local love options. She couldn't truly get behind any
romance for herself. Sometimes things weren't fair. Like maybe it wasn't
about the location. Maybe it was about the fact that Charlie hadn't let
any guy in since her divorce. She simply couldn't. It was too difficult to
decipher their intentions. Did they like her for her? Or did they like her
for her trust fund?

"Not fair," Charlie said. "Maybe it's been bad timing for me. I really
haven't tried too hard. It's been difficult to trust anyone since my divorce,
so maybe I'm the problem and the scene is just fine."

Paul cleared his throat and held up a hand. "You're not the problem,
Charlie," he said, covering her hand with his own. "Your asshole ex is. So
let's take jerks like him out of the equation for the benefit of this piece."

Whatever. She needed to relax. And just flirt. Like Kat and
Paul were doing.

"This is a very incestuous organization," Charlie said, pointing from
Paul to Kathryn to the door. "Between you two and the accounting
department, a tree house should be the official headquarters of *City
Wings*. You're all too tight."

The conference room filled with laughter. Paul and Kathryn had known
each other forever, so they had no problem teasing or hitting below the
belt. When it came to Charlie, they treated her with kid gloves. As if her
divorce had been the end of her life. It hadn't. It had actually opened her
eyes to what she really wanted. More than anything, she was so over the
money-grubbing scumbags of the world.

Charlie was ready to move on from sitting-duck status. She was
doubly ready for a real sex life—something she hadn't had with the ex—
but she needed to learn how to compartmentalize physical and emotional.

Shit. Shit. Triple shit. She had to stop thinking so hard. Everything
she wanted would come, after she had her byline. First, she had to prove

herself as a competent and successful writer to her family. It was a matter of professional and personal honor.

"We're looking for love, not sexy interludes," Charlie said, an idea sparking in her mind. "Sexy interludes. But. Fine. Okay. Got it." She placed her palms flat on the table and stood. "If we're really looking for the perfect place to find love, why not a cruise ship? It's textbook romance. What about one designated for singles? Passengers board with an agenda. Just think how much fun we'll have writing about a cruise."

"Nope. There is no 'we.' You can sail away on a Love Boat, and Kathryn will fly off and take her chances in Paris," Paul announced. Kathryn tried to argue that he should reverse the assignments because she was nervous about running into a past fling, but thankfully he didn't budge. Paul insisted that Kathryn would benefit from a personal tour with Marko Renard, the man she'd placed above all others for years. He assigned her Paris. Charlie got the cruise. She sent up a silent prayer of gratitude. She didn't need the added stress of flying if she was going to concentrate on her feature.

"Good," Paul said. "Time for you ladies to bring out the claws and get down to work. You each have your assignment. Your expense accounts will be adjusted and ready to go by noon. See Justin for the details. Get me your stories by next Wednesday. I'll decide which one gets published in the Valentine's issue."

"On what criteria will the winner be chosen?" Kathryn asked.

"Whatever I want," he said with a devilish grin. "I'm the boss."

* * *

Two thousand dollars was more than enough money for roundtrip bus or train fare and a reservation on Lovers Sail Tours. Just over a day on the bus, then she'd sail out from Miami on Thursday. Then off to romantic Cozumel; add the singles on board, and she was sure to get enough material for a winning feature.

Charlie reserved an inside cabin on the sixth deck and booked a port excursion. Lovers Sail recommended the "romantic" experience, and was even willing to pair them up if needed. Partners would be determined once on board.

After clearing her immediate departure from the office with Paul, Charlie went home to pack.

* * *

With her expandable carry-on-size suitcase and leather backpack ready by the door, Charlie grabbed her cell, opened the Seamless app, and repeated the last order of shrimp pad Thai, red curry beef, and two orders of the crab Rangoon appetizer. She finished verifying payment just as the front door crashed open.

"Charlie, I'm home," Kathryn called, her forehead wrinkling as she took in the packed bags.

"Aowww." Charlie pretended to rush and hide the luggage in the closet. Relieving her friend of the large brown bag, she peaked inside and squealed. "Fuck-me boots! Way to go, babe."

"Got you something, too." Her friend dangled a smaller bag, stuffed with tissue paper, and dropped on to the couch. Kathryn patted the cushion at her side, but didn't offer her the gift. Instead, in a very animated and exuberant manner, she did the honors herself.

Charlie sat and clasped her hands between her knees. She watched her roommate pluck tissue paper from the bag and fling the sheets extravagantly over her shoulder. Amused with Kathryn's stripper imitation, Charlie covered her mouth with her hand and made her eyes extra big with excitement. "Should I blush before or after the big reveal?"

"I'm sure you blushed enough while you were packing," Kathryn said, pulling out a package of batteries and waving them in the air.

Charlie burst out laughing and grabbed the batteries. "Thank you. These are much appreciated and will be put to good use."

"I hope not," Kathryn said, lifting a red lace thong from the bag. "I think you could get more use out of these." Next came the black lace and lastly, the silk.

"You're too much," Charlie said. "You do know this is a work trip?"

"So what?" Kathryn replied, shaking her head. "A good reporter explores all avenues. *All.* Figured you could wear the granny panties the first night, but you'll need these for the next three."

Kathryn had assumed correctly. She had packed nothing but cotton underwear. Shaking her head, she stood and reached for the new lingerie. "For your information, I don't wear granny panties. They're cotton bikini panties. Practical. Pretty and sexy, too."

"Sure, if you're in high school." Kathryn scrunched her nose. "I take that back. Have you seen what those girls wear?"

"These are adorable," Charlie said. "Thank you." She walked the few steps to her suitcase and folded the new underwear into the outside pocket.

"Wait. One more thing," Kathryn said, dangling a skimpy, pink string bikini from her fingers as she walked toward the closet. "Pack this."

"No way," Charlie protested, sliding her palms over her hips. "Have you seen *these*?"

"I certainly have. You have a rockin' bod. You're not covering it with that stuffy one-piece you've had forever." She fit the bikini into the same pocket Charlie had placed the underwear in, then propped one hand on her hip and held out the other. "Give me that fugly suit."

"I like my fugly suit," Charlie replied, laughing and waving a dismissive hand through the air. The intercom buzzed. "Saved by food delivery. If you want dinner, you'd best be nice to me."

"I am nice," Kathryn insisted. "Didn't I just give you a sexy bikini and killer panties? Do I need to deliver a ripped man to your bed?"

"That would work," Charlie answered, plucking a five from her wallet for a tip and sashaying to the door.

Once they'd devoured the appetizers, finished half of each entrée, and switched dinners, Charlie confessed to packing mostly conservative outfits.

"My cruise-appropriate clothing is pre-divorce," she explained. "They're a little traditional, considering my mother had a hand in selecting every piece, but they're fine. I'm not cruising as a participant. I'm cruising as a professional observer."

"Seriously? You packed *those* clothes?" Kathryn placed the red curry beef on the coffee table and stood. She disappeared into the bedroom, clearly on a mission, leaving Charlie cringing on the couch from the noise of the massive storage bins being dragged out of the closet.

"I can't fit into your clothes," Charlie called, imagining her friend tossing short and skimpy dresses over her shoulder. "Don't bother. Even if I could get your miniskirts over my hips, they'd reach my knees."

"I'll admit we have different shapes. You're blessed with knockout curves, I have more height, but we're almost the same size," Kathryn said, emerging with her arms full of casual, bright-colored clothes.

"They still have tags on them," Charlie said.

"I picked them off the clearance racks at the end of the season and haven't had a chance to wear them yet." Kathryn held up a neon-green tank top printed with a phrase about giving her coffee before speaking. "These will help with getting people to talk openly with you. They invite conversation." She held a pink one up to her chest. It read, *Ask Me.* "If being a non-intimidating professional is your goal, these will work in a casual setting. You could wear them by the pool bar."

"Yes," Charlie conceded, reaching for the tanks. "They're good, non-intimidating, and cute. If you don't mind me being the first to wear them, I'll take them."

"I don't mind," Kathryn replied, holding the bright-colored shirts high. "On the condition that you agree to take these dresses with you." She held up a barely-there little black number. The plunging halter matched the nonexistent back, which matched the tiny skirt.

"That's not enough material to cover my hips." Charlie held up a hand in protest. "Even if I'm five inches shorter than you, it's barely going to reach past my underwear."

"Don't wear any." Kat handed her the items in order. Colorful tanks. Miniskirts. Skimpy and fun sun dresses.

Sighing, Charlie stuffed them in her case and returned to the couch. "You need to look at it from my point of view, Kat. This assignment means something different to me than it does to you."

"What are you talking about?" Her friend gave her a sobering look and sat beside her. "It means a byline to me and to you. We've worked hard for our own features. Plus, it's an opportunity to break out of our loveless ruts."

"Kind of." Charlie reached for the electronic cigarette and took a long drag. "I'll admit that what you're saying is mostly on target. However, there's never been a doubt in your ability to make it as a writer. Your parents supported your career goals—maybe not financially so much, because they couldn't, but they always cheered you on. Paul hired you because he knew you were a capable writer. He had proof from your school days." She puffed on the pink stick and chased the vanilla-scented vapor with a waving hand.

"You're a great writer," Kathryn insisted.

"Thank you," Charlie said, folding her hands between her knees. "I like to believe that, but my family doesn't. According to them, the only reason for me to attend Columbia Journalism School was to find the right husband, which I recklessly overlooked during my undergraduate education. They think I was there for my M.R.S. degree."

"You are so much more than pretty wifey material," Kathryn said, her pitch a bit higher than typical. "You're such a talented writer, not to mention someone that I would always want at my side. Dependable, smart, hardworking, stable—"

"It doesn't matter." Where her family was concerned, her main objective had been to find the proper husband to grow her inheritance. Her shoulders dropped in defeat, but her determination rose in opposition.

"Okay. Let's talk about how this week will make a difference." Kathryn covered Charlie's hand and squeezed in support. "I'm here for you. Let's brainstorm the best avenues to prove that you're more than a pretty face."

Relief and gratitude flooded Charlie. She was so lucky to have a friend who believed in her. "I'm going back to the basics. Starting with the five *W*'s every investigative reporter asks: *Who, what, when, where, why* . . . I'm going forward with my intentions from the moment I embark. I'm going to interview all of my fellow passengers that are willing to share."

"Don't forget the *how*," Kathryn added, folding her feet under her bum. "I got it. Let's come up with all your key questions over a bottle of wine. That way, you're guaranteed not to miss anything you could use."

"Can't," Charlie said, checking the time on her phone. "I need to get to the Port Authority. My bus leaves in a little over an hour."

"Bus?" Kat shrieked. "Are you out of your mind? That's going to take forever."

"Twenty-six hours, to be exact. The same amount of time you'll have on the ground in Paris." Charlie winked and stood. She carried the dinner containers to the kitchen and set them on the counter. "If I take a flight, I'll arrive totally wrecked and the first two days of the cruise will be ruined. The load of meds I'd need to get my butt on a plane would take a huge toll on my body. I'll bus it."

Shaking her head, Kat gazed at the floor. "You're going to regret getting stuck—wait!" She looked up, excitement playing in her eyes.

Charlie looked at her friend, wondering what exactly the massive brainstorm was. "You know I'm on a tight schedule, right?"

"I got it," Kat said, holding an index finger in the air. "I have twenty-six hours in Paris. You have twenty-six hours on the bus. So you need twenty-six interview questions for the cruisers." She clasped her hands together and rolled her shoulders. "Trust me. It's our lucky number. Twenty-six! Everything twenty-six."

"Okay. If you insist." Charlie stretched up and wrapped her arms around Kat's shoulders. "I really have to go. I'll work on the questions while someone else drives. You never know who may be on that bus."

"You never know," Kat agreed.

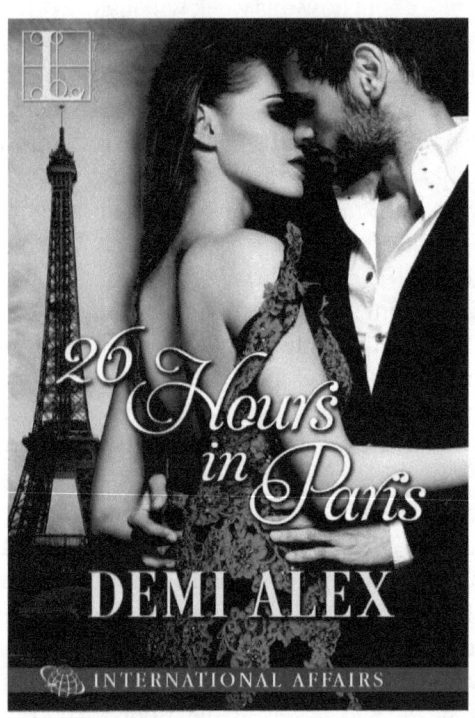

One day to see the sights.
One night to change your life…

Magazine writer Kathryn Taylor is traveling from New York to Paris for work. But the flirtatious Frenchman she left long ago is waiting at the airport—and he wants to play…

No one can guide Kat through the sensual city's delights like Marko Renard. He let her get away once, and now he's determined to make her stay—even if he has to tie her down. He will wrap her in cashmere, tease her tongue with chocolate, and take her to the peak of the Eiffel Tower…But can he convince the bohemian beauty she belongs with him, in his luxuriously decadent world? In business, he's the master—but it's Kat's body and soul he truly longs to rule. He has just enough time to show her the pleasures of the boulevards, the boulangerie—and the bedroom. To finally get her to just say oui, he'll have to seize the day—and the night…

Demi Alex writes steamy romances, blending emotional fulfillments of the heart and carnal desires in her work. Born in Athens, Greece, and raised in her own version of a big fat Greek life in New York, Demi was infected with book and travel bugs early, and currently admits the only therapy for this condition is to combine the two in fictional stories that allow her characters to let loose and experience all they crave. She attended SUNY at Stony Brook, and after changing her major numerous times, graduated with a degree in Public Policy and International Studies. Her characters are loosely based on people she encounters while she travels or during the time she spends matching homes to owners as a Realtor. She simply has a passion for matchmaking that can't be put to rest. Readers can visit her online at www.demialex.com, on Facebook, and on Twitter @DemiAlex2U.